GW00391139

EARTH'S FURY

OBSIDIAR FLEET BOOK 4

ANTHONY JAMES

© 2018 Anthony James
All rights reserved

The right of Anthony James to be identified as the author of this work has been
asserted by him in accordance with the Copyright, Designs and Patents Act, 1988

The characters and events portrayed in this book are fictitious. Any similarity to
real persons, living or dead, is coincidental and not intended by the author

This book is sold subject to the condition that it shall not, by way of trade or
otherwise, be lent, resold, hired out, or otherwise circulated without the publisher's
prior consent in any form of binding or cover other than that in which it is
published and without a similar condition including this condition being imposed
upon the subsequent purchaser

Illustration © Tom Edwards
TomEdwardsDesign.com

Follow Anthony James on Facebook at facebook.com/AnthonyJamesAuthor

WORLD'S END

Judged purely on that most superficial of attributes, *beauty*, planet Atlantis had been the jewel in the Confederation's crown since the first moment one of humanity's scout craft emerged into high orbit and sent news of the discovery to its home world. Amongst the enormity of the universe, habitable worlds were few and far between, a rarity even when spaceships were capable of crossing colossal distances at high multiples of lightspeed.

Viewed against the backdrop of space, its sun a distant circle of vibrant yellow, Atlantis was close to romantic perfection. The planet's deep seas, lush forests and temperate climate had once attracted artists and poets from across the Confederation, along with millions of tourists, who flocked here to escape the dreariness of New Earth, Pioneer, or any of the other highly-industrialised economic powerhouses in human-held territory.

The good times for Atlantis were a thing of the past. Following the arrival of the Vraxar, the Confederation Council had authorised a full evacuation. Billions of the planet's inhabitants were loaded onto vast interstellar craft and taken away to the comparative safety of deep space or one of the other worlds in the Confederation. Of course, not everyone was willing to leave. A few million were content to ignore the warnings, or were simply too frightened of the unknown to be cajoled into accepting the promise of a new life elsewhere.

It wasn't exactly lawless, since the Space Corps was obliged to leave enough personnel to impose a minimum level of order, but as far as the Confederation was concerned, the people of Atlantis had been provided with ample opportunities to make the right choice and leave.

As well as reduced levels of personnel, the Space Corps no longer provided significant air support. At one time, there would have been anything from a handful, to many dozens of heavily-armed spaceships either in orbit or undergoing routine mainte-nance on the surface facilities. Now all that remained was half a dozen old freighters, suitable for carrying off anyone who changed their minds about staying, and a single Crimson class destroyer.

Even at peak numbers, the fleet once stationed here wouldn't have been nearly enough to divert the incoming disaster.

At an altitude of eighty thousand kilometres directly above the day side of the planet, a cloud of fission energy appeared - energy which heralded the imminent arrival of a spaceship. Far below, the skeleton staff left to run the Tansul military base comms hub registered the arrival. They didn't need to check the Space Corps flight database – they knew nothing was due for weeks. An automated warning was sent across the planetary network to the other populated bases, and a further alert was sent to New Earth via a deep space monitoring station.

With an emotion closer to resignation than fear, the men and women on these bases left their posts as part of a well-rehearsed routine and made their way towards a series of newly-constructed bunkers which were several thousand metres below the surface and accessed via battery-operated airlifts.

One woman, a comms lieutenant called Katia Springer, didn't join the others. She wasn't content to leave the Tansul mainframe to do all of the work and she stayed, watching and relaying the information onwards to New Earth.

The spaceship which burst out of lightspeed was like nothing which had come here before. The vessel was an elongated ovoid, covered in turrets, domes, antennae and countless other structures. It was *Ix-Gorghal* – one of the Vraxar capital ships. At six hundred kilometres in length and three hundred at the greatest part of its Y-axis, there was nothing to compare to it in the Space Corps.

Ix-Gorghal came to a standstill and for a time measured in minutes, it remained in place, its propulsion systems inactive while Atlantis rotated serenely beneath. A scattering of still-operational ground batteries launched a few dozen high-impact missiles, the warheads detonating fruitlessly against the immense spaceship's energy shield.

Lieutenant Springer watched it on a feed from the Tansul comms hub sensor array. The nose of the enemy ship was aimed directly at the planet, affording her an excellent view of a circular hole in the black-metal armour which covered *Ix-Gorghal*. This hole had a diameter of two thousand metres, with four pyramid structures arranged near the edges. The comms hub's sophisticated sensor array was able to register the sickly green light somewhere deep inside the Vraxar spaceship.

This green light grew slowly in intensity, until it was difficult to look at directly. Then, it fired.

Atlantis was destroyed, shattered into a hundred trillion pieces by the Vraxar weapon. Fragments of the planet were hurled outwards in defiance of gravity. The world which had been threatened with destruction so many times before was finally reduced to rubble and scattered, sent tumbling for an eternity towards the edges of space.

Many hours later when the majority of the planet's remains had dispersed, there was something left behind. *Ix-Gorghal* was in the exact location it had been when the weapon was fired. Its energy shield was so immense, not even the ruins of a planet were sufficient to make the Vraxar ship retreat.

Eventually it *did* move. Its fission engines spent a short time accumulating energy and then the huge alien spacecraft vanished into lightspeed, its course unknown to the Confederation. In its wake, it left nearly six million dead and no clue as to why the Vraxar had decided it was time to kill instead of convert.

CHAPTER ONE

IT WAS three weeks since the loss of Atlantis and there was no sign of the panic dying down. On the New Earth Tucson military base, Fleet Admiral Duggan was finding it hard to remember what it was like to have more than three hours sleep in a single twenty-four-hour period. His medical staff were in regular attendance, monitoring his diet and keeping him topped up with whatever drugs they deemed necessary to keep him alert and capable of making vitally important decisions. If things ever blew over, he knew it would take days for him to recover.

"It's not like I'm a young man anymore," he muttered to himself, long past bitterness at the inexorability of time. Duggan was in his eighties and whilst medical advances meant an average human could expect to live beyond 130 years, he was long past the bloom of youth.

The most frustrating part was that Duggan knew he was struggling to do anything more than deal with issues and problems as they came to him. He was reduced to a wholly reactionary state and no matter how hard he tried to change the situation - to allow himself to look ahead instead of at the present day - he found himself thwarted at every turn. The *now* had taken over and he couldn't find enough time to handle everything. The failure was his and he knew he couldn't let the situation persist.

In his office, he mulled over the most pressing issues in the war against the Vraxar. The biggest lead they had from the first encounter with *Ix-Gorghal* was a recording of a fission cloud from the alien cargo vessel believed to be carrying the wreckage of the *ES Determinant*. A combined fleet of human and Ghast spaceships had followed the trail, only to find it go cold. There was no sign of the enemy cargo ship and no further clues as to where it had gone.

After that, Duggan was left to rely on the remaining unencrypted data arrays of the *Valpian* – an Estral cruiser captured years ago. In the end, it was fruitless. The *Valpian* had evidently been built prior to the Estral engagement with *Ix-Gorghal*, so there was nothing the Space Corps could learn about the enemy capabilities.

He shifted in his chair and sighed. The desk in front of him was covered in an ever-growing pile of what he colloquially referred to as *crap,* though he didn't refer to it as such in front of anyone except his wife and one or two trusted friends. In truth, this *crap* was produced by the finest minds in the entire Confederation – men and women who were able to perform wondrous feats using only the few pounds of grey mush which they kept safely inside their skulls.

He picked up a folder and spent a few seconds looking over the contents. He guessed this final report on the nature of fission engine efficiency had taken a million or so manhours to compile and he felt a pang of guilt that it was a low priority for his attention.

With a practised flick of his wrist, Duggan cast the folder onto the far-left corner of his desk, upon which was his unofficial

I'll get around to this later pile of other brown folders. He reached for the next report, only to be interrupted by his personal assistant, Cerys.

"Councillor Stahl wishes to speak with you, Fleet Admiral. He would also like to know why he's been denied direct access to your communicator when he's part of the organisation that pays your damned wages."

Cerys was back to speaking in its usual business-like female tones. Only a few months ago, the computer behind it had decided for whatever reason, to talk like a seductress. It had left Duggan somewhat puzzled and he was relieved when it had reverted to normal without any apparent explanation.

"Those were his words?" Duggan gave a half-smile. Councillor Stahl could be a pain in the backside, but the man had shown himself able to make the tough calls when it was truly necessary.

"His exact words," said Cerys.

"Bring him through."

The desktop communicator hummed softly and the display indicated it was connected to a hub on planet Charing in the Origin Sector. Stahl spent much of his time on Old Earth, but, like most of the Council, he often found his presence required on several different planets at the same time.

"Fleet Admiral."

"Councillor Stahl."

Neither man was interested in wasting breath on anything beyond the tersest of greetings and Stahl got straight on with it.

"How are the preparations for Last Stand?"

"There were unforeseen issues with the construction of Benediction. The last one proved to be the hardest to complete. Nevertheless, it is finished and I signed it off yesterday. It is being moved into position."

"I thought we were building from a blueprint. Why were there problems?"

"We are not talking about the creation of children's toys, Councillor. Benediction is an advancement of the design and with a greater yield than the others. A far greater yield."

The words were an understatement.

"Why not save the modifications for later models?"

"I didn't expect delays, else I would have denied the request to make design changes."

"New Earth is the last?"

"Yes, Councillor. The other planets are already part of Last Stand."

Stahl sighed, giving an indication of the weight bearing down upon him. "I hope to hell we never need to put it in motion."

"On that we agree. Have you reached consensus on the protocols?"

"No one wishes to take responsibility."

"It needs more than one man."

"I have put myself forward, so you will not be alone, Fleet Admiral. However, the Council are still arguing over how many more need to be involved. If we decide authorisation requires a majority decision..."

"Last Stand will never be activated," finished Duggan.

"This is where the responsibility of the Council ends and that of the Space Corps begins," Stahl replied. "To ensure we don't find ourselves in a situation where we need to sacrifice billions of our own people."

"Agreed."

"Can we defeat *Ix-Gorghal* and *Ix-Gastiol*?"

Duggan was aware that it was frowned upon in the lower ranks of the Space Corps to sound negative about anything, even when it was glaringly obvious that failure was inevitable. Fortunately, it took little skill to identify the buzzwords used to cover up such nonsense and it was equally lucky that Duggan felt no compulsion to call a turd anything other than what it was.

"It'll need a miracle to destroy just one of those two space-ships," he replied.

"And presumably a miracle to destroy the second. Does that make it a miracle squared or simply two miracles added together?"

Stahl was attempting a clumsy joke.

"Somewhere in between, Councillor."

"I've been keeping up to date with the progress on *Earth's Fury.*"

"It is going well, though it won't be ready as soon as I would like."

"I trust we aren't putting all of our eggs in that particular basket?"

"No, Councillor. The Space Corps has several promising new designs undergoing testing."

"Fine, keep me informed."

With that, Stahl was gone.

Duggan stared at his desk for a few seconds. He wasn't fond of inaction, so he stood and stretched the aches and pains from his muscles.

"Cerys, I'm going to check on the progress of *Earth's Fury.*"

"Would you like me to send advance warning?"

"No. And make sure I'm not interrupted unless it's of abso-lutely vital importance."

"Yes, Fleet Admiral. Will you be gone for long?"

The computer knew damn well how long he was likely to be gone and was trying to act like it had human uncertainties.

"Use your best estimate."

He left his office. His appearance surprised a few of his staff who worked in the open plan area outside and they prepared themselves to follow. He wasn't in the mood for their questions and he waved them to their seats.

"I'll be back shortly," he said.

A few minutes later, he was outside. He took one of the boxy, utilitarian pool cars and gave its onboard computer directions. With barely a murmur, the vehicle pulled out of its parking place and entered the traffic of the base. The cloth interior of the car seats smelled of damp and the navigational screen flickered.

Outside, there were trees and a few grassy areas, in stark contrast to most other bases in the Space Corps where greenery was unheard of. It was late afternoon and the sky was grey, though for once there was no sign of the drizzle which was a seemingly permanent feature on this part of New Earth. Duggan's mind was elsewhere and he didn't notice any of these things, and was only dimly aware of his transit through the wide streets of the base.

The car emerged from the shelter of the buildings and continued onto the flat, concreted landing field. Several warships were parked further along the strip – there were four Crimson class destroyers in a neat row, along with one Imposition class cruiser. The sight pulled Duggan from his reverie and his eyes roved over the warships. They were beautiful, terrible constructions built to defend humanity and it saddened him to think how powerless they would be against the might of the Vraxar capital ships.

This part of the landing field was several kilometres across and it took the car a few minutes to pass the docked spaceships. It entered the shipyard and there was a marked increase in ground traffic. The car weaved its way between three huge gravity cranes and was forced to stop to allow an immense flatbed gravity crawler to go by. The crawler was several hundred metres long and it carried a half-billion-tonne cuboid block of Gallenium. A team of anxious-looking technicians walked alongside, checking their diagnostic equipment for any sign of malfunction in the crawler's engines.

The crawler's destination wasn't hard to fathom – a new Hadron battleship was ninety-five percent complete in Trench One. The *Ulterior-2* was so long they'd needed to do additional work on the docking trench in order to fit the hull inside. The battleship loomed hundreds of metres above the sides, its armour plating dull in the artificial light. Construction robots filled the skies, dancing a computer-controlled dance with two huge lifter shuttles. Everywhere around, thousands of technicians hurried about their business.

The *Ulterior-2* was an evolution in design – it was still identifiably a wedge shape, but it was proportionally bulkier than most other warships in the fleet. A few last-minute alterations had allowed the shoehorning in of a secondary Obsidiar core and there were immense layers of shielding between the engine sections to try and limit the effects of the Vraxar Neutralisers. This shielding was of unproven worth and Duggan had been initially reluctant to sign off the design without greater research.

The secondary Obsidiar core wasn't the only significant update. Space warfare was changing and Lambda missiles were no longer as effective as they had once been. The Vraxar could jam their guidance systems, which meant Duggan had been forced to explore new methods of delivering high-impact punishment to the enemy. The *Ulterior-2* was equipped with hardly any Lambda tubes, relying instead on the more effective and proportionally more expensive Shimmer missile system. It had new-design comms and sensor arrays, as well as heat-dispersing armour plates. Most importantly, the battleship was designed specifically to carry the first working prototypes of the new Havoc cannons, and the huge, squat turrets of the four upper guns were clearly visible.

The Havocs had a twenty-metre bore. They could rotate 360

degrees and launch a sphere of hardened Gallenium at a speed in excess of two hundred thousand kilometres per second. The power of the guns had produced all manner of knock-on problems which had been exceptionally difficult to resolve. Duggan felt immense pride to see how far the Corps scientists had come in such a short time.

Gradually, the gravity car left the Ulterior-2 behind. The vehicle picked up speed as it moved towards Trench Two. There was as much activity here as there was around the battleship. Trench Two had also required modifications, though in this case it was for width instead of length.

Once again, the gravity car was required to wend steadily through the construction traffic, which increased in density the closer it came to the focus of the activity. Duggan knew who he was looking for and used the onboard communicator to speak to Cerys.

"Locate Project Manager Peterson and point this car in the right direction."

"Certainly, Fleet Admiral. PM Debbie Peterson is seven hundred and three metres to your left."

The car changed course and its speed decreased to little more than a walking pace. Duggan was impatient, but he had no desire to injure someone because he wanted to reach his destination two minutes sooner. Eventually, the car pulled to a halt near a group of men and women who were in a heated debate over something. Duggan recognized Peterson, since she'd overseen at least a dozen high-end construction projects. She was in her middle years, with sharp eyes and a permanent frown. She saw Duggan emerge from the car and came to meet him.

"Fleet Admiral, I wasn't expecting you." She was too much a professional to sound disapproving at this unscheduled visit.

"PM Peterson, I have come to see how the construction is proceeding."

She turned towards the vessel nearby. "We are mostly on target, sir."

Duggan bent his neck in order to see the details of *Earth's Fury*. The lower three-quarters of the spaceship were slab-sided and plain, with thick armour plating. The Shield Breaker was mounted on top. This experimental weapon was an intricate construction of beams, with a long, slender barrel in the centre. The gun was delicate and not designed to move quickly or to have a wide arc of fire.

Earth's Fury wasn't really a spaceship as such – it had a gravity engine and a backup Obsidiar core, which were only intended to take it as far as one of the planets in the New Earth solar system. It was designed to scrape into a low lightspeed, though additional drive modules could be fitted if it ever needed to go faster.

"Is testing complete on the loading mechanisms?"

"As much as we're able to, sir. We've test fired several hundred dummy projectiles, which doesn't give us much information about how it'll work when we send Obsidiar through it."

"You can appreciate we won't be testing it extensively with live ammunition," said Duggan. "I don't have Council agreement for many trial shots."

Peterson was a pragmatist. "We'll work with it. The field generators are functioning fine, and testing on the heat-exchangers finished an hour ago." She crinkled her nose. "How the hell do they figure this stuff out in the first place?"

Duggan smiled. One of the labs on Pioneer had discovered that if you spun a piece of Obsidiar at high speed through a powerful magnetic field, heated it to near melting point and then cooled it as low as it would go, the substance became temporarily unstable. It was a vaguely similar principle to how the Obsidiar bombs were detonated, but the major difference was that *Earth's Fury* could repeat the process. It was nothing like as efficient as a dedicated bomb, yet the Shield Breaker could fire a four-metre Obsidiar sphere at high velocity and with what were *assumed* to be devastating consequences for anything unlucky enough to be hit. *Earth's Fury* was originally conceived to knock out Vraxar Neutralisers. Now, the intentions were different.

"It's what our research labs are there for," he said. "Believe it or not, there are a few of my best scientists who freely admit they can't tie a shoelace. Like it's a badge of honour."

"Yet they can design something like this."

"I'm a firm believer that everyone's got a talent and the more talented you are in some areas, the less talented you are in others."

"The great scales of existence."

"They don't always balance and I don't know if that's good or bad. How long until *Earth's Fury* is ready for flight?"

"I've got five weeks on the plan. In truth, we're going to see a few days slippage on one of the engine modules. This is totally new, so everything's custom and we're having to change half of the components on the fly."

"We can't afford delays, PM Peterson."

"I know, sir. I'll do what I can to minimise or eliminate."

Peterson was one of the best and Duggan knew the job was in capable hands. He took his leave and returned to the car, unsure exactly why he'd made this trip in the first place. The car pulled away and he leaned back in the seat, making its cheap foam filling squeak. The answer to his question came to him – *Earth's Fury* and the *Ulterior-2* represented humanity's hope for the future. They demonstrated that the Confederation would never give up fighting. Even project Last Stand was a statement of the same intention, albeit one which would have appalling, unthinkable consequences.

Atlantis was gone. The planet had seen far more than its fair share of conflict both against the Vraxar and, long ago, against the

Ghasts. In a way, his experiences in and around Atlantis had contributed a lot to making Duggan into who he was today. Though the Vraxar had destroyed the planet, Duggan realised he was still attached to his memories by countless invisible threads which held him back and clouded his vision.

He closed his eyes and allowed himself to feel the pain for this one last time. Then, he cut the threads and felt them drift away, vanishing into his past and leaving him feeling momentarily bereft. The sensation passed and his determination returned. Clarity of thought came with it and he was angry to have allowed this weakness to have affected him so much.

A gentle beeping from the car's navigational system caught his attention.

"You have arrived. You have arrived. Please exit the vehicle."

Duggan complied. With purpose to his stride, he returned to his office with the intention of shaping the future instead of being constrained by his past.

Inside, he was too invigorated to sit and he paced his office, deep in thought. After a period, his eye was drawn to a new folder on his desk, which had evidently been placed there during his absence. He picked it up and read the title. *ES Determinant Memory Array – Projections Team Update 23-13d.*

He swore under his breath before he even bothered opening it. The captured data on the *ES Determinant*'s memory arrays had been hanging over the Confederation like some kind of shit-coated sword of Damocles and every time one of these Projections Teams updates arrived it reminded Duggan how tenuous was humanity's grip on survival.

The contents of the folder were far worse than he'd anticipated and the details threatened to overcome his new-found strength. He read the overview section and then studied the figures. With a grimace, he put it back on it desk.

CHAPTER TWO

THE SOUND of his door opening caused him to look up. There weren't many people allowed access to his office and in this case, the new arrival was his wife.

"John - I thought I'd find you here."

"Where else would I be?"

"In bed, perhaps? Where I told you to go ten hours ago."

"There's no time for bed, Lucy."

"Cerys tells me you've been out to look at the *Earth's Fury*."

"I needed to clear my head."

"And?"

"Now it's clear."

"You're worried about something."

"I've just received the latest Projections Team update on the *ES Determinant*. They reckon there's a 92.3% chance the Vraxar have cracked the static arrays."

"How the hell did they come up with that? Wasn't it only 31-point-something percent last week?"

"The information we have on *Ix-Gorghal* suggests it has

vastly greater processing capabilities than anything else in the Vraxar fleet."

"You look like you've already lost."

"You know I'll never accept defeat. It would be nice if there was some good news for a change. How many people are there in the Confederation? Nearly four hundred billion at last count, and every single one of them could be dead within the year. Within months. It's a lot to bear."

His wife was definitely the only person allowed to sit in his seat, and she did just that, leaning back with her hands behind her head in mimic of Duggan's thinking pose. She grinned suddenly, unexpectedly, reminding him there was more to his existence than presiding over endless death.

"What are you going to do about it?" she asked.

"We need to find the Vraxar and kill the bastards."

"That's the sum of your thoughts so far? What happened to the John Duggan who was never short of a plan?"

"It's been hard these last three weeks," he admitted. "I'm ashamed I didn't figure out what was wrong sooner. Atlantis had a hold on me. And then this new information from the Projections Team."

She studied him carefully, understanding exactly what he meant. "Is the hold gone? Are you ready to guide the Space Corps? You're the best they've ever had."

"I'm not the best. That was Malachi and always will be. He could wrap a plan within a plan and if those failed, he'd have a dozen viable backups waiting to take their place."

Lucy Duggan's dark eyes gleamed dangerously. "Admiral Teron had Captain John Nathan Duggan at his disposal. Without you, those plans would have come to nothing."

"Maybe. I try not to think about it too much."

"You were never a good liar."

"No."

"The Vraxar are coming, John, and you're the only one who can stop them."

He ended his pacing and leaned against his desk, rubbing one stubbled cheek. He started counting off on his fingers. "We've got two – possibly unstoppable - Vraxar capital ships somewhere in Confederation space. We don't know where they are or when they'll put in another appearance, but it seems likely they'll come for our planets one at a time. In order to stand any sort of chance, we need to find them before they find us."

"Tell me how to find the Vraxar," she prompted.

"We have a fairly good idea of their aims now. They want to convert humanity into Vraxar, they want to destroy the Ghasts and then they want to move onto the next species on their list."

"The Antaron."

"So we believe. I've spoken with my officers about all of this, without being able to figure out a way to put our guesswork to good use."

"Their main fleet is still in Estral space. Won't their priority be to bring them here? Perhaps they can open another wormhole or something. Their fleet is surely more important to them than anything else. If they know where our planets are, they don't need to rush."

There were several other wormholes in Confederation Space, each of which had been traversed several times during the last four decades. As far as it was possible to tell, none of them led to populated areas of the universe. The only certain thing was that the other ends of these wormholes were so far distant they rendered the Space Corps' star charts useless.

"They can't simply open another wormhole anywhere they choose. In theory, they could make another attempt to reopen the Helius Blackstar."

"Which they haven't done."

"We have Obsidiar bombs ready to deploy."

"I'm not convinced that's enough to put them off," said his wife.

"I agree. It seems more likely they don't have another Gate Maker, which is why they haven't tried again."

"You'd imagine they'd carry a few around with them, considering how important it is for the Vraxar to keep moving."

"They've been travelling for a long time and they've come a long way. Perhaps they've lost them through attrition."

His wife had the familiar serious expression which indicated she was thinking hard about something. "Don't you ever wonder how they achieved this?"

"Achieved what?"

"Everything we know indicates they have spent hundreds or more years going from place to place, killing as they go. Yet...they never once saw the need to make use of the captured ships of their enemies. Where do they get their resources from? How have they survived the constant whittling away at their fleet, particularly against the Estral?"

"They could turn out dozens of ships every year from *Ix-Gorghal* alone."

"What happens when they run out of Gallenium or Obsidiar?"

"Are you suggesting they have a home world, somewhere out there?"

"I don't know. You might be right – they could simply plunder each race they conquer and store a hundred trillion tonnes of raw materials in their capital ships."

"It would be another limitation which would have the effect of providing impetus to their progress."

"Have you tried contacting the Antaron?" she asked.

"It's not a risk I am willing to take. I am old enough to assume every species out there is as hostile as the next one."

"What if there's an exception?"

"It makes no difference – we don't know where to aim our broadcast. Even if we did, I still wouldn't sanction it."

"The enemy of my enemy is still my enemy, huh?"

"Show me evidence to the contrary and I'll generate you lunch from the replicator outside."

She laughed. "I already ate." The smile faded quickly. "Maybe it's time we did the same as the Estral. Put as many people as we can on our Interstellars and head out into the depths."

"We don't have nearly the capacity with our existing fleet and I think we've run out of time to lay down new hulls."

"I can see it in your eyes – you think it would be a declaration of failure."

"There's always a time to run – we did it often enough in the past. The trouble is, you reach a point where you can't run any more. When the enemy reach your door, it's time to fight with everything you have."

"The rules don't apply when the enemy are firing missiles through your window from forty thousand klicks."

There was little useful to add to the conversation and Duggan reclaimed his chair.

"Time for me to go?"

"I've got a lot to do."

His wife left the office and Duggan returned to business. He took a deep breath before issuing his next orders.

"Cerys, please make the information contained in report 23-13d available to everyone of appropriate rank. Afterwards, I want you to ensure every warship and every planetary base, every defence emplacement is on maximum alert."

It took the Cerys node of the Tucson base a few seconds to acknowledge. By the time it spoke again, the sound of the Tucson siren was already audible through the thick panes of Duggan's window.

"Your orders have been disseminated and I have received confirmation from each warship in our fleet."

"Good. Please cancel all scheduled leave, except where the reason is related to health or bereavement."

"Done."

"I would like the Confederation Council to be aware. As soon as they learn about it, my communicator is going to light up. Please make sure I am not interrupted."

"Is that wise, Fleet Admiral?"

Cerys didn't usually offer advice, and Duggan hoped it wasn't about to go through another of its funny periods.

"Allow me to make that decision, Cerys. After you are finished, I would like you to connect me with Subjos Kion-Tur."

"Certainly."

Duggan found himself becoming increasingly at ease with his Ghast counterpart. It wasn't long until an image of Kion-Tur appeared on one of the desktop viewscreens. The presence of screens and consoles in the background suggested the alien was onboard one of his fleet's Oblivion battleships.

"What can I do for you, Fleet Admiral Duggan?" rumbled the Ghast.

"Have your warships reported any new sightings of the Vraxar?"

"There has been nothing in the thirty minutes since we last updated the Helius database."

"We believe there is a high chance the enemy have unravelled the contents of the *Determinant*'s arrays."

"How high?"

"92%"

"That is high. Do you know the Vraxar's likely first target and have you ascertained their intentions?"

"We don't know where they will come or when. As for their intentions, death would be preferable to conversion."

"What action should we Ghasts take under the terms of our joint agreement?"

"I would like your warships to reinforce our planets. I will have my personal assistant send over relevant details."

"We will be spread thinly."

"There is no choice. I will not ask any captain to throw his ship at the enemy. We must do our best to engage cautiously and hope we can gather sufficient numbers to finish the bastards off."

"Very well. I will pass on the orders."

"There is something important you should make your captains aware of. If the Vraxar come to our worlds, there may come a time when we send notice concerning the activation of Last Stand. When that warning comes, your warships should enter lightspeed immediately."

Subjos Kion-Tur narrowed his eyes. "Very well. If we hear mention of Last Stand, we will break off any engagements and go to lightspeed."

"Thank you."

The Ghast's good humour returned at once. "No, Fleet Admiral Duggan! It is we who must thank *you* for this opportunity to crush the maggot-like Vraxar. We will succeed where the Estral did not and the annals of history will record our victory!"

"I am glad we are no longer enemies, Kion-Tur."

"As am I. The universe will lay [*translation unclear: baskets of fruit*] at our feet once we have eradicated the Vraxar!"

Duggan ended the connection and turned his attention to the information on his desktop console. Status reports rolled up the main screen as each warship in the fleet provided updates on locations and new flight paths. The network of military bases throughout the Confederation were now running on Obsidiar backup power.

Sitting at his desk in his quiet office, it was difficult for Duggan to envisage the enormous activity his few simple words had triggered. *Maximum alert.* Those words meant there would be somewhat more than a million Space Corps personnel looking for guidance and direction. For the vast majority, this would be the first time they'd been asked to respond to such a command.

He rotated his chair in order to see out of the window – there were red lights visible amongst the artificial daylight which covered most of the base. Below, people ran to places unknown, and overloaded vehicles sped to their destinations along the crowded roads. The rain had started and it fell from the blackness of the sky, making patterns through the light and spattering the pavements at the end of its journey.

A shape rose into the sky, the vast, grey underside of an Imposition cruiser cast in relief against the darkness. The warship hung in the air for a second and then it accelerated, creating a series of hollow sonic booms, its immense engines exerting only a tiny fraction of their full thrust. It climbed vertically, gaining speed at an increasing rate as it left the Tucson base far below.

Moments after the cruiser was gone from sight, the first of the four Crimson class destroyers rose from the ground. The second followed and the third, until every one of the parked warships was in the sky, ready to face whatever might come. Duggan closed his eyes, wishing he was with them.

It was not to be, and with a gentle push of one foot on the floor, he propelled the chair into a full rotation until he was once again facing his desk. The communicator was covered in red lights – seventy admirals and members of the Confederation Council who wanted to speak to him. His brain selected one at random – Admiral Tamiko Kruger – and his finger moved towards the comms button.

"Research Lead Marion Norris requests entry into your office," said Cerys.

Duggan's finger stopped.

"What does she want?"

"She says it's important. Very important. The feed from your door sensor suggests she is in a state of great distress."

Duggan withdrew his finger from the communicator. Marion Norris was the second most senior member of the Projections Team and he had a good idea what she was here for.

"Let her in."

The door opened and RL Norris spilled through the opening. She was young, pretty and blessed with wild hair and a brain that could solve certain types of theoretical mathematical conundrums faster than an Obsidiar processor. Duggan had seen her do it – it was like the answers just popped into her head. Norris carried a brown folder, from which sheets of ill-arranged paper protruded. She was flustered and she stumbled across the floor towards Duggan.

"You don't need to bother with greetings, just tell me the facts," said Duggan.

"We ran the *ES Determinant* numbers again, sir. The chance of a data harvest went past 100 percent ten minutes ago. They know where to find us."

"92% was enough to make me issue a Confederation-wide full-scale alert, RL Norris."

"I realise that, sir," she said, still trying to catch her breath.

"Now you're going to tell me you've put a percentage to something additional. Something I don't want to hear."

"Sorry, sir. The modelling we use required a 100% certainty before it could begin populating the second stage."

Duggan was aware of the prediction model's second stage – once it had achieved certainty on stage one it could begin guessing at the Vraxar's first target.

"Where are they going to show up?"

The answer was exactly what he'd expected. Duggan was a man whose entire life had been a series of progressively higher, thicker walls for him to climb over or simply break his way through. It appeared as though fate wasn't done playing tricks on him, even in his later years. *Death always wins.*

"Here, sir. We expect the Vraxar will come here to New Earth. I have derived the percentages and created a table for you to look at."

"Thank you, RL Norris, that won't be necessary."

The voice of Cerys intruded upon the meeting and there was an urgency to the tones which Duggan had never heard before.

"Fleet Admiral, the Retulon base reports the arrival of an unidentified vessel in New Earth orbit. I recommend you follow emergency protocols and make for your command bunker."

The words sunk in like the serrated claws of a wild animal through the still-living flesh of its prey. Just hours ago, Duggan had been filled with new energy to face the Vraxar threat. In a short time, that optimism had been torn up, shredded and rubbed in his face as a mockery of his efforts to bend the future to his will. Far from being bowed by this new calamity, Duggan found himself laughing in bitter defiance. Whatever twists fate planned for him, he would meet them head-on and do whatever it took to come out on top.

Death might always win, but it's damned well going to happen when I choose it.

"What was that, sir?" asked Norris.

The question was nearly as shocking to Duggan as everything else which had happened. *She can almost hear me think.*

"Nothing, RL Norris. We're under attack. Do you know the routine?"

She nodded and hurried from the office, leaving the folder behind her.

"Cerys, order Tucson ground personnel to the shelters. Then, get me through to Colonel Stinson on the Retulon base."

"The comms link is down, Fleet Admiral."

"Is it the link or have the Vraxar destroyed the base already?"

"I don't know the answer to that."

"Find out and tell me, damnit!"

There was something wrong with Cerys. The voice of his personal assistant suddenly became much slower, as if there was something chewing up so many of the node's processing cycles it had none left to formulate a response.

"I...will...keep...."

"What is happening?" he asked, knowing it was a waste of breath.

As he anticipated, there was no further response from his personal assistant. Whatever was affecting Cerys was also working on his desktop console. The real time updates on the screens slowed to a crawl and then stopped entirely. He tried to access another of the base's many processing nodes, this time on a separate core cluster. The result was the same.

There was a muted pounding on his office door, the sound of fists striking thick, dense metal. Duggan ordered it to open. Outside was his security team, fully armed and dressed in protective suits. Lieutenant Tom Richards was with them and from his manner he wasn't in the mood to argue, even with the most senior officer in the Space Corps.

"Sir, we're leaving. Now."

It looked as if the short war was already entering its final phase and Duggan had no idea what the next hours would bring. He nodded at Richards and allowed himself to be led away from his office and towards the secure bunker many hundreds of metres below the surface. The bunker wouldn't help him if the Vraxar did the same to New Earth as they did to Atlantis, but if they planned a longer visit it might buy him the time needed to have a say over what was coming.

CHAPTER THREE

THE MOOD WAS SOMBRE on the bridge of the Galactic class heavy cruiser *ES Lucid*. The air was cold, the lights slightly too bright and the crew said little. The deep fission engines thrummed, their soothing sound completely at odds with the urgency of the situation. Captain Charlie Blake paged through status reports from the warship's critical systems, killing time rather than doing anything useful.

A few minutes after the system-wide comms alert had gone out ordering them into a state of battle-readiness, the reports of *Ix-Gorghal*'s arrival at New Earth had come through. There were more than thirty Space Corps warships stationed in or around the planet, and the *Lucid* was amongst a small group of others which were a short lightspeed distance away.

Blake had checked the records – each and every one of his crew had family on New Earth, himself included. There were more than one hundred soldiers in their quarters below and sixty of those also had family. New Earth was a big planet – easily the most populous in the Hyptron Sector - and many people could trace their history back there. In the circumstances, it was incredible how well they were keeping it together.

"How long until we enter local space?" he asked. The countdown timer was on a screen in front of him, but he felt an urge to break the silence.

"Less than one hour, sir," said Lieutenant Jake Quinn.

"It should only take a few seconds for our databanks to receive the newest information once we exit lightspeed," said Lieutenant Caz Pointer.

The ship's systems couldn't update during lightspeed travel and it was usual practice to have a series of short breaks on the way in order to establish a connection to the Space Corps network.

"Then we can be on our way for the final ten-minute leg of the journey," said Quinn.

"I hate the waiting," said Blake. "I could handle it in the past. Now it's the worst part."

"I've never liked waiting," said Lieutenant Dixie Hawkins. "Particularly when I know the end of the waiting will see me dumped face-first into a heap of crap."

"I wonder how our fleet is getting on," said Pointer.

"Best not to think about it," said Quinn.

Blake didn't usually tolerate overt expressions of pessimism, but today wasn't a day for pretence.

"They'll hold back until they believe they have a chance to score a kill."

"What happened to sending in the damage soaks and following up with overwhelming numbers?" asked Hawkins.

"That was in the days when your enemy warships weren't the size of a small moon." Blake thumped his clenched fist down hard on the arm of his seat. The padding denied him the distraction of pain and he growled in frustration. "I can't see a way out of this."

"The Ghasts will help, won't they?" asked Pointer. "Imagine what three or four Particle Disruptors will do to *Ix-Gorghal*'s shields."

"The Ghasts have plenty of battleships, however I don't think they're all equipped with Particle Disruptors. The *Sciontrar* was new, and the Kalon-T7 with it."

"Well just damned incendiaries then!" said Pointer, showing the depths of her own frustration. "There's got to be something that can bring down *Ix-Gorghal*'s shield."

"Ideally, something with more finesse than detonating an Obsidiar bomb next to one of our home worlds," said Quinn.

"They won't let a bomb off, will they?" asked Pointer. She, at least, hadn't yet given up hope. It was early days yet.

"There's only one on New Earth," said Blake quietly. "That's classified information, by the way. I don't think it matters anymore."

"Can they launch this bomb?"

"It's not designed for launch, Lieutenant. I'm not even sure if it's ready yet."

"If it's not designed for launch, what did they hope to do with it?" asked Pointer. "Drop it from a heavy lifter onto the enemy shields?"

"It's called Benediction. A bomb designed to save us even as it turns us to cinder."

The meaning wasn't lost on any of them.

"They'd really do that?" asked Hawkins.

"There may be no option, Lieutenant. Which alternative would you prefer?"

Hawkins sniffed and Blake realised she was close to tears. "I was hoping it wouldn't come to this. That we'd somehow find a way."

"Don't write us off yet." He hesitated, wondering if it was worthwhile giving them false hope. "We have *Earth's Fury*."

"What's a deep space monitoring station going to do for us?" asked Quinn.

"That's what they're pretending it is these days?" said Blake. "It's not a monitoring station – it's an Obsidiar gun, designed to fire unstable Obsidiar projectiles at near-light speeds."

"Will they use it against *Ix-Gorghal*? Can we expect to receive the all-clear when we enter local space?"

"It's not ready yet," said Blake. "It's close. Maybe they can get it operational in time to give us some support when we attack the enemy."

"Forgive me if I don't sound too enthused, sir," said Hawkins. "If it's unfinished, I assume it's on the ground and if it's on the ground, then it needs a firing angle to hit the enemy. The chance of that happening seems remote."

"Well, it's something," Blake replied. "It's better than triggering Last Stand."

"Last Stand?" asked Pointer. She narrowed her eyes. "You mean there's an Obsidiar bomb on every Confederation planet?"

"Yes, there is. Benediction was the last to be signed off, the others are ready to detonate."

"Shit luck for humanity," said Hawkins.

"Shit luck for the Vraxar," Blake replied. "They've found a species which is willing to take whatever action is necessary to ensure either victory or mutual destruction."

Pointer didn't look assured. "Will Benediction be enough to kill the Vraxar at the same time as it kills us and destroys our planet? Or will we simply be killing ourselves in order to avoid conversion? *Ix-Gorghal*'s shield was strong enough to withstand the destruction of Atlantis."

"I don't have the answers you're looking for, Lieutenant. I wish that I did."

"We're guessing, sir. We need more than guessing."

"You know more about Fleet Admiral Duggan than I do, Lieutenant. Is he a man who likes to guess?"

Pointer slumped in her seat. "No. Not according to the records, he isn't."

"In that case, you need to rely on history to make your judgement about the present." He waited until he caught her eye. "And maybe you need to rely on your crew to pull something out of the bag. We've done it before."

She opened her mouth to respond. The anger was gone and she kept the words to herself. Blake trusted his opinion of her and was sure she'd channel her hatred of the Vraxar into action when the time came.

The minutes ticked away and the seconds followed. The countdown timer reached zero and the *ES Lucid* ripped through into local space, entering an area of Confederation territory which was devoid of planets or any other notable features. The near and far scans were a priority and Pointer finished up quickly. The Space Corps number crunchers were sure the Vraxar had only a handful of warships left in human-held space, so the chance of a random engagement was infinitesimally small.

While Pointer did her job on the sensors, Blake prepared to sift through the expected flood of new information, keeping his fingers crossed there'd be a team working to issue summary data and save him from the hours it would take to separate out the chaff. It wasn't looking good.

"There's still no contact with New Earth," he said. "Nothing in, nothing out."

"Another Neutraliser? I thought we got the last one," said Hawkins.

"We *think* we got the last one in Confederation Space," Blake corrected her. "This doesn't look like a Neutraliser, so much as a total comms lockdown."

"*Ix-Gorghal* did that to us before," said Quinn, remembering the time the Vraxar capital ship had kept the *ES Abyss* and the Ghast battleship *Sciontrar* held in a stasis beam. The Vraxar had blocked communications using an unknown technology.

"Lieutenant Pointer figured out a way to reach the *Sciontrar*," said Hawkins.

"That was a very slow signal," said Pointer. "It was fast enough for our needs. It wouldn't travel fast enough for interplanetary communication."

"What about the fleet?" asked Hawkins suddenly. "Have we heard from the New Earth fleet?"

Blake continued reading, his eyes skimming over a series of reports whilst his chest constricted until it was an effort to suck in the chill air. "They're gone," he said, his voice hollow.

"Destroyed?"

"I don't know. None of the local defence fleet is showing up on the Space Corps network."

"You're shitting us?" said Quinn in disbelief.

"I thought they were meant to sit back and observe?" said Pointer. "What the hell were they playing at?"

"We don't know what happened, Lieutenant. It could be that *Ix-Gorghal* has a hundred warships in its hold, or it may have simply forced a confrontation."

"What are we going to do?" asked Quinn.

"We're going to find out who's running the show and we're going to speak to them."

"Admiral Morey on Prime is dealing with fleet orders, sir."

"Can you reach her?"

"She's busy."

It was understandable and Blake didn't want to put his foot in the door just to ask how things were going when it was clear everything had gone to shit. Instead, he applied himself to figuring out how he could put the ES *Lucid* to best use in order that he could bring his recommendations to Admiral Morey when it was his turn to speak.

"We're at the vanguard, folks," he said. "The next warship after us is due in six hours."

"Six hours?" asked Hawkins. "Why so long?"

"The fleet is spread out, Lieutenant, with most of our ships assigned to a specific world. It leaves fewer floaters to call upon. We've prepared as well as possible, but anticipating where the Vraxar would strike was always going to be a struggle."

"What about the Ghasts?"

"Checking...the next ship is actually a Ghast vessel." Blake laughed with disbelief. "Well I'll be - it's the *Sciontrar*. Tarjos Nil-Tras will be positively ecstatic to have another go at the Vraxar."

"And I'll be positively ecstatic to have a Ghast Oblivion flying with us," said Hawkins.

"I'd trade it in for another ten," said Quinn.

"We can't sit here for six hours," said Blake. "We've got stealth modules and they fitted fission suppression units when they fixed the *Lucid* up after our first encounter on Atlantis."

"The stealth units didn't help us much last time," said Hawkins. "Sixteen of the fleet at New Earth had them too."

"We don't know what happened to the fleet. If they were required to fight, they'd have revealed themselves to the enemy. We need to act."

It had been hard work in the past for Blake to persuade his crew that he wasn't an over-confident glory-seeker. He felt he'd finally got them on side and earned their trust. He tried to gauge their reactions and was pleased to find there were no signs of doubt at his determination to act.

"Well someone's got to do something," said Hawkins.

"We've got to the front of Admiral Morey's comms queue, sir. It doesn't sound like she's in the mood for small talk."

Blake waved his hand in acknowledgement and Pointer brought Morey through. The comms channel carried the background noise of many people in a state of near-panic as the personnel on Prime tried to bring some measure of control to the situation.

"Admiral Morey, we are unable to see the New Earth defence fleet on our network and I have read the early, worrying reports."

Morey had the clipped tones of a person who was naturally short of patience. She spoke brusquely. "Those warships are gone, Captain Blake. Destroyed to the last, as far as we know."

The confirmation drove home the enormity of the loss.

"How?"

"The enemy vessel initiated hostile action, directed at New Earth. We could not allow them to proceed without responding. Our hand was forced."

"What about New Earth? What kind of hostile action?"

"We don't know exactly. *Ix-Gorghal* began deploying a series of craft into New Earth's upper atmosphere."

Blake breathed out. "They didn't destroy it."

"Not yet, Captain Blake. I think we can safely assume they haven't come to party."

"Did we achieve anything with the attack on *Ix-Gorghal*?"

"We don't have a lot of intel. We're working on the assumption the enemy is fully operational. I have ordered Monitoring Station Sigma to turn its lenses towards New Earth. The recalibration will take several hours to complete and then we will have a way to track the Vraxar activity."

"What weapons did *Ix-Gorghal* use against our warships? Did we learn anything about its capabilities?"

Morey gave a short, barking laugh. "Overwhelming firepower

and a shield that can absorb a hundred thousand conventional missiles."

"Did the nukes work?"

"No. The enemy shield generators are either unaffected by gamma radiation or the radius of the shield is such that our warheads can't detonate close enough to shut it down. Either way, we're screwed."

"Admiral Morey, I would like to bring the ES *Lucid* out of lightspeed a suitable distance from New Earth in order to act as a remote observer of the Vraxar."

"That's a negative - we can't afford to throw our fleet piece-meal at the enemy. I am in the process of pulling together a new fleet from those stationed elsewhere. We will join with the Ghasts and act according to circumstances."

"How long will that take? And what do you mean *according to circumstances*?"

"The travel time to New Earth from Truth, Prime and Old Earth is several days. The *Maximilian* and *Devastator* are preparing to leave for a new rendezvous point, along with eleven Galactics and twenty Impositions, plus destroyers. We can't risk stripping away any more from the defence of these other worlds."

Blake shook his head angrily. "Several days? There'll be nobody left to save when they get here!"

Morey adopted the knowing tones of someone talking with a wayward child. "And what exactly do you propose, Captain Blake? Should we throw more ships after those we've lost? Or should we take stock and provide a measured response on our own terms?"

"The enemy is here and now, Admiral!" Blake felt realisation thunder into him like a right hook from a champion boxer. "You've given up on New Earth."

There wasn't a hint of shame in Morey's voice when she

responded. "Our intel suggests New Earth is a lost cause. This battle is already over, Captain. There will be another."

"The new fleet isn't coming?"

"It will remain in the Origin Sector to defend our home worlds. One of my team is sending coordinates to your navigational system. You will leave your current location and travel at maximum lightspeed to join with Defence Fleet Epsilon."

Blake was shocked to his core. "You don't have the authority to abandon New Earth, Admiral."

"Fleet Admiral Duggan is not available to command. It falls to me to make these difficult decisions."

"Does the Confederation Council know?"

"Enough! The decision is made, Captain Blake. You will bring the ES *Lucid* to the rendezvous point. That's an order! Do I need to make it any clearer?"

"No Admiral, I hear you well enough."

"Good. You will receive further orders once you reach your destination."

The comms channel went dead and the sudden absence of background chatter from Admiral Morey's office made the *Lucid*'s bridge as quiet as a morgue.

"She can't do this!" Blake roared, breaking the silence like a hammer blow against a glass pane. "Of all the stupid, cowardly, idiotic things!" He stood and kicked at the unyielding metal side plating on his console.

"We can't give up on New Earth," said Hawkins, shaking her head in shock.

"I know that!" shouted Blake in fury. He closed his eyes and took a series of slow, deep breaths, while the crew watched. "I'm sorry, Lieutenant. I should not have directed my own anger towards you."

"Don't worry about it, sir."

"We've received the coordinates for Defence Fleet Epsilon,

sir," said Pointer. "It's kind of at an intersection between Old Earth, Truth, Charing and Prime."

Blake sat for a time, resting his chin in the palm of one hand.

"Sir?" asked Quinn. "Would you like me to warm up the fission engines?"

"Who wants to join the defence fleet?" asked Blake.

"We've been ordered, sir," said Quinn.

"I know it was an order. Who wants to join the defence fleet?"

"I'd feel like a coward," said Pointer.

"Me too," said Hawkins.

Quinn wavered. "If we go to New Earth is there anything we can do, given that an entire fleet got shot down?"

"We won't know if we don't take a look," said Hawkins.

"I suppose there's a lot more at stake than our careers," Quinn replied with a nervous smile.

"Any objections to us seeing what we can do to help the people of New Earth?" asked Blake.

"I guess not," said Pointer.

"I always liked the rain," added Hawkins.

Blake nodded at his crew in turn. Ensigns Toby Park and Charlotte Bailey kept their heads down. In a way, Blake felt sorry for them – he'd put them in a really bad position. The reality was, they'd signed up to a job which would put their lives at risk and this was what it came to.

"Take us to New Earth, Lieutenant Quinn. Make sure the fission suppression system is working when we arrive and don't bring us in too close."

"Yes, sir. I'm preparing the jump."

It was a comparatively short journey and the *ES Lucid*'s processing cores made quick work of the computations. The heavy cruiser re-entered lightspeed, heading towards New Earth. With his course set, Blake didn't waste energy asking himself if he was doing the right thing. There was an excellent chance he'd be court-martialled for this, even if the Confederation Council adjudged Admiral Morey to have exceeded her authority. There were some things more important than a career and a gold-plated watch at the end of it.

The *ES Lucid* flew on into the unknown.

CHAPTER FOUR

FLEET ADMIRAL DUGGAN was blessed with eyesight which showed no signs of degeneration. This perfection of his physical vision meant it was all the more difficult to cope with the blindness he was experiencing in the bunker beneath the Tucson military base. It made a change for the power to be running freely during a Vraxar attack and the thousands of high-tech control consoles in the facility gave every appearance they were fully-functional. Looks were deceiving and everything was running at a crawl. In addition, the Vraxar had completely locked down the comms – there were no messages in and no messages out.

Duggan felt caged and he strode about the main command and control room, occasionally stopping next to one of the operators to ask for an update. His personal team waited anxiously and offered ideas and suggestions where they thought it appropriate.

"Is there anyone here with good news?" he asked in exasperation.

He cast his eyes around the room. There were upwards of one hundred people inside – many of them technicians trying to get things running smoothly again - and not one of them dared meet his gaze.

"I do *not* want silence!" he shouted. "Someone tell me what we're doing to fix this! You!" he said, pointing at a random officer.

The bald-headed man swallowed. "Well, sir, we've successfully completed our emergency response procedure. Every one of the two thousand expected personnel are now in this bunker. We are attempting to find out if the rest of the base personnel are in the other bunkers. The lack of comms is making it difficult."

"You!" said Duggan, pointing at an older man in the far corner.

"We're trying to figure out what's eating the base mainframe processing cycles, Fleet Admiral. It's slowing everything down and there's a chance it may be part of what's holding up the comms."

"That's more like it!" said Duggan approvingly. "What are you doing to fix it?"

"I'm working with the comms hardware technicians to find out how to get a signal out. If there's a problem with the hardware, we might be able to switch in replacements from the stores. If it's software, we need to squirt in some new code to bring it back to normal. If it's something else entirely – something unknown..." he shrugged to show he didn't have any idea what this potential *something else* might be.

"Keep at it. You!" said Duggan. This time his finger aimed unerringly at a huddle of red-uniformed officers.

It was a grey-haired woman who answered. "We are collating data to build a picture of what's going on. This bunker is ancient and they never removed the hard links to the surface, so we can speak to certain other areas on the Tucson base. As you've been informed, there is still no sign of a Vraxar ground incursion."

The news only added to Duggan's sense that he was huddling away like a coward. He was wise enough to know the reality was rather more nuanced. Gone were the days when he was required to throw himself directly into the fray.

The officer he was speaking with appeared to know her stuff, so he pressed on.

"Where do these hard links go? Can we communicate with Retulon base, or connect with a piece of ancient hardware somewhere which isn't affected by the jamming? Maybe get a signal off world or to our defence fleet?"

"I don't know, sir. We've had about a thousand system upgrades since the last hard links were installed and now it's almost impossible to manually route a comms message. The comms hub does all the hard work."

"No manual routing? Who the hell was responsible for that decision?"

"It likely seemed a reasonable idea at the time, sir."

"Does this hard link reach the main comms hub on Tucson?"

"Yes, sir. I assume you want to find out what's coming through the sensors."

"That would be nice."

A man from the same huddle spoke up. "We've been getting a feed ever since we came down here, sir. The trouble is, the lack of spare processing resource from the base mainframe means we aren't receiving anything useful."

"Keep working on it and tell me as soon as anything changes." Duggan raised his voice. "The most important things I want to know are these. One: what are the Vraxar doing? Two: what happened to the New Earth defence fleet?"

Once again there was silence.

"Find out and tell me!" he roared.

The activity in the room increased markedly at this demonstration of fury. In the centre of it, Duggan seethed. It felt like a game of chess where the opponent had already declared checkmate in three. He beckoned over a few members of his team and also Research Lead Marion Norris who had accompanied him into the bunker. Without further word, he took one of the passages leading from the command and control room, with the others following.

"At least the damn doors work," he said.

Parts of the Tucson bunker were more than two hundred years old. The Space Corps had kept it up-to-date when it came to technology, but the place still reeked of age. After years of service on fleet warships, with their tight corridors and claustrophobic rooms, Duggan felt at home and the dull thump of his footsteps on the metal-tiled floor gave him solace. His anger slipped away, leaving the cold, calculating part of his mind spinning, seeking the traction which would generate a plan of some kind.

The destination wasn't far. He glanced once over his shoulder and saw the nervous expressions on the faces of several of his team as if they feared being so far beneath the surface. *Are we getting soft?* came the unbidden question in his mind.

Duggan knew it was unfair to judge – the Confederation had been at peace for a long time and gradually the Space Corps began attracting people who expected a comfortable life, safe in their offices, with a food replicator at the end of the corridor and the certainty of a warm bed at the end of it. Duggan had tried to keep them tough with regular off-world training exercises, but he was fighting the inevitable. The three Fleet Admirals proceeding him had been little more than mouthpieces for the Confederation Council, only too willing to accept cutbacks and to introduce new lines of research with no benefit to the war fleet.

Part of Duggan longed for the old days – longed for them more than anything. His brain reminded him how conflicted he'd been back then and how much he'd craved the quiet life at the same time as he brought death to his enemies. A smile tugged the reluctant corner of his mouth upwards. *I've always been too old to fool myself.*

"Is my wife settled?" he asked.

"Yes, sir," answered Lieutenant Charissa Paz.

"Did she give you a hard time?"

"She was reluctant to accept assistance, sir. She's probably clocked more flight hours than I've lived. I can understand it."

Paz was easy company, competent, and with a dry sense of humour which never overstepped the mark.

"I'll speak to her later," he said with a chuckle.

"If she doesn't hunt you down first, sir."

They located a meeting room and Duggan's head swum when he saw the number on the door.

"Is there any meeting room throughout this entire organisation that isn't numbered 73?"

"I am not aware of any specific directive which insists upon conformity, sir," said Paz.

"My whole life seems to be spent in meeting rooms with the same damned number on the door."

"Confirmation bias, sir."

Duggan pressed the access panel and the door opened, allowing him across the threshold. "Is that what it is?"

The meeting room was a fairly standard affair, with a wood-veneer square table and mismatched chairs, suggesting they'd been borrowed in the past and the wrong ones returned. There were one or two pictures on the wall, mercifully devoid of motivational exclamations. There was a large viewscreen in the far wall and several desktop communicators. Duggan had seen images of such rooms from eight hundred years ago and the basic layout hadn't changed. He felt a passing shame that he'd been Fleet Admiral for so long yet had failed to instigate a programme of improvements. It was way down the priorities list.

His chosen seat scraped roughly across the floor when he

pulled it out. His staff followed his lead and Duggan found himself facing their expectant faces. He was sitting opposite some of the brightest human minds in the universe, but in this conflict, they were lost children.

Duggan got the ball rolling.

"Well folks, we're in the shit."

"I'm glad I'm not the only one thinking it," said Lieutenant Allison Jacobs.

"I'm going to run through the main problems and after that, I'll be grateful to hear anything you might have to say and I don't care if you think it's foolish or if it subsequently turns out to be foolish."

"Blue sky thinking," said Paz with a twinkle in her eye, knowing Duggan passionately hated buzzwords.

"Thank you, Lieutenant. The situation isn't so parlous that I won't dismiss you from my staff if it becomes necessary."

"Yes, sir."

"As I was saying, we're knee deep in it," Duggan continued. "We're comms blind and we don't have any way to find out what the enemy are up to. However, these are the Vraxar, so we can be sure their aim is to kill us. The more we learn about how they intend to achieve that, the greater our chances of stopping them."

He paused to let the words sink in. He didn't need to spell out that a *greater chance* still meant there was effectively no chance at all. He continued.

"We don't know what happened to our fleet. There were thirty-two vessels in New Earth's upper atmosphere, with three Galactics amongst them. I would dearly like to know what the man in charge - Admiral Nathaniel Bunch - is planning. Without comms, I have no way to give instructions."

"There is an eighty-three percent chance the fleet is destroyed, sir," said Research Lead Norris, her eyes staring into the distance.

"You modelled that in your head?"

She smiled unhappily. "It just came to me now, sir."

Every fibre of Duggan's being wanted the New Earth defence fleet to have beaten the odds. He'd worked with the Projections Team for so long he couldn't easily discount Norris's conclusion. He swore and crashed his fists onto the table top with such ferocity, a few of the others jumped.

"Sorry, sir," said Norris.

The possibility of the defence fleet's destruction was something Duggan had already considered, yet never allowed himself to think of as a high probability. In his mind, the Space Corps warships were conducting a series of careful hit-and-run sorties against *Ix-Gorghal*, keeping the Vraxar distracted and buying time for Admiral Morey to organize a large-scale response. The notion all thirty-two warships were gone was more than he could bear and Duggan bowed his head for several minutes.

Eventually, he settled himself and raised his head.

"It's not something to apologise for, RL Norris," he said. "What other possibilities have you considered?"

"Nothing yet." Norris lifted her palms upwards in a gesture of uncertainty. "I don't have much control. I guess some part of my mind thinks about stuff away from my consciousness. Every so often, I get an answer, sometimes to a question I wasn't aware I'd asked."

Duggan was keen to keep the meeting on track, but he couldn't help pursuing this diversion.

"Don't you even use a computer? I thought that's how the Projections Team worked – the computer did the maths and you applied a humanness to the results."

"Sometimes that's what happens. A few of us just see the answers and use a computer to record them or to obtain a second opinion on what we already worked out." She looked scared. "You're not going to put me in a lab for study, are you?"

41

"It's hardly the time, RL Norris. If we get out of this alive, we'll speak further, but I promise nothing will happen without your agreement." He put the matter to one side and addressed his staff. "If the fleet is gone, our options are limited to say the least. Now, tell me your ideas."

"We should attempt to make contact with Retulon, sir," said Lieutenant Joe Doyle. "I used to work on comms hardware and I'll bet there are still three or four intact hard links under the sea. The Pilast, Lander and Rion bases should be hard linked as well."

"What benefits does it bring to reach these other bases?" asked Duggan. "There were two warships docked at Retulon and three more in early-stage construction. I assume the *Spinebreaker* and *Meteor* were lost along with the rest of the fleet. The others were little more than empty hulls and weren't due for completion until early next year."

"We need intel, sir," said Paz. "We don't know what the hell is happening and it would be nice if we weren't so much in the dark."

"It still feels as if we're focusing on the little details," mused Duggan. "Let's say we establish comms with Colonel Stinson at Retulon and he tells us some things. We still don't have a way to respond against the Vraxar."

"What if they tell us the Vraxar are killing everyone?" asked Jacobs.

The question hung in the air for a time. Eventually Duggan acknowledged it with a grunt.

"You're right, Lieutenant. We should prepare for the possible use of Benediction. Where is it now?"

"I don't think anyone knows, sir," said Lieutenant Jacqui Gallant. "It was in transit when the Vraxar came. There's a chance the responsible team continued with their orders and finished the operation or are in the process of doing so."

"Or it could be sitting out there on the landing field somewhere," said Duggan. He had another thought. "I'm the only one with the codes to detonate it."

Jacobs guessed what he was leading to. "Except you can't make the command remotely since the comms aren't working. You'd need to be at the panel on the bomb itself."

Lieutenant Doyle wasn't part of the team who got a full briefing on the details of Last Stand. "Doesn't this need multiple codes to activate?" he asked.

"No, Lieutenant. I'm the only one with the code for all of the bombs."

"Isn't that a bit...?"

"Yes, it is. The Confederation Council still haven't sorted their crap out. Once they do, I'll gladly share the burden with whoever they nominate. Until then, there's only me."

"My sympathies," said Doyle.

The words were genuine and Duggan acknowledged them. "I wish it were otherwise."

"It's too early to contemplate using Benediction. Isn't it?" said Paz.

"It's too early to use it, but definitely not too early to *contemplate* using it," said Duggan. "We need to locate the bomb and we require a plan that will allow me to access it at short notice if it becomes necessary."

"Will it take out *Ix-Gorghal*?" asked Doyle.

"We had a breakthrough a few hours before I signed off the construction orders for Benediction. Against my better judgement I allowed a series of design alterations to be included. The Obsidiar is unpredictable, however the weapons teams told me the detonation of Benediction will produce a blast sphere large enough to encompass the explosions of every other Obsidiar bomb we've ever made."

Doyle gave a low whistle. "There'll be no pain when it goes off, then?"

"You won't feel a thing, Lieutenant. More importantly, you won't experience a thousand years in the hold of a Vraxar ship with a metal bar in your spine and a collar around your neck."

"I'd still rather explore other avenues that might lead to my living through this crap," said Paz.

"Of course, Lieutenant. We're simply discussing our options."

"Good, because as far as I was aware, we still have a Hadron battleship and a mobile Obsidiar cannon sitting out there."

"Neither of which is finished, and both of which are easy targets for an aerial bombardment if the Vraxar choose to do so." Realising he was being far too negative, Duggan went on. "They're both close to completion and there's a chance they might fly."

"Great, let's get them warmed up," said Paz.

Paz was fully aware it wasn't as easy as flipping a switch and having the two spaceships ready to go.

"The *Ulterior-2* is missing one of its main engine modules," said Duggan. "They were bringing it in on a crawler this afternoon. There's a chance they got it fitted, but no way they got the plating on top. As for *Earth's Fury*, there're still five weeks remaining on the programme. I don't know what the hell it's missing – they don't even have the life support units tied in. One thing is for definite – it's got no ammunition, since that's in the secure Obsidiar Storage Facility."

"Problem on top of problem," said Paz. "At least we know what's ahead of us."

"We need to find the Obsidiar bomb, figure out a way to put an experimental gun into operation and then fire it at the biggest damn warship humanity has ever faced," said Duggan. For some reason, laughter seemed the only possible response to the difficulties. He tried and found it came easier than expected.

The whoosh of the meeting room door caused everyone in

the room to turn. A man came in - it was one of the technicians from the command and control room who'd been working to identify the cause of the Tucson processing cluster slowdown. Duggan couldn't recall the man's name and didn't know if he'd ever been told. What was abundantly clear was that this technician was about to deliver some bad news.

I should have known better than to laugh, Duggan thought sourly.

"What is it?" he asked with greater anger than intended.

"We've managed to get the sensors working better than before, sir. There's an old mainframe in this bunker – fifty years old it is and it still works – and it seems to be shielded from whatever the Vraxar are doing to the main cluster. We managed to tap into it and…"

The man was babbling and Duggan interrupted him.

"I can see this is important. Please get to the point."

"Yes, sir. The Vraxar have put satellites in orbit. We don't know exactly how many - we're limited by line of sight since the comms links to our own satellites are offline. What we *do* know is that these alien satellites are doing something to the New Earth atmosphere."

This was it. Duggan could tell he was about to learn something big about why the Vraxar were here.

"What are they doing?"

"They're taking out the oxygen – burning it up, turning it into something else – we don't have specifics. We only just noticed. New Earth's atmosphere is usually 21.6% oxygen. Now it's 20.9%."

"There's no chance of error?"

"We triple-checked before I came, sir."

Lieutenant Jacobs recited some figures from her head. "At between 12 and 15% oxygen the human body doesn't work too well. Once it drops below 10%, that's when we start dying."

"How long?" asked Duggan.

The technician looked at his feet. "We don't know."

"Guess."

"Hours. Less than eight and more than four. Don't expect to do any running two or three hours from now."

"Thank you...?"

"Hampton, sir. Lead Technician Fred Hampton – Sensor Maintenance."

"Thank you, Lead Technician Hampton. When you return to your duties, tell the most senior officer you can find that I'm exceptionally displeased that they saw fit to leave it to you to bring me this news."

Hampton backed out of the room. "Yes, sir."

And that was it – the door closed leaving Duggan and his staff shifting in their chairs, desperately trying to think of something useful to say. The Vraxar *were* going to kill everyone in a way which would leave the bodies intact. The command bunker was sealed and self-sustaining, so there was no immediate threat to those inside. It wasn't much consolation – Duggan had no desire to hide away while billions died.

"Is this why they haven't attacked the base?" asked Paz.

"Yes, Lieutenant – it looks like they can do exactly what they want without bothering themselves to initiate a ground deployment."

"We should be pleased they don't know we have fifty percent of the Confederation's Obsidiar stashed away on Tucson."

Duggan requested silence in order that he could think more clearly. It didn't take long for him to understand the height of the mountain before them. If there was a way out of this, he didn't have any idea what it was.

CHAPTER FIVE

THE BRIDGE on the *Earth's Fury* was different to that of most other warships. It was fitted with later-model control consoles, four exceptionally comfortable chairs and a replicator which could produce food better than mother ever used to make. The lighting was perfect and the temperature was suitably cool, yet for some reason, it still felt rudimentary. Old, almost.

Perhaps it's the smell, thought Lieutenant Maria Cruz. There was an oiliness to the air. When she was young, her father had kept a couple of old combustion-engined motorbikes in his garage. He never managed to get them going, but it didn't stop him trying. The *Earth's Fury* had that same smell of oil-stained rags and grease, mixed with something much newer – electricity and perfectly-machined metal.

Coming back to the present, Cruz checked her diagnostic tablet again. It had gone screwy several times over the last few days and it was probably time to get a replacement from the stores.

"Is yours playing up as well?" asked Lead Comms Technician Ashlea Dubose, brandishing her own tablet.

"I don't know what it's doing," said Cruz, tapping the screen hard with a fingertip. "It's dropped its connection to the comms console again."

Technology wasn't renowned for its positive response to force and the tablet restarted itself, treating her to a black screen with a winking cursor. She poked it again.

"I'd say we're just about ready to request a final sign off, don't you?" asked Dubose.

Cruz nodded. "Everything's testing just fine apart from this tablet. Five weeks until this spaceship flies."

"That's what they say."

"You don't believe?"

Dubose was middle-aged and with an excellent ear for base gossip. "I pick things up here and there. They were late bringing in the life support modules – something went wrong in the factory and yadda yadda. They don't like to warm up the engines without the life support systems fully tested and online, so we've ended up with a delay to the entire project." Dubose had taken a shine to Cruz and she smiled sympathetically. "I bet you wish you were anywhere but here."

"They needed someone with flight experience to test the live systems. I was on the ground at the right time and here I am."

"Well, Lieutenant, I'm going to tell Lady Peterson that the comms systems on the *Earth's Fury* are as ready as they'll ever be." Her face hardened. "Now we move to the *Ulterior-2* and the hard work really starts."

"We've got three days, haven't we? That's enough for testing if we put in the hours."

"We've been given less than three days. I got a memo earlier this evening telling me they want final testing complete in thirty hours. I hope you don't need much sleep, Lieutenant."

Cruz was happy to step it up. "Thirty hours should be enough."

"Haven't you read the briefing?"

"What briefing?"

"Maybe I forgot to copy you in. Never mind, I'll tell you about it now. The *Ulterior*-2 isn't like the *Earth's Fury*. This spaceship we're on here is little more than a..." Dubose waved her arms around, trying to pick the right phrase, "...gun with an engine. The *Ulterior*-2, now that's meant to fight for fifty years and be a platform for every new weapon we can come up with during that time."

Cruz nodded – she knew this already. "The Space Corps makes new stuff all the time."

"The *Ulterior*-2 has completely updated comms and sensor arrays."

"I know."

"With a totally new interface."

"That I didn't know."

"That's why thirty hours is going to be tight. I have no idea why they prioritised the *Earth's Fury*."

Cruz checked her watch – it was already two hours past the end of her shift. The shipyard was on a rotating round-the-clock shift pattern, but for whatever reason she found herself doing more than her fair share of hours.

"I can get started now."

"You should get some sleep instead. Come back in the morning."

"Then there will be closer to twenty hours to finish the testing."

Dubose cackled evilly. "You're a good Space Corps officer, Lieutenant Cruz."

Cruz wasn't sure what to make of that particular statement, but luckily she was saved from having to provide a response. Unfortunately, what saved her was the sounding of the bridge emergency siren. The lighting turned a deep red, ensuring there was no possibility of missing the alarm.

For once, Dubose was lost for words and she began spluttering, while her head jerked left and right. "What's going on?"

Cruz didn't answer immediately. The comms console – along with every other console on the bridge – displayed the reason for the alarm.

"The base has been placed on maximum alert. Priority 1."

"That means we have to get out of here," said Dubose. "We're not allowed to remain onboard an unfinished warship unless we're given specific instructions to do so."

"I'll check," said Cruz. "Nope, there's nothing asking us to stay. Let's go."

She grabbed her tablet and ushered Dubose off the bridge ahead of her. The corridor outside was bathed in the same red light and the siren was painfully loud. The bridge was in the upper central area of the spaceship, close to what was called the *nose,* though *Earth's Fury* didn't really have a nose as such.

After a two-hundred metre run along a wide corridor, they reached a pair of airlifts. The left one was still in place from when they'd arrived a few hours earlier. Inside, the siren was muted and Cruz found herself able to think more easily.

"I'm out of shape," gasped Dubose. "This is the first Priority 1 alert in the twenty-eight years I've worked here. They picked a fine time for a drill."

"I don't think this is a drill."

Dubose gaped stupidly. "Then what?"

"Vraxar."

"Don't say that. You're scaring me."

Cruz didn't want to mollycoddle so she didn't say anything else. The lift reached the bottom of its shaft and they headed for the rear boarding ramp. There were a few others ahead of them - members of the other teams testing the internal systems.

The exit ramp wasn't steep and they walked quickly towards the bottom of the trench. From here, Cruz could see there was a crowd gathered around a huge bank of airlifts, waiting their turn to get up to the surface. There was a palpable feeling of panic and it infected Dubose before they were even halfway to the end of the ramp.

They passed a team of soldiers at the bottom, led by an officer Cruz recognized as Corporal Eddie Sullivan. The squad was assigned to guard against intruders and they were armed with gauss rifles. From the soldiers' expressions, Cruz got the impression they wished to be on their way as soon as possible.

Corporal Sullivan also recognized Cruz and he stepped forward to greet her.

"Good evening, ma'am. Are you the last?"

"I don't know, Corporal. Don't you have a roster?"

"Lieutenant Griffin is in charge tonight. He went off a while ago and hasn't come back." Sullivan did his best to smile. "He's taken the security handheld with him."

It was no wonder Sullivan didn't look happy. Without the security tablet, there was no way to be sure if anyone was still working on the *Earth's Fury*. Even worse, there was no way to close up the ship without confirmation everyone was accounted for.

"Where's the backup?" asked Cruz. "Who's covering the *Ulterior-2*?"

"Lieutenant Griffin, ma'am."

There was something shifty in the man's responses, though Cruz couldn't quite put her finger on what it was. "A single officer for both ships? There should be one assigned to each and a third as backup."

"Not tonight."

Cruz pointed at the visor perched up on top of Sullivan's head.

"Can't you get Lieutenant Griffin on the comms?"

"He's probably on his way."

Cruz knew the routine. In order to close up the *Earth's Fury*, Lieutenant Griffin required both his security tablet and his personal authorisation codes. He couldn't enter the latter remotely, so he would need to come back to the warship to seal it.

"Someone's head will roll for this, Corporal. I'm sure you already guessed that."

"Yes, ma'am."

Cruz and Dubose joined the rapidly-thinning crowd at the bottom of the airlifts. When their turn came, they piled inside along with fifteen or twenty others. The entrance doors were transparent and as the lift climbed, Cruz saw a few stragglers coming down the *Earth's Fury* boarding ramp. The base-wide alert was doing an excellent job of highlighting a multitude of failures in this section alone.

Once they reached the surface, Cruz and Dubose looked for a vehicle to get them back to their designated muster points. The base was working a rotating shift, but this emergency had depleted the ranks of pool cars, leaving none remaining. Evacuating workers were meant to wait until their vehicle was full before driving off. In this case, it appeared that panic had set in, resulting in many cars being driven away only half loaded. It was a long run back to the main part of the Tucson facility and there were upwards of forty people left stranded.

In the artificial light, Cruz saw dozens of fleeing vehicles in the distance as they sped past the *Ulterior-2*'s construction trench.

"So much for discipline," said Dubose.

There were four soldiers nearby, doing their best to keep everyone calm while they tried to arrange for transportation. A few of the technicians called out angrily, demanding answers the soldiers couldn't provide.

"Listen up everyone!" shouted one of the R1Ts. "We've got a transport on its way with room for everyone and it'll be here in a few minutes."

"Why can't we just go in yours?" asked one of the lead weapons technicians, pointing at the single vehicle nearby – it was a twelve-seat gravity truck designated specifically for the soldiers.

"It won't fit everyone," said the soldier. "The transport will be here soon."

"How long is soon?" called out another technician. "I can't see it coming."

"I'll check."

The soldier lowered his visor, evidently meaning to speak to the driver on the comms. Cruz watched the soldier tap his finger-tips against the side of his head. He lifted the visor again and spoke to one of his colleagues.

"Something's wrong," said Cruz.

"Like what?" asked Dubose.

"His comms."

On a whim, Cruz pulled the diagnostic tablet from her pocket and took a look. It was still connected to the *Earth's Fury* main comms array by short-range wireless and it didn't take long to realise there were problems. She frowned and double-checked.

Dubose had her own tablet, but made no effort to look at it. "What can you see?" she asked.

"The comms aren't sending or receiving," Cruz replied. "I've just instructed the *Earth's Fury* to contact the Tucson main comms hub and it's failed. The spaceship hasn't received a ping from the main hub for the last two minutes either."

"You said Vraxar, didn't you? Maybe you're right," said Dubose, making no effort to keep her voice low. She used a hand to shield her eyes and looked upwards, as though she'd seen an alien warship hovering over the base.

A few of the others overheard the words and they began muttering amongst themselves. Many of them squinted upwards in a search for hostile craft.

"We need to get away," said one voice.

Soon there was a clamour of frightened men and women and the panic in their voices rose by the second. They were only technicians, given basic training and then assigned to non-combat roles. Nevertheless, their reactions angered Cruz.

This is the damned military, she thought. *What the hell did they expect? A lifetime of peace?*

She didn't say the words. Instead, she tried a few different ways to connect with the Tucson comms hub. Unfortunately, the diagnostic tablet was only designed for testing a limited number of scenarios and she ran out of options quickly. She tapped the screen in frustration and the image wobbled threateningly.

"Don't you dare," she muttered.

The tablet's screen stabilised, just as another thought came to her. She logged out of the *Earth's Fury* comms and tried to connect to the *Ulterior-2*. For security purposes, the diagnostic tablets and personnel using them were usually locked to a single warship. Since she was due to start testing on the battleship, Cruz kept her fingers crossed that she'd been given approval to access the *Ulterior-2*'s arrays. The range was extreme and the link, when established, was tenuous.

"What's going on here?" she asked herself.

Dubose had drifted away, no longer even pretending to be interested. Cruz didn't spare her a second thought and she made a few tests of the *Ulterior-2*'s comms system. The results were inconclusive and before she could try again, her tablet's link dropped out and then the tablet itself shut down. It was tempting to let it fall to the ground and stand on it. In the confusion it would be easy to claim it was an accident. The tablet survived and Cruz dropped it into the pocket in her uniform.

She located Dubose in the crowd and put a hand on the woman's shoulder. Dubose turned, her expression distant and her mind clearly elsewhere.

"I'm going to the *Ulterior-2*," said Cruz.

She wasn't even sure if the other woman heard the words. If she did, she gave no acknowledgement. Cruz left her and ran for the *Ulterior-2*, setting off at a fast pace that would see her exhausted by the time she reached her destination. No one asked where she was going or told her to stop.

While she ran, Cruz reflected bitterly on how poorly the people on the Tucson base were reacting to the situation. If this was indeed the Vraxar, they'd find very little to stop them doing whatever it was they'd come to do. Cruz had no intention of meekly accepting her fate and she increased her pace, the rhythmic pounding of her feet loud in her ears.

The ES *Ulterior-2* was even more impressive from close up than it was at a distance. Cruz descended in the airlift to the bottom of Trench One and emerged, gazing at the sheer walls of the battleship's rear section. A few of the missile hatches were visible from here, as well as the aft underside particle beam. To her right, she could see one of the flank Havoc cannons – the barrel of the gun pointed towards the battleship's nose and she briefly wondered if the weapons were online.

She hurried onwards, until she was amongst the shadows beneath the hull. The vessel was supported by countless thick landing legs, each one strong enough to hold the largest skyscraper from any of the Confederation's major cities. For a moment, she thought Lieutenant Todd Griffin had got here before her and closed up the spaceship. Then, she spotted one of the central ramps through the forest of support legs – it was a few hundred metres away and rested on the ground. To reach it, she was required to pass directly below another particle beam dome and she heard the humming of its overcharge power units.

There were soldiers here – six in total. They were jumpy and watched her approach with suspicion.

"Who's in charge?" asked Cruz.

The squad leader identified herself. "I am. Corporal Jennie Baker, ma'am."

"Lieutenant Cruz. No sign of Lieutenant Griffin?"

"No, ma'am. The comms went dead ten minutes ago and we don't know what the hell is going on."

There was the same evasiveness in Corporal Baker as Cruz had detected in the soldier earlier at the *Earth's Fury*. She stared long and hard at Baker. Baker didn't flinch.

"I'm going onboard the *Ulterior-2*."

"There's a full alert, Lieutenant. No one's allowed back inside."

"We're under attack and this battleship has the only functioning comms array on the base."

"Attack?"

"I am certain the Vraxar have come."

Baker looked like she didn't believe it, as if this was part of a big practical joke played by senior officers. For a moment, Cruz thought she was about to get an argument from a junior officer. In the end, Baker didn't give a challenge.

"It's all yours, Lieutenant. We think everyone already left, so you'll be all alone."

"Do you have a way of sealing the ship?"

Baker shook her head. "Only Lieutenant Griffin."

"I might wring his neck when I see him," said Cruz with feeling. "You'd be better off somewhere inside as well. I don't have any idea what's coming, but you can be sure it won't be pleasant."

"We'll stay here for the moment, ma'am."

Cruz didn't waste time attempting persuasion. She jogged up the ramp, through the airlock room at the top and into the main personnel area of the battleship. Cruz hadn't been on the *Ulte-*

rior-2 before and she certainly hadn't seen the design plans. Even so, her feet knew the way to the bridge and they guided her along wide corridors, through two open areas and onwards to a flight of steps which took her to the blast door protecting the bridge. To her relief, the door slid open when she pressed the access panel and allowed her into the room beyond.

The *Ulterior*-2's bridge was a large, square area, with sixteen consoles arranged in clusters of four, each powered up and left in diagnostic mode. The captain and commander's consoles were set apart and positioned at the front, directly before the main bulkhead screens.

Much of it looked new and unfamiliar. The consoles themselves were different in appearance to those on every other Space Corps warship – the first in a new generation of technology come too late to be fitted throughout the fleet.

It was eerily quiet, like a ghost ship from an unknown civilisation found drifting through space. When she concentrated, Cruz picked up the faintest of background humming noises, hardly detectable over the rushing of blood through her ears.

Shaking her head clear, Cruz approached the comms cluster and dropped into one of the seats. There was an additional screen with a menu of options that made little sense. The panel itself was arranged differently to anything she was used to and again, it had a variety of new options specific to the battleship's sensor arrays.

It only took a minute for Cruz to realise the scale of the challenge before her, especially since the sensor arrays weren't even fully powered up. It appeared Lead Technician Ashlea Dubose hadn't been exaggerating when she mentioned how difficult it would be to complete testing in the thirty allotted hours. Cruz wasn't easily put off and she got on with the task of figuring out firstly how to bring the sensors online and then to see what they were capable of.

CHAPTER SIX

LIEUTENANT ERIC MCKINNEY flexed his right arm and suppressed a shiver. The underground room wasn't cold as such, in spite of what was stored a few hundred metres below, and he was sure the tiny fragments of Obsidiar which powered his new heart and flesh-covered alloy arm were responsible for his recent susceptibility to the cold.

He rotated both forearms slowly, trying for the thousandth time to detect any difference between the two. The new one looked exactly the same as a normal arm, though at the moment his spacesuit covered the skin. He had no difficulty in concluding the surgeons had done an excellent job and there was no discernible difference. *Except for this damn cold,* he thought.

The far door opened and Sergeant Johnny Li walked in, back from his visit to the central admin building. He was wearing his suit as they all were, and with his visor on top of his head. There were a few others inside the guard room, but Li's eyes found McKinney.

"Hey, Lieutenant! Any news?"

Li was usually upbeat and nothing seemed to get him down,

not even a full-scale planetary alert and a Vraxar capital ship with a billion alien soldiers onboard.

"What do you think?" grunted McKinney. "Anyway, you're the one who's been outside."

"You've got the knack, Lieutenant. If a mouse takes a crap in the armoury, you're always the first to know." Evidently dissatisfied with McKinney's answer, Li's eyes searched out his next target. "Corporal Bannerman, my friend!"

Corporal Nitro Bannerman was sitting at the lone, fixed metal table, with his comms pack in front of him. He didn't look up and continued poking at the pack's innards with a slender metal probe. "What can I do for you, Sergeant?"

Li used his gauss rifle to point. "The good lieutenant knows shit, so I thought maybe you'd have something for me. What's happened while I've been away?"

"Same old same old. The comms are dead except for the hard links. I couldn't even get a message to your visor from here. There's not even static."

"Any update to our orders, Sergeant?" asked McKinney. Li's demeanour had given him the answer already.

"Keep doing what we're doing, Lieutenant. There are some angry people out there. I hear Fleet Admiral Duggan himself has strangled a dozen people with his bare hands because they didn't think to cover the base with hard links."

The hard links reached across much of the Tucson base, but they didn't extend as far out as the Obsidiar Storage Facility. This was one of the newest areas on the base and fitted with internal backup cables, but they hadn't thought to link them to the main command and control. It was as though the pursuit of technology made the designers sneering of anything so old fashioned as physical cables.

"Yeah, right," said Bannerman.

"What are you doing to that pack anyway?" asked Li, taking a greater interest. "That's expensive military equipment and you're sticking your nail file into it."

Bannerman paused in his tinkering. "These packs are made to survive in all the same places as a soldier in a spacesuit and they're meant to be field serviceable at a pinch. So I'm having a look to see if there's anything I can change in order to get a signal in or out."

Ricky Vega was lounging in one of the other chairs. "He's pissing about, Sergeant, in the hope he gets a medal for solving the base comms problems before the Vraxar blow us to pieces from orbit."

"There'll be nothing left to pin a medal onto when those alien bastards are finished with this place," said Martin Garcia. He lifted his rifle and looked along the smooth barrel. "Maybe they'll show their faces and we'll get to shoot a few."

"That's the spirit!" said Li. "And then when they turn you into a walking corpse you'll have some good memories to keep you going during your thousand years of servitude."

"Maybe a few of us will get through this," said Huey Roldan. "Just think of the prize - a chance to shoot Garcia the Vraxar in his face."

"I'll be aiming for his balls," said Vega.

Jeb Whitlock joined in. "You're not that good a shot."

Garcia didn't like the banter too much when he was on the receiving end. He swore and raised his middle finger to the others in the room, which only made them laugh more.

McKinney chuckled and picked up his rifle. "Play nicely while I'm gone."

Li was the curious one. "Where are you off to, Lieutenant?"

"I only stopped by here for two minutes to make sure everyone knows what they're doing."

"Guarding the interior until it's our turn on the wall or until the Vraxar do something," said Vega.

Li addressed the others as if McKinney was already out of the room. "The man runs a tight ship."

"Don't you forget it, Sergeant."

McKinney exited the guard room through one of the two doors. There was a passage outside, stark metal walls dull against the blue-white light cast from tiny globes in the ceiling. A ceiling mounted mini-gun whirred softly as it turned sluggishly towards the movement of McKinney's stride. He did his best to ignore the nine barrels spinning softly in preparation to mow down anything the OSF defence computer didn't like the look of. Whatever it was affecting the main base cluster, it was also making the independent systems here operate at a fraction of their usual speed.

The guard room door opened again. "Mind if I tag along?" asked Bannerman. "My eyes can't take much more close-up work."

"Sure, come and stretch your legs."

The two of them set off. The Obsidiar Storage Facility was a fairly straightforward place to navigate. The above-ground part of the building was low, square and with thick walls of concrete-clad alloy. It was surrounded by two separate walls, each with wide gates, unsmiling guards and the kind of city-levelling multi-barrelled chainguns the Space Corps mounted on the latest generation of Colossus tanks.

The Obsidiar itself was stored far beneath the surface in a huge room which reminded McKinney a little of the storage areas in the Tillos underground bunker on Atlantis. There was a single main lift to bring the Obsidiar to the surface, this lift kept operational by its own Obsidiar-driven gravity engine. Once the cargo arrived at the surface, it was carried towards the nearby shipyard on the back of one of the dedicated OSF crawlers.

Throughout the facility there were fully-armed soldiers and numerous automated emplacements. After a recent disastrous inspection report on the organisation of the soldiers, McKinney had been drafted in to sort things out and he'd brought a few of his experienced men with him.

The pair walked in silence for a time. They passed other soldiers and McKinney occasionally stopped to ask questions. It was obvious Bannerman had something to say and eventually he spoke what was on his mind.

"When will they come for us, Lieutenant?"

"Soon. Hours." McKinney shrugged. "I'm surprised we're still alive."

"Maybe they've got something in mind for us."

"You know what they've got in mind."

"Yeah. I thought they'd be a bit more interested in what we've got in this building."

McKinney stopped. "Who's to say they aren't?"

"Why would they hang around? If they know what we're holding."

"Maybe they've got more Obsidiar than they know what to do with. Every time they run out, simply blow up a few planets and get some more."

"You just implied they'd be coming here."

"Whatever they do, we'll be ready for them."

"Unless it's death from above."

"If they want this Obsidiar I can't believe they'd be stupid enough to level the place with missiles. If the Vraxar know it's here and they want it enough, they'll land with a hundred thousand of their rotting corpses and send them inside to take it."

"And we'll kill every last one of them."

"You're not normally one for bravado, Corporal."

Bannerman grinned. "I've been around the others too long. It's affecting the way I think." His smile faded. "We've been dealt another shitty hand."

"I'm beginning to wonder if there are any aces in the pack. If there are, I can't remember holding one."

"I'm surprised we haven't been reinforced."

"There are two thousand men and women guarding this place. We could add another sixty thousand and it wouldn't be enough if the Vraxar were determined to get what they wanted. And the lack of comms has screwed everything up."

They reached one of the interior airlifts and stepped inside. It was colder here and the lift descended silently to the lowest level. The door opened onto another square room and Bannerman smiled uncomfortably when the three ceiling guns spun towards them. There were no soldiers present – an automated check-in console was fixed to the floor and there was a single metal door in the far wall. McKinney knew from experience this door was about seven metres thick and it was currently closed.

The internal comms system was working fine, but McKinney was still obliged to enter his details into the check-in console. A tiny sensor in the unit scanned him, confirmed his identity and also that he wasn't acting under duress.

After a long pause, the square door rose until it vanished into the ceiling. A squad of six soldiers waited on the opposite side, with rifles at the ready. McKinney gestured for them to lower their weapons and they did so. He walked towards the group.

"How's it going, Corporal Evans?"

Evans lifted a hand in greeting. He could have given the standard answer that everything was absolutely gleamingly perfect, but chose otherwise. "The guys are getting jumpy, sir." He indicated those around him. "They reckon they're going to die down here."

"Is that right?" asked McKinney, fixing one of the soldiers with his gaze.

"Not me, sir," said the man. "I've got a date tomorrow and I don't want to miss it."

"A date with his dead grandmother's best friend," said a woman standing to one side.

"Nah, I told you it's with the goat farmer's three-titted daughter," said another.

McKinney had heard enough and he pointed through the doorway. "Get back to your duties," he said. "I don't want any more pissing around." He turned to Bannerman. "Come on."

They walked quickly through the passage into the next room, conscious that several thousand tonnes of door hung overhead – a door which relied on a faulty computer system to keep it in place.

"Lower it," Evans ordered when everyone was through.

McKinney took in the details of this new room – it was fifteen metres to a side and with a three-metre-high ceiling. A window took up much of the far wall, made of a substance much more durable than glass. There were more gun emplacements in the ceiling, as well as a couple of trapezoidal four-barrel mobile repeater turrets which were as nasty in operation as they were in appearance.

"Any problems?" asked McKinney in a low voice.

Evans grimaced. "They're crapping themselves, Lieutenant. What you saw a minute ago? That was just for show to make you think they're on top of it. None of them wants to die and they're all sure it's coming to them soon."

"What do you think, Corporal?"

"I think it's coming to us soon as well, Lieutenant. It's just that I've faced it before and I'm not scared anymore."

"We have a lot of spaceships guarding New Earth."

"That's what I keep telling myself. And then I ask why we're still down here with no word about what's happening. If the enemy was gone, everything would be working again and we'd have someone telling us on the comms what a good job we'd done and that we could stand down."

There was no point in arguing the point and McKinney

wasn't even inclined. "Keep them distracted, Corporal. If we get a chance to fight I'd like to know there are people at my back rather than looking for some place to hide out."

"I'll do my best, sir."

McKinney didn't stick around to chat any longer. He walked over to the window and looked through it for a moment. The main Obsidiar storage area was brightly lit and there were few shadows. Cubes and cylinders of pure black were everywhere, some of them in piles, others alone. There was no apparent method to the arrangement of the Obsidiar blocks – they were kept away from the central gravity lift platform, but that was the furthest the organisation went.

"Humanity's salvation," said Bannerman with a note of bitterness.

"It might still be."

There was ongoing activity inside the storage area. A series of specially-built robots continued doing exactly what they'd been instructed to do before the base went on alert. They cut the blocks into the required shapes and carried them to the transportation crawlers for delivery to the surface. McKinney had been told that the Estral had done much of the cutting work already and many of the blocks required little or no modification.

One of the cylindrical robots drifted past, floating serenely through the air a hundred metres from the window. Six multi-jointed laser cutting arms protruded from opposite sides of the robot's main body and green lights from its status screens made the ice-rimed metal glisten. It was well below freezing in the storage room and McKinney shivered again at the sight.

"Let's get moving," he said.

They left the room and eventually found themselves in one of the technical control offices. This was a comparatively cramped space, made smaller by the densely-packed banks of monitoring equipment. There were five technicians keeping an eye on things and they all looked up at the arrival of the two soldiers. McKinney recognized the fleeting hope in their eyes at the thought he might be bringing them good news. It seemed best to tell them up front.

"No change, ladies and gentlemen."

"Figures," said one. McKinney struggled to remember her name – Bobbi Melton.

"Lieutenant McKinney will keep us safe, won't you?" said another, giving him an exaggerated wink.

"Sure will," he agreed. He wasn't here for small talk. "Just passing through, folks. You'll be the first to know if anything changes."

The technicians were clearly desperate for news and it was difficult to leave without answering at least a couple of their questions. McKinney tried his best, whilst walking slowly towards the exit.

"No, there's no word from high command and no I don't know where the defence fleet is," he said.

"Blown to crap," said Amie Horvath.

"Shut up," said Melton, clearly sick of hearing her colleague parrot the same line.

"Whatever."

Horvath turned back to her console and began looking at a series of status graphs relating to something McKinney neither knew nor cared about. He was hopeful of making a getaway when Melton brought him short with another question.

"Next time you send someone out to a place where the comms are working, will you ask if they can speak to one of Fleet Admiral Duggan's team about this latest shipment we were meant to be getting out?"

"What shipment?" asked McKinney, impatient to be on his way.

"It's classified," said Melton. "They'll know which one I mean."

Horvath turned her head. "We've got twelve Obsidiar projectiles awaiting transportation to that new spaceship they're working on. They were finished a week ago and we were told to hold onto them but keep them ready. They're sitting on the main crawler next to the lift. They were officially signed out and so we can't touch them until someone tells us they're our responsibility again."

"We need that crawler for the next Obsidiar core they're due to deploy in a couple of weeks," added Melton.

McKinney shook his head at this sudden shift in priorities. "The Vraxar are here," he said.

"Yeah and we might be dead tomorrow," said Horvath. "Until then, we've got work to do – it keeps us occupied."

"No promises. I'll do my best."

The two men hurried through the exit before the technicians came up with any more questions.

"I thought we'd never get away," laughed Bannerman.

"We got lucky to escape when we did. It must be lonely in that room – I once got stuck talking to them for half an hour."

"I thought you were blunt when it came to crap you don't want to hear."

"I don't like to be rude," said McKinney.

"I've heard you say all sorts to the men!"

"There's a difference between rudeness and discipline."

"Fair enough. Where to now, Lieutenant? By my reckoning we've seen just about everything."

"I'm going to take a look outside and make sure there's no one sleeping when they should be patrolling. You don't need to come."

"What else am I going to do?"

The journey didn't take long. The Obsidiar Storage Facility

was large but well-designed. There were other places on the Tucson base which were rabbit warrens of interconnecting passages. Here it was straight lines and airlifts.

There was a total of four pedestrian exits from the building, each of them sealed by a guarded door thick enough to withstand thirty minutes of mobile repeater fire or several rounds from a medium tank. McKinney and Bannerman left by the front entrance which was to one side of the main transportation doorway.

It was dark overhead, though the base lighting made it feel as though they were standing in daylight. When McKinney looked up, he was reminded how strange this contrast between artificial day and night had been for the first few weeks on base, way back when he was a new recruit.

Bannerman shifted his weight from foot to foot. "Which way?"

McKinney paused for a moment in thought, trying to plan the most efficient route which would allow him to speak to as many of the facility soldiers as possible. He looked around - the first of the two surrounding walls was a couple of hundred metres away and it loomed overhead. To the right, the immense outer main door was sealed. It was opened only when absolutely necessary and rumour had it Fleet Admiral Duggan was made aware every time it was activated. There was a second door beyond it and a particularly nasty surprise waited behind the inner door – an additional defence in case it was ever needed.

"Let's check out the wall gate station," said McKinney.

There was a total of eight rooms in each of the two perimeter walls – four rooms on each side of each gate. These guard stations were warm, comfortable and gave an impression of remoteness. A soldier had once been found asleep in one of these rooms.

The ground was covered in thick plates of perfectly-joined metal, which McKinney presumed were meant as added protection from aerial bombardment. He walked quickly – there was no give beneath his feet and his steps gave off hardly any sound. The metal could have been fifty metres thick for all he knew.

They didn't reach the gate station. The soldiers had gone little more than halfway across the open space when McKinney heard a noise – it was a kind of pulsing fizz that pounded his eardrums and made him grit his teeth. He spun, raising his voice to speak a question he knew was pointless.

"What the hell?"

Bannerman pointed towards the roof of the main building. Several of the facility's fixed gun emplacements were firing. McKinney could see the low, squat turrets with wide-bore barrels protruding from the centre. Three of the ten were visible from this angle and they thumped out a steady stream of projectiles which streaked away into space, leaving their bright trails behind.

"Something's coming," said McKinney.

"Yeah."

McKinney lowered his visor across his eyes and used it to enhance his vision. Like everything else on the base, it was running much slower than normal and it took seconds to adjust. He saw a huge, ugly spaceship made up from a series of different-sized blocks. It was high above and descending at speed.

"Where're our ground-to-airs?" he muttered. "They should have lit that bastard up by now."

Eventually, a few base missile emplacements fired their rockets. McKinney heard the shriek of their propulsion systems as they hurtled into the sky. One or two of them detonated against the inbound spaceship. It didn't have an energy shield, but the impacts weren't enough to knock it from the sky.

"There are about a hundred multi-launchers around Tucson," said Bannerman. "What's going on?"

"I don't know," said McKinney. "Maybe they can jam those too."

Whatever the Vraxar were doing, it wasn't enough to completely negate the Tucson automated batteries. Another high-yield missile exploded against the incoming craft, leaving a deep crater in its armour.

"We're going to get those bastards!" said Bannerman, clenching one fist.

At that moment, the artificial daylight was increased tenfold by a thousand huge explosions. Protected by the walls, neither McKinney nor Bannerman could see the blasts directly. A second after the light came the sound. It thundered and rumbled, shaking the ground and forcing them to lower their visors to block out the sound. The rumbling went on and on, like it would never stop.

McKinney grabbed Bannerman by the arm. "Move!"

They ran for the facility door. McKinney glanced upwards as he ran – the incoming spaceship was damaged and its hull glowed with heat. No more missiles exploded against it and it was only a few kilometres above the base. He knew exactly what it was coming for.

"Looks like they had mammy to protect them," gasped Bannerman as they reached the door.

McKinney gave the access panel a hard slap with his palm. "Was it ever in doubt?"

"Maybe for a moment."

It had only been a short run, but McKinney found he was out of breath. They stopped for a few seconds, panting.

"There's more bad news," he said.

"What's that?"

"When I had my visor down it gave me an alert – the atmospheric oxygen levels are dropping. If it keeps going down, billions of people are going to suffocate."

Bannerman took it in his stride. "We'd better stop them, eh, Lieutenant?"

"With our gauss rifles and endless determination."

"That'll do it."

"Come on, we need to plan our defence."

They ran for it, bringing whoever they met with them. The Vraxar had decided to pay the base a visit and McKinney was in no doubt what they wanted, since they'd left the OSF intact. Obsidiar was the most valuable substance known to exist, so it made sense the enemy would send their troops to pick it up. McKinney hated the aliens more than ever and told himself he'd do whatever it took to throw a spanner in their works. *With rifles and determination,* he repeated in his mind. McKinney grimaced and ran on through the corridors of the facility.

CHAPTER SEVEN

SINCE THE VRAXAR bombardment of the surface a few minutes ago, activity within the underground command and control bunker had increased markedly. Groups of personnel ran here and there, doing their best to collate information in the hope of sifting a clear picture from the ruins of a chaotic situation. Within the main command and control room, the various teams did their best to keep everything moving and ensure everyone was working towards the same goal. Through it all, the base technicians tried to get the comms working and to fix whatever was wrong with the Tucson processing clusters.

In the centre of the room, Fleet Admiral Duggan stood, doing his best to exude calm. His fists kept clenching of their own accord and it was a constant effort to keep himself from folding his arms across his chest.

As soon as news came of the missile attack, Duggan had organised a team and sent them to the surface. He wasn't sure exactly what he hoped to achieve with this action, other than doing *something* instead of nothing. In fact, he already had a fairly good idea of what had happened and he crossed over to the comms team for the second time in five minutes.

The grey-haired woman he'd spoken to earlier was Lieutenant Priscilla Montgomery and she continued to impress with her attitude. She noticed his approach and broke off conversation with another member of her team.

"I was just about to bring you an update, Fleet Admiral." She ushered him towards one of the consoles nearby.

Duggan found his eyes roving over three of the display screens, trying to make sense of what they saw. "What's this?" he asked.

"As you're aware, we've been tapping into that old processing box here in the bunker," said Montgomery. "It's old but it was still a dedicated unit, so we're able to get some use out of it."

"Yes, yes," said Duggan.

"We've been clearing up the sensor feeds. Just in time to catch the attack, as it happens. I'll show you an overlay of the damage shortly. Before that you need to be aware we saw something coming down during the bombardment."

"What was it?"

"A spaceship, sir. We didn't get a great view of it since we were focused elsewhere – I'll show you the replay."

Montgomery pressed at the console and a recording played on one of the screens. The image wasn't razor-sharp, but it was good enough for Duggan to make out a boxy spaceship dropping from orbit.

"Here's where we got a few missile strikes on its hull," said Montgomery.

Duggan watched the low-resolution feed of missiles exploding against the Vraxar spaceship.

"And then the bombardment started," said Montgomery.

"Did you see where the attack came from?"

"There was a sensor ghost."

"You're sure though."

"Yes. Here."

This time there was no recording to look at, simply an enormous table of numbers. Montgomery had found a pen from somewhere and she drew an imaginary circle around a section of the screen.

"*Ix-Gorghal*?" Duggan asked.

"Yes – a huge object flew overhead, travelling in a slow orbit at an altitude of approximately forty thousand kilometres. Its arrival ties in with the appearance of this other spaceship as well as the missile attack."

"Are we still visible to them?"

"We will be for another few minutes. Their speed indicates they'll complete each full orbit in approximately two hours." There was more bad news. "They've left another warship behind."

"For certain?"

"More or less – I wasn't going to tell you until I knew for definite. You're here now, so I thought I'd better fill you in. Whatever this new vessel is, it's larger than the *Ulterior-2* – first guess is it's eight kilometres long and displaces thirty percent more. It's just as likely a source of the bombardment."

"A Vraxar battleship."

"I'm sure you know better than me."

"It's not what I wanted to hear." He didn't want to dwell on it, so pointed at another screen on the console. "Show me the damage we've sustained on Tucson."

"Using the positional readings from the sensors, we've generated this overlay upon the base map," she said.

It wasn't a pretty sight and Duggan swore.

"They've hit every single one of our ground launchers as well as a few hundred of our other buildings."

Montgomery pointed at several different places on the overlay. "We believe they completely destroyed the weapons lab, the north-west warehouse and the plant storage facility amongst other things." She took a deep breath. "And the entire barracks areas to the south, the west and the north."

"That's all the barracks."

"Yes."

The Vraxar weren't exactly known for their compassion when it came to the lives of others.

"Can you tell if their warheads penetrated to the areas underneath?"

"I don't have that information for you, sir."

Even if the Vraxar missiles hadn't breached the reinforced shelters beneath the barracks, it seemed certain the casualties would be in the thousands. If they'd used armour-piercing warheads, the number of deaths would be into the tens of thousands.

Duggan leaned forward and tapped at one particular area of the screen. "This area is undamaged."

"We detected no missile strikes close to the Obsidiar Storage Facility, sir."

"What about the Vraxar spaceship - the one you saw dropping from orbit?"

"It landed on this area of ground near the OSF, sir."

"I thought as much. This map doesn't show the shipyard."

"Without a link to our satellites, we can't get a clear picture through all these buildings on the base," said Montgomery. She shrugged. "The Tucson array was designed to look into space, rather than at the ground."

"Did you detect missile blasts in that area?" Duggan persisted.

"No, sir."

Montgomery clearly didn't have anything more to offer on

the matter, so Duggan changed the subject. "How are efforts proceeding to establish a hard-linked comms network?"

"We've got people working on it elsewhere in the bunker, sir."

"How far are they getting?"

Montgomery was experienced enough to know when there was no point in attempting to massage the truth. "We have yet to establish a single additional link, sir, and there is no guarantee that a single success will lead to more rapid progress."

"Thank you, Lieutenant."

Duggan left Montgomery to get on with her work. He was aware the members of his personal staff needed to hear this latest information, but since he required time to think he meandered his way slowly around the room.

The situation was grim, though no more so than expected. Once *Ix-Gorghal* arrived, there was no amount of death or destruction which would have surprised or shocked Duggan. He paused at an empty chair and sat in it, trying to ignore the noise and activity in the room.

The Vraxar had neutralised the New Earth defence fleet and isolated the entire planet from the rest of the Confederation. From there, they had destroyed the ability of the Tucson base to respond to an aerial threat and then sent a dropship, presumably with the intent of stealing the contents of the Obsidiar Storage Facility. With the oxygen levels falling, the enemy would soon kill everyone who didn't have access to a sealed refuge.

"Sir?"

He looked up, to find Lieutenant Paz nearby with concern on her face.

"What is it?"

"We've found Benediction."

"Where?"

"The deployment team just returned. They got it in place and then came home. They arrived a little while before the

Vraxar missile strike, found a hard-linked comms station and reported in."

"I'm impressed with their efficiency."

"What did Lieutenant Montgomery tell you, sir?"

"A few things I had already guessed and one I hadn't. We've got thousands dead from the missile attack, there's the start of an assault on the OSF, and finally, we have no progress in resolving our technical problems. On top of that, it appears the Vraxar have left a battleship in stationary orbit over the base." He gritted his teeth.

"That's bad."

"The most galling part of it is, even if we somehow managed to get everything working and somehow against all the odds got a signal off-world, there's no way Admiral Morey could get a fleet here in time."

"Norris could be wrong, sir."

"I don't have a choice other than to act as if she is right, Lieutenant. If our warships were still up there, they'd have done something by now. I can't see a way to salvage anything good from this."

"Does that mean...?"

"I'm still thinking on it," he said. He scratched at his stubble. "Tell me, Lieutenant Paz, why would the Vraxar leave the *Ulterior-2* and the *Earth's Fury* intact?"

Paz furrowed her brow. "I can think of three reasons they might do that. The first reason: they wish to steal those warships. The second reason: neither the *Ulterior-2* or the *Earth's Fury*'s engines are online and the Vraxar might assume both are nowhere near completion. The fact they weren't part of the defence fleet kind of gives it away."

"What's the last reason? I probably know it."

"The last reason? They're just too damned big to care. They've wiped out our fleet and they're not worried about a single battleship or a mobile gun, even with a huge barrel on top of it."

"Why take a gamble?"

"Is it really a gamble, sir? Besides, they might change their minds whenever they feel like it. They're the ones controlling the show."

"You may be right."

"You don't sound convinced."

"It's my job to sound unconvinced. If you thought I accepted everything you said, there'd be no encouragement for you to improve."

"Really?"

Duggan grinned. "Now it's you who sounds unconvinced."

"Touché." Paz wasn't one for giving up and it was clear she was thinking. "Why don't you activate the *Ulterior-2* and the *Earth's Fury* anyway, sir? We should be able to find enough people to fly them. What is there to lose?"

Duggan was the only person on New Earth with the authority to sign off a fleet warship in order for its full operational potential to become available. "There're no comms, so I can't do it remotely. I'd have to personally sign in to the captain's console on the bridge of each one. Even if I did so, I'm not sure what good it would do – the *Earth's Fury* isn't carrying any ammunition for its cannon and the life support system isn't due to be brought online for another two weeks."

"What about the *Ulterior-2*, sir? I'm sure some of the entry points for this bunker would bring you out close to Trench One. With the right team we could get you there."

Doing his best to ignore the aching in his joints, Duggan pushed himself upright. "I think I've made my mind up. Come on."

"You're going to the deployment site instead?"

He didn't answer. Instead, he beckoned Paz to follow and made his way to where the other members of his staff waited.

"I will go to Benediction and make preparations to activate it."

The others exchanged glances and RL Norris looked at her feet.

"This is it, then?" asked Lieutenant Doyle.

"I haven't quite given up yet."

"Are you sure, sir?"

"If I'd given up every time the odds were stacked against me, I'd have died sixty years ago, Lieutenant."

"My apologies, Fleet Admiral."

"You were right to ask; however, the time is running out for me to act. The Vraxar have taken a greater interest in the Tucson base and I believe they're in the process of landing a large number of their troops. If I stay in this bunker, it may end up impossible to reach the bomb."

"You're leaving at once?" asked Lieutenant Jacobs.

"In minutes, once I assemble a suitable team."

"What if we get things working here again, sir?" asked Doyle.

"If I thought it would make a difference, I'd wait it out."

"You're just going to set it off as easy as that?" Doyle understandably didn't look pleased.

"Nothing so straightforward, Lieutenant. I would prefer to be near it in case the decision becomes unavoidable."

"How will you know? What if something new comes up?"

"You said you used to work in comms, Lieutenant. That puts you in an excellent position to oversee matters here."

Doyle rubbed his face. "I know we agreed on this." He took a breath. "I need something else. A hope, no matter how remote."

"There is hope." Research Lead Marion Norris spoke for the first time.

"What is it?" Duggan urged.

"I don't know, sir. A number came into my head – the chance of an unknown influence upon an apparently certain outcome."

"What is the number?"

"Four percent, Fleet Admiral."

Duggan turned his head towards Doyle. "There you go, Lieutenant. Four percent. Is that enough hope for you?"

Doyle smiled unexpectedly. "Looks like it'll have to be, sir."

"Four percent is almost a certainty when it comes to Fleet Admiral John Duggan," said Paz, winking at Doyle.

Her words, spoken as they were in jest, caused Duggan's stomach to knot. Though he'd escaped from more than his share of bad situations, he made sure he never called luck to his aid. Somehow, he felt as if Paz had unwittingly spurned that tiny chance and doomed them to death.

Trying his best not to think about it, Duggan ran through the list of people he wanted with him on his coming journey to find Benediction.

CHAPTER EIGHT

TWENTY MILLION KILOMETRES away from New Earth, the heavy cruiser *ES Lucid* emerged from high lightspeed. A spaceship this size would have usually created an immense cloud of fission energy, though in this case, the vessel's advanced fission suppression system concealed the giveaway signs of an inbound craft. In theory, twenty million kilometres was more than enough to ensure their safe arrival regardless of fission suppression, but with the fate of his ship and potentially the entire population of New Earth at stake, Captain Charlie Blake wasn't in the mood to take chances.

The moment he felt the deep fission engines cut off, he grabbed the control bars and aimed the *Lucid* towards New Earth, at the same time shouting out a series of orders.

"Lieutenant Quinn, activate stealth. Lieutenant Pointer, if there's even so much as a pebble out there, I want to know about it. Lieutenant Hawkins, be prepared to fire the overcharged particle beams upon sighting of a target."

The crew weren't rookies and didn't need these instructions. Nevertheless, Blake felt better giving the orders and his crew felt better hearing the words. It didn't take long until the crap started overflowing.

"I've got Admiral Morey on the comms," said Pointer.

"I want you to finish your scan as a priority. Cut her off."

"Done."

Admiral Morey wasn't to be so easily dissuaded. She had the authority to simply force open a connection to the *ES Lucid* and she did so. Her voice came through the bridge speakers, dripping with sarcasm and fury.

"Captain Blake, you appear to have taken a wrong turning. Perhaps my orders were not clear enough for you?"

"Your orders were clear enough, Admiral Morey."

"That's *Acting Fleet Admiral* Morey. Why have you chosen to ignore my orders?"

"I don't believe you have taken sufficient action to secure the safety of the citizens on New Earth. Equally, I don't believe you are acting with the sanction of the Confederation Council."

"I will not get into this discussion with you, Captain Blake!" hissed Morey. "You will rendezvous with Defence Fleet Epsilon and there you will relinquish command of your vessel to an officer who can follow orders!"

"Negative, Admiral. I will not leave New Earth until I have done what I came to do."

"And what exactly is it you hope to achieve with a single warship, where thirty-two have already failed?"

"The *ES Lucid* will remain hidden and take advantage of whatever opportunities might arise, Admiral. We will not come to an agreement here and I suggest you turn your energies elsewhere."

"Consider yourself removed from command as of this moment, Charlie Blake."

"As *acting* Fleet Admiral, you lack that authority, ma'am. You will require formal signed approval from three other admirals in addition to yourself. Even then, I will not deviate from my chosen course."

The channel went dead.

"She cut you off, sir," said Pointer. "In the meantime, I've finished my near scans and we're clear. It's going to take me a while to see what's happening on New Earth – it's a long way away."

"Keep at it." Blake paused in thought. "Can you prevent Admiral Morey from opening a channel like that again? I don't need the distraction."

"It's easily done, just completely against protocol."

"I don't think we – I - need worry about that any longer. Do it."

"We're all in it together, sir," said Hawkins. "Don't think for one moment that if we get out of this I'm going to stand in front of the court martial judges telling them how I was an unwilling participant. I'm sure I can speak for the others when I say we've each made our mind up about this one."

"Thank you, Lieutenant, that's good to know. When it comes to it, there's a good chance they'll show leniency to everyone except the ship's captain. They're especially likely to show sympathy to officers of ensign rank and lower."

"There's no need to try and keep us onside, sir," said Ensign Charlotte Bailey. "We're adults the same as everyone else."

The words went only a small distance to assuaging Blake's growing sense of guilt at what he'd dragged them into. It was a matter for later.

"Lieutenant Pointer, anything to report?"

"In terms of comms, New Earth is completely and utterly silent. There are signs of a few crude low-speed signals going from place to place on the surface, but it's nothing we can tap into. It's civilian kit from what I can gather."

"It's what we were expecting," Blake replied.

"There's a lot to collate. I wish Lieutenant Cruz was still onboard. Rescuing her is just another reason to come here and try to do our part."

Blake shared the sentiments – there were others on New Earth he very much wished to be given a chance at life. However, he didn't need to hear about it at the moment. "Answer the question, Lieutenant. Is there any sign of the enemy?"

"Yes, sir. I haven't found *Ix-Gorghal* yet. However, there is a series of satellites arranged in a band around the centre of New Earth."

"What sort of satellites?"

"It's difficult to be sure from here. They're large – I'd guess close to a thousand metres in length and they look a bit like cigars. Extrapolating the known data, I estimate there are thirty such satellites in a fixed orbit at a height of about two hundred kilometres from the surface."

"Two *hundred*? That's low."

"Yes, sir, it is. It's not clear what they are there for."

"Lieutenant Quinn, do you have any idea? Could they be part of a monitoring or comms network?"

"I'm still checking, sir. It seems logical they would contain both monitoring and communications elements, however..."

"Out with it."

"They're far bigger than necessary and they're giving off large power readings. As Lieutenant Pointer said, we're too far out for certainty."

"I think you've said enough for me to be sure these satellites are an important secondary target." The possibilities were worrying. "You remember that device they left under the sea at Atlantis?"

"That reactor we heard about from the old man on his boat?" said Hawkins. "Hard to forget."

"It was intended to kill everyone and I think we can safely assume these satellites have a similar purpose."

"We can knock out the visible ones with the Shimmers from here," said Hawkins. "Seventy-nine minutes travel time."

"Want me to plot a course that will allow us to get a lock on the others, sir?" asked Pointer.

"Thank you, the plan is a good one, but I'm not going to act on it immediately. I don't want to give the game away until I've decided how much we can snatch off the Vraxar. I want to hurt these bastards as much as possible."

Blake's conviction wasn't in doubt and none of his crew made any effort to persuade him to make an early commitment to destroying the satellites.

"Most of the important stuff was based out of Tucson," he said. "Work out the most efficient course that will give us a view of the base and send it to my console."

"On its way, sir. I've added in trajectory links to each of the other bases on New Earth. If you want details of the capital cities, I'll add them too."

"We'll check out Tucson first."

The main military base was a third of the way around New Earth. The ES *Lucid* was so far out it would take a good number of minutes to bring it into view. The warship flew and the crew did their best to uncover as much information as possible about what the Vraxar were planning. The closer they came, the more hints they found.

"Something's disturbed the Postern Ocean," said Pointer. "There are a series of overlapping ripples with several points of origin. There's a huge cloud of steam coming from an area to the north."

The sensor image appeared on the bulkhead screen. New Earth lacked the vibrancy of colour which had been so abundant in Atlantis, and every shade was dull as if seen through a filter.

The visible land mass was greys mottled with greens and whites, while a range of mountains extended for thousands of kilometres to the north and south, the hostility of their peaks tangible even across the huge intervening space. The Postern Ocean was a patchwork of blues and greens, which covered twenty percent of the planet's surface. The crew watched the image intently.

"Any idea what's going to happen when those waves reach the shores?" asked Hawkins.

"It's not going to be good," said Quinn. "I don't have the core cycles spare to do the model."

Blake stared miserably at the screen. "Does it matter? One million or five million dead. The numbers begin to lose meaning."

"You know it matters," said Pointer.

"Yes, I know." Blake shook himself. "No distractions. Can't let it get to me."

Pointer told the others what they already knew. "There's an object on the ocean floor beneath that cloud of steam. It's a piece from one of the defence fleet spaceships, about a billion tonnes in weight. It's going to take a long time to cool down."

"Keep an eye out for other wreckage. If there're pieces still due to come down I'd like to add them to our targeting system. We'll shoot them down if we can." He had another idea. "Also watch for another of those Vraxar reactors – not just in the ocean, but anywhere on the planet."

Pointer gave a loud exhalation of pent-up breath. "I've found *Ix-Gorghal*," she said. "I'm updating the viewscreen feed."

The all-too-familiar image of the Vraxar capital ship drifted across the screen, travelling high above one of the most densely-populated areas of the planet. It was exactly as Blake remembered it; the ovoid shape, monumental gun turrets, the towers, the complicated sensor arrays. Details etched into his mind forever.

"At least they don't have their stealth system activated," said Quinn. "That's one spaceship I don't want sneaking up on me."

"It's holding an altitude of forty thousand klicks, sir, and it's travelling directly over the ring of satellites."

"That's going to make it a little harder to bring them down," said Hawkins. "It limits the opportunities for a surprise attack."

"Send this data to the main base on Prime."

"Taron, sir."

"Yes, Taron. I'm sure they'll be grateful."

Blake kept the *ES Lucid* on course, bringing it steadily closer to New Earth. *Ix-Gorghal* disappeared from sight, its vector putting it on a two-hour full orbit. It showed no sign it had detected the heavy cruiser; even so, it was a relief when the alien craft vanished around the cusp of the planet.

"I know what those satellites are there for," said Quinn suddenly. "They're screwing up the composition of the atmosphere."

"In what way?"

"The oxygen levels are going down and the nitrogen levels are going up."

"Are the changes significant?"

"Significant enough to kill everyone on the planet in a few hours, sir."

Blake scowled. "That's a good way for the Vraxar to ensure they have endless undamaged bodies to choose from."

"I'm still trying to work out how they've locked down the comms," said Pointer. "At first, I thought it was the satellite ring. Now I'm not so sure."

"New tech," said Hawkins. "The Vraxar have developed kit that enables their style of warfare. I'd like to know what it is."

"Me too," said Blake. "The more intel we gather, the better a chance we have next time."

Following Quinn's discovery about the enemy satellites, Blake once more considered his decision on destroying the satellite network, finally rejecting it for the second time. Even if the

ES Lucid was successful in bringing them down, there was nothing to stop the Vraxar deploying more. *Or just blowing the planet to pieces and moving on to somewhere else.*

The discovery of the Vraxar's intentions was a sobering one, though ultimately not something unexpected. It made each passing moment feel like a wasted chance to act and it took all of Blake's inner strength to resist the urge to launch missiles at the Vraxar satellites and deal with whatever might come afterwards.

"Tucson is just coming into view now, sir. We'll be able to see it directly in a couple of minutes," said Pointer. "And there's an enemy battleship directly overhead."

"Figures," said Hawkins.

"It's just another bump in the road," said Blake. "Give me the stats."

"Another new shape, sir. It's seven-thousand-eight hundred metres long and two thousand on its Y-axis. There's not enough data to tell you what sort of tricks it has up its sleeve."

The Vraxar battleship was V-shaped, with a squared-off nose. It tapered slightly from nose to tail and its hull was near-black metal. No matter how hard he tried, Blake was unable to decide whether the enemy ship was a new design, an old one, or neither. With the Space Corps and the Ghost fleets, there was a clear evolution between each new generation of warships. The Vraxar were different and Blake was curious to know why.

"Check to see if there are any signals coming from the Tucson base," he said. "Maybe they've worked out a method that gets around whatever the Vraxar are using the jam the comms."

The *Lucid* was still ten million kilometres from New Earth and Blake knew it was hard work for his officers to provide any degree of certainty. Even so, there were no complaints about his orders.

"There're no comms signals in the sky, sir." Pointer fell silent.

"What is it?"

"They've been attacked. There is extensive damage across most of the facility."

The bulkhead view changed again, showing the Tucson base as a bright patch of light amongst the darker towns and cities in the surrounding area. Smoke poured upwards, obscuring much of the view.

"That must have been a couple of thousand missiles," said Hawkins.

Blake spat angrily. "Most of them on the barracks area."

"There's a Vraxar craft on the ground. It doesn't look much like a warship."

The enemy vessel was a series of mismatched cubes joined unevenly together. It was approximately eleven hundred metres long and rested on an open area of ground a short distance from the nearest building. The distance was too great to make out any of the details.

"It's a transport," said Blake. "I'd bet a month's pay on it."

"You've been sacked, sir."

"Not yet, I haven't!"

"There's plenty of comms activity on the base itself," said Pointer, working hard. She was in sore need of a backup officer. "It's shielded traffic, so they must be using some of the old hard links put in when they first built the place."

"Can you intercept what they're saying?"

"No, sir."

"I thought as much." Blake got up from his seat and walked closer to the main screen. He indicated one or two places on the image. "Interesting what they left intact."

"I've never been to Tucson," said Quinn. "I don't know what they keep in those areas."

"This building here with these big walls around it is by far the largest single storage facility for Obsidiar in the whole of the

Confederation. We hold more than fifty percent of our remaining stocks here."

"It's got ten gauss emplacements on the roof," said Pointer. "They appear to be firing at the battleship."

"With no sign they've got enough grunt to take down its shields, or indeed the battleship itself even if it didn't have shields," added Quinn.

"And those other areas you were looking at are the *Ulterior-2* and the *Earth's Fury*," said Hawkins. "Still intact as well."

Quinn was busy checking. "Both spaceships are offline. There are a few modules with power flowing through them, which is to be expected when the construction is at such an advanced stage. They're not going anywhere in a hurry."

"That's got to be why they're still in one piece, eh?" asked Ensign Toby Park. "Why destroy something that can't fly?"

Blake wasn't convinced. "The Vraxar don't usually act in a rational manner. There's no way they don't know about those two spaceships, so I'm stumped. If it was me, I'd make absolutely certain and hit them with a few hundred missiles."

"They might not care anymore," said Quinn shrugging.

With a grimace, Blake backed away from the screen and returned to his seat. The closer they came to New Earth, the clearer it became how little they could do to influence the final outcome. Whatever they did, however well they played the limited cards in their hand, there was one thing against which they had no hope. As long as *Ix-Gorghal* remained close by, the death of everyone on New Earth was assured. To cap it off, it was going to happen in the coming few hours.

He drummed his fingers against the arm of his seat, lost in thought. His mind turned over each problem, hunting for a new approach that might extract a better result from the situation. *Not necessarily a good result,* he reflected. *Right now, I'd settle for something other than a total disaster.*

It was no use and his brain refused to offer anything incisive. At the moment of despair, something new came.

"Sir?"

It was Lieutenant Pointer, clearly excited.

"Tell me."

"I've got Lieutenant Cruz on the comms. She's on the *Ulterior-2*!"

Blake felt a spark ignite inside him, though he was as yet uncertain if this development was in any way significant. He waved frantically and Pointer opened the channel.

CHAPTER NINE

"LIEUTENANT CRUZ, it's good to speak to you," said Blake.

"And you, sir."

"We'll save the details for later. How come you're able to speak to us?"

"The *Ulterior-2* has new sensor and comms arrays, sir. Whatever the Vraxar are using to jam everything else it isn't working against this battleship."

"Have you spoken to anyone? Is Fleet Admiral Duggan alive?"

"I haven't spoken to anyone else. Every receptor is open, but they're all quiet. I'm using the sensors to see what's going on around me, but the view isn't great from this trench."

"Have you attempted to make contact with these receptors?" asked Pointer. "The *ES Lucid*'s comms are working so the interference is local to the planet. I can't see any receptors on the surface, so whatever they fitted to the *Ulterior-2*, it's the only vessel currently able to talk on the whole of New Earth."

"I've linked, but there's no handshake at the other end. That's as far as I've taken it."

"There's a chance they can hear you without being able to respond," said Pointer.

"I considered that. I'm not sure what I can do to help the situation. The *Ulterior-2* is mostly offline and even if it was capable of flight I couldn't personally get it off the ground without flattening what's left of the base in the process."

"And you don't have clearance to pilot it anyway," said Blake. "The ship wouldn't accept your request for it to take off."

"Yes, sir. I'm stuck."

Blake scratched his chin in thought. "Do you have access to the construction progress reports? I'd like you to send them over."

"There are parts of the files I can't access, but I'm able to send them. They're coming to you now."

Blake turned to see Pointer lifting a thumb in the air.

"We've got them, thanks."

"What now, sir?"

"I need some time to think. In the meantime, I'd like you to collate a list of the receptors available to you. Send a message to the local command and control immediately, telling them your status. I'll get back to you shortly."

"Okay, sir."

Blake closed the channel and turned his attention to the construction progress reports. He had the beginnings of an idea, though it was far too early to know if it was feasible.

His intentions were evidently clear to his crew. "Do you think you can get those new spaceships up in the air?" asked Hawkins.

"I'm not thinking anything at the moment, Lieutenant."

"Yes, you are," said Pointer accusingly. "Don't keep it quiet – you never know, we might have something to offer."

Blake sighed and leaned back. "I wasn't intending to keep anything to myself. In fact, I think I tell you far more than I'm meant to." His eyes roved over the top-level plan for the *Ulterior-*

2, following the project's critical path from start to end. "Assuming this plan is up-to-date, the Hadron could fly right now. Everything is fitted except for the armour plates covering the final engine modules. They haven't done extensive testing however, and they're running late with it."

"Is that a problem?" asked Quinn.

"I personally wouldn't like to fly an untested battleship," said Blake. "Ah! Here's why they've left off the testing. There are problems with the *Earth's Fury* and they diverted several teams from the battleship to help out on this one."

"What's wrong with the *Earth's Fury*? You said it was just a big gun, right?"

"That's more or less right, in the same way that a Colossus tank is just a larger version of a child's plastic tank."

"Fine, it's a *really* big gun," huffed Pointer.

"A really big *experimental* gun, Lieutenant." Blake corrected her. He read through the series of problems. "No life support, incomplete engine installation, they haven't installed three of its four Obsidiar cores yet. The list goes on. The comms and sensor arrays were due to finish their testing a couple of hour ago, so anyone onboard will be able to call in their food order since they haven't installed the replicators either."

"Does the main armament work?" asked Hawkins.

"It's been test-fired only at this stage. Obsidiar is a little too valuable to start hurling balls of it towards random moons. I don't know for definite where the live magazine is. However, it's almost certainly in the Obsidiar Storage Facility."

"Could you take control of *Earth's Fury* from here and launch a few pot shots at the battleship with conventional rounds?"

"Not without comms I couldn't. From memory, those conventional rounds aren't anything more sophisticated than balls of Gallenium. *Earth's Fury* wasn't meant to use anything other than specially-designed ammunition and I doubt it'll be effective without it."

"We've got to do something with the *Ulterior-2*, then," said Pointer firmly. "I've had a look at the specification documents, or at least the non-detailed version they allow officers of my rank to look at, and those Havoc cannons seem like they'd go clean through a thousand metres of armour."

"They performed a lot better than that in final testing," said Hawkins. "I get to hear a few things."

Blake didn't like to bring the mood down, especially since he often called others out for doing the same. Nevertheless, he felt obliged to inform his crew of the difficulties.

"We have no crew for the *Ulterior-2* and no way to organise a crew. In addition, it might require anything from fifteen minutes to an hour for its engines to wake up and be ready for flight. Lastly, it's not going to face any Vraxar until Fleet Admiral Duggan signs it off."

"I'm sure he won't mind if it flies without signoff, given the circumstances, sir."

"Without his direct approval, the battleship will remain in maintenance mode, Lieutenant. Its weapons will only fire after its crew jump through additional hoops and its engines will only permit full power in very short bursts, such as would be necessary for testing purposes."

"I see," said Pointer. "You live and you learn."

"Does this mean we're going to do absolutely nothing?" asked Hawkins.

Blake smiled. "No, Lieutenant. What it means is that we are going to do *everything*. We're going to do whatever we can and hope that somehow everything comes out all right. What do we have to lose?"

"The worst outcome is that everyone dies anyway," said Quinn.

"I haven't worked out the details yet, Lieutenant. First things first: get me Lieutenant Cruz again."

The connection took hardly any time, which was unsurprising given Cruz wasn't exactly overburdened with other tasks.

"Have you got me that list of receptors?" asked Blake.

"I certainly have, sir. I have also sent a message to the command and control bunker to let them know where I am and also about the *ES Lucid.*"

"Excellent. I've received your list."

Blake mumbled quietly while he checked the many open receptors on the Tucson base. There was a lot to get through and he heard Cruz stirring uncertainly on the *Ulterior-2.*

"Sir?"

"That's it!" exclaimed Blake. "I see our old friend Lieutenant McKinney is still assigned to the task of whipping a sense of duty into the soldiers on the Obsidiar Storage Facility. Corporal Bannerman's pack is showing open and available."

"Yes, sir."

"I have two messages for you to send, Lieutenant Cruz. Listen up."

Whilst Blake recited the details he wanted relayed, the rest of the crew listened with open mouths and a growing sense of disbelief. The level of trust involved was going to be such that even the slightest misstep or misunderstanding would cause everything to fail.

There were occasions when you just had to go for broke and Blake did exactly that.

———

THE SITUATION in the Obsidiar Storage facility was a poor one and about to get considerably worse.

Lieutenant Eric McKinney was in one of the two security

control stations in the central building, pondering his options. The front wall of the room was covered in screens and most of the floorspace was taken up by a control console.

A few of McKinney's men were with him and together they watched the unfolding events through the network of monitoring sensors in the outer wall. Corporal Bannerman had ousted the previous occupant of the central chair and he operated the monitoring system with ease.

"There's their dropship," he said. "Makes it sound small when you call it that."

"Four hundred metres away from the outer wall," said McKinney. "And big enough to fit a million troops onboard if you packed them in."

"It's going to look like a piece of cheese when the perimeter chainguns run out of ammunition," said Ricky Vega.

The OSF outer guns had maintained a constant barrage against the Vraxar dropship from the moment it landed. They sprayed it with hundreds of thousands of high-velocity slugs, which drummed against the damaged metal plating. The automatic defences were programmed to fire continuously until their targets were either neutralised or the guns reached at certain temperature, at which point they would drop to a reduced rate of fire and maintain it till their magazines ran dry. Meanwhile, the roof emplacements were unable to hit the dropship once it descended beneath their firing arc.

Garcia snorted. "They haven't got the penetration to get through something as big as that dropship."

It was difficult at the best of times to agree with anything which came out of Garcia's mouth, though there were times it was unavoidable. "You're right," said McKinney.

"Do you think they're going to sit it out, Lieutenant?" asked Huey Roldan.

"They'll be waiting a while if they do," said Bannerman.

"The OSF is equipped with the best shit the Space Corps can make." He waved a finger over the six topmost displays. "There's not one gun exceeded fifty percent of design tolerance for heat and each one could chop a hundred thousand Vraxar into rotting chunks of rat food."

"What about the ammo?" pressed Garcia. "They can't fire forever."

Bannerman shook his head. "Sometimes I ask myself if you'll ever be happy, Garcia. We've got enough in the magazines to keep this up for another twenty minutes."

"Yeah, but twenty minutes and then they come for us."

"Send him to the perimeter wall, Lieutenant. I'm begging you." said Jeb Whitlock. "Or if you don't send him, send me so I don't need to listen to his crap any longer."

"Whitlock's right. Put a sock in it, Garcia," growled McKinney. "I don't want you going out there and telling all these inexperienced guys how they're about to die."

"Point taken, Lieutenant. I'll only sing happy tunes from here on."

McKinney sighed in irritation and didn't pursue it. "Corporal Bannerman, can you get me a visual on the defence squads?"

"Certainly can. We've got five hundred stationed on the eastern outer wall, with another five hundred on the inner." The sensor view showed the soldiers standing on top of the wide perimeter wall. There was plenty of cover, so in theory they would be able to fire freely into any approaching force.

"Doesn't look like many when they're all spread out like that," said Roldan.

"Movement on the dropship!" said Bannerman.

McKinney watched the feed carefully. Along the length of the Vraxar dropship, wide sections of the hull opened outwards.

"Anyone behind those doors isn't going too last long," said Vega.

"There's no way they'll let..." McKinney started.

Without warning, a dozen of the external feeds shut off, whilst several of the remaining ones lit up in pure white. The security room was dimly lit to begin with and the glare caused the men to squint or shield their eyes.

"What the hell?"

Bannerman was on it at once, trying his best to get the sensors online again.

McKinney felt empty. "Don't bother trying."

"Huh?"

"Look."

It took a few seconds for the light to fade on the main building east wall sensors. When it did, there was no mistaking what had happened.

"The bastards hit us from orbit."

McKinney's anger overflowed. He swore loudly and it was hard not to punch one of the blank screens in front of the security console. Leaving those men on the walls had always been a gamble, but one which he'd felt pushed into taking. The perimeter guns were dumb tools and no replacement for the eyes and judgement of a trained soldier. Somehow, he'd convinced himself the Vraxar wouldn't risk an orbital strike against the OSF and would rely on ground artillery backed up with overwhelming numbers.

Both the outer and inner east walls were smashed and ruined. There were two gaping holes in the outer wall and further to the north it had collapsed in parts. The inner wall was even more badly damaged and had been reduced to a pile of rubble and scattered everywhere. Here and there, the stone continued to burn in testimony to the heat of the plasma warheads which had struck the wall.

"Crap, they got all the east side guns," said Bannerman. "Some of the north and south ones too."

"Did they strike this central building?"

"Not as far as I can tell, Lieutenant. We're holding the prize and they don't want to blow it up."

The sensors fixed to the main facility building were undamaged and through them, McKinney watched six huge doors on the dropship's flank fall to the ground, forming ramps for the occupants to disembark.

"What's that?" asked Roldan. "Doesn't look much like soldiers."

"It isn't," said McKinney. "They're bringing out the heavy stuff."

"They aren't going to risk losing all this Obsidiar, are they?" asked Vega. "There's no way they're just going to blow the walls open and hope for the best."

"Just when I think I'm learning something about our enemy, they show me how mistaken I am," said McKinney.

From each of the six doors came an artillery piece, their armoured metal frames floating a few inches above the surface. They were of a similar size – each about three metres square from the front - though with differing functions. Some had multi-barrelled guns, others had a single, larger bore cannon. A third type had a compact missile cluster mounted on top.

"What are they doing?" asked Garcia.

"Those ones are heading into the main area of the base," said Roldan.

"What about us?"

"I'm sure we're going to find out."

There was little choice other than to watch. More of the artillery emerged from the depths of the dropship. McKinney was granted a side view of the mobile weapons and saw that each was eight or nine metres long. Smaller shapes were visible on the artillery - Vraxar soldiers stood on purpose-built platforms which offered shelter from any small arms fire which might come from the front.

Dozens upon dozens of weapons left the dropship. More and more foot soldiers came after – tens of thousands, who walked in the sheltered centre of the artillery formations. To McKinney's surprise, the majority of them ignored the storage facility and moved out of sight behind the damaged walls, many heading south and the rest dispersing to the north and west.

"Most of the south wall sensors are still operational," said Bannerman. "We'll pick them up in a few seconds."

Sure enough, the Vraxar artillery came into the sight arc of the first functioning south wall sensor. The enemy streamed by – sixty or more heavy mobile weapons, accompanied by a swarm of hulking Vraxar soldiers. The image was clear enough for McKinney to determine that nearly all of those on foot were Estral in origin. They strode without hurry, yet easily kept pace with the gravity-engined guns around them.

"They're going for the *Ulterior-2* and *Earth's Fury*," said McKinney.

"How do you know, Lieutenant?"

"What else is there across from the landing strip?"

"They don't usually bother stealing spaceships," said Sergeant Li.

McKinney was hit by another illuminating thought. "Maybe they only capture the spaceships that are good enough for their fleet. The *Ulterior-2* was meant to be the most powerful warship in the whole Space Corps."

"What about the *Earth's Fury*?" asked Webb. "I was told it was some kind of new souped-up monitoring station."

"With a gun on top?"

"Maybe it needs to shoot asteroids or something," said Webb.

"You've said nothing all the time we've been in this room and then you come out with that crap?" laughed Roldan.

"Webb. you'll believe any old shit," said Whitlock.

Li didn't want to miss out on the fun. "Someone's got to be a gullible bastard, otherwise there'd have been no need to invent the word, would there?"

"Enough," said McKinney quietly. "We've just lost hundreds of men and most of our defences. We're holed up with nowhere to go and we're facing that."

He aimed a thick finger towards the eastern wall sensors. Eighteen artillery weapons remained, a mixture of all three types. There were plenty of converted Estral soldiers and they remained in cover. Behind, there were more – thousands more – and they kept flooding off the dropship. Some followed the others towards the *Ulterior-2*, whilst others remained facing the Obsidiar Storage Facility. In terms of what they required to break into the OSF, it was overkill.

"It's not all good, Lieutenant," laughed Bannerman sarcastically. "Now we know they've left a warship in space somewhere above the base. Even if we made a run for it, they'd turn us to cinder before we got two hundred metres away from here."

McKinney picked up his rifle, intending to check if each of his teams was in place. The interior of the OSF was designed with defence in mind, though he sincerely doubted the Space Corps had anticipated it would ever be assailed by such an excessive force.

Corporal Bannerman jumped as if he'd just noticed a fifteen-legged tropical Atlantis tarantula running along his arm. "Wait up, Lieutenant!"

McKinney turned in puzzlement while Bannerman reached beneath the security console for his comms pack.

"Is it picking something up?"

Bannerman didn't answer immediately. He turned one of the dials and moved a couple of the sliding tuners.

"It's the *Ulterior-2*!" he said in disbelief. "Lieutenant Maria Cruz."

"What's your girlfriend doing on the new Hadron?" asked Roldan.

McKinney gave him the finger and elbowed his way next to Bannerman.

"How is she?" The question wasn't likely relevant to the reason she'd made contact and he corrected himself. "What does she want?"

"I can't ask, sir. The *Ulterior-2* must have new super-duper comms. I can hear what she's saying, but I can't give a response."

"How are we going to..."

"Shhh, Lieutenant. She's speaking."

McKinney listened in. What he heard was about as unpleasant as he'd expected and when he stopped for a second to think about it, realised what a truly awful position it put him in.

CHAPTER TEN

THE TUCSON BASE had been built on land specifically chosen for its stability and lack of seismic activity. The reinforced landing strips had enough to bear carrying thirty billion tonnes worth of Hadron battleship without them having to also contend with underlying shifts in the tectonic plates.

As a consequence of this necessary stability, there wasn't a mineshaft – either active or abandoned - anywhere within twenty kilometres of the base. This presented a problem when it came to the Last Stand project. In order for the blast of an Obsidiar bomb to be properly channelled, the geologists, engineers and experts in theoretical explosives, decided it would be best for the devices to be stored deep underground in order to guarantee that a dud bomb which exploded with less than expected force would still kill everyone living.

Obsidiar bombs were new technology and came with a certain degree of uncertainty and unpredictability, hence the reason for this concern. However, Benediction was so far removed from everything before it, even if its blast realised only a few percent of its expected median diameter, it would be more than sufficient to destroy New Earth several times over.

Unfortunately, the design advancements on Benediction came several months after Fleet Admiral Duggan had ordered a suitable shaft dropped into the earth for the storage of the device. The bomb was inside Facility LT3 now, deactivated and awaiting someone with the necessary authorisation to arrive and allow it to fulfil its terrible potential.

Duggan was that man and though he hated it, he would have given the responsibility to no other.

The airlift doors leading to the surface above the command and control bunker were ahead of him. Duggan stood straight in the confines of the room, while the men and women around him finished their preparations.

"Sir?" asked Lieutenant Tom Richards. His earnest face and confident manner made him an ideal officer.

"Are we ready?" asked Duggan. He rolled his shoulders, feeling the unfamiliar weight of the spacesuit's material resisting the movement of his limbs. Duggan wasn't out of shape but there was no way his body could compete with that of a younger man. He was especially glad he wasn't carrying one of the plasma repeaters which many of the others wore as if they were no more of a burden than an extra cotton shirt. R1T James Lopez carried the plasma tube and he leaned against it with the kind of nonchalant air which was common amongst soldiers trained to use this particular weapon.

"Yes, sir. We need to move. We don't know if the Vraxar attack on the OSF is the extent of what they intend."

"Have you planned a route which takes us away from the OSF?"

"As best we can. It's three klicks and keeps us under cover most of the way. Facility LT3 is to the north-east – we're going to pass within a thousand metres of where the dropship came down.

If they're only interested in the OSF, we've got nothing to worry about. If they've got bigger plans, we should be able to get through before they secure the area. As long as we move fast."

"Three klicks on foot," said Duggan wryly. He lifted a hand, forestalling the response. "I'm aware we don't want to be hit by a missile from that battleship."

"No, sir. The more of us we bring, the better the chance they see us from the air. Particularly if we're in a vehicle." Richards took a gauss rifle from one of his soldiers and handed it to Duggan. "I hear you can shoot."

Duggan reached out and grasped the barrel. A feeling of excitement rushed through him like a drug and for the tiniest of moments he knew *exactly* what it was to be young again. "That I can, Lieutenant. I hope I won't be needing it."

Lieutenant Edwards was admirably thorough and he repeated the mission instructions for anyone who'd been thinking of lunch when he'd spoken them the first, second and third times.

"Listen up! I don't want any pissing around on this. We're going to move straight to the objective, following the route I've given you. Part of this route takes us through an area hit by enemy missiles so the going is likely to be tough. Keep under cover where you can and with any luck we'll be able to stay inside for most of the journey."

A few of the assembled soldiers nodded and muttered their acceptance. Richards continued.

"The comms aren't working, so we're going to leave our visors up as much as possible. Only use them if you get lost and need to refer to your map, or if there are toxins in the air. We have Fleet Admiral Duggan with us and I want you to do your utmost to impress him with your skills and your professionalism. Is that clear?"

The response was loud and enthusiastic. "Yes, sir!"

Someone spoke up from the back. "Can you tell us what this is all about yet, sir?"

"Negative, soldier. What I know is that this is a top-priority in our efforts to repel the invaders."

The words made Duggan feel even worse than he already did, like he was personally stabbing each of these soldiers in the back. Giving his approval for the Last Stand project was far and away the hardest thing he'd ever done and it wasn't about to get any easier.

Lieutenant Richards was evidently satisfied and he called for the airlifts. There were four in this bank, with plenty of room inside for fifteen soldiers, Duggan and finally, Lieutenant Paz. The lift ascended in silence, with not a single one of the men or women inside moving or speaking. The door opened and they gathered at the top in a room identical to the one below.

"Move out, people," said Richards.

He set off at once, choosing one of the three exit corridors, which led through a series of secure blast proof doors, up a single flight of steps and eventually into the reception area of the central administration building for the Tucson base. It was deserted here, though the lights were on and each console was fully operational. Several sets of clear doors led outside, where the base lighting did its best to fool the eye into thinking it was daytime.

Richards didn't pause and he set off across the reflective marble-tiled floor, his feet producing a crisp sound on the surface. The other members of the squad spread out in loose formation and followed, keeping Duggan and Paz close to the centre.

The Vraxar had landed a short time ago and it was important for the squad to reach Facility LT3 before the enemy could sweep through the base. In truth, Duggan could only guess at what the aliens planned and how they would achieve it. The main sensor array had detected the incoming dropship and after that it was down to guesswork.

"I'll be glad if they settle for the OSF," Duggan muttered.

"What else is there for them here?" asked Paz.

"Two unfinished warships."

"Which are in the opposite direction."

"I don't need reassurance, Lieutenant. Whatever comes, we'll deal with it – if we hide in the bunker we're failing everyone in the Confederation."

"Just a shame for the people on New Earth," she whispered.

"Not everyone is lucky enough to have a say in the method of their death. If I thought there was another way…"

"I'm not judgemental, sir, and I know what it costs you to do this."

"Have you been talking to my wife again?"

"I've worked with you long enough to know how you think."

The squad approached the exit doors. They had a reflective outer coating to stop people staring in, so there was no danger an enemy sniper could pick them off while they remained inside. Richards motioned everyone to a stop and then he advanced in a crouching run with his rifle in hand, lowing his visor with the other. He stopped behind one of the doors and spent a few seconds checking the street outside.

"Clear," he said.

Richards opened the door and the soldiers hurried outside. A flight of wide, stone steps led to the parking lot in front of the building. A pavement went to the left and right. The main street was a hundred metres away, directly across the parking area. A few birds, their body clocks tricked into thinking it was morning or evening, trilled from the rooftops. Otherwise, this usually-busy area of the Tucson base was empty, with the personnel presumably following procedure and keeping low in the below-ground bunkers built for just such an emergency.

On any other day, the familiarity of these surroundings would have blinded Duggan's eyes to the details. Now he found himself seeing little things he couldn't remember – two well-tended trees next to the Space Corps flag at the bottom of the steps, a manhole cover on the pavement. Even the squat research building opposite – a place he knew well - seemed oddly unfamiliar.

Not everything was normal. Thick smoke billowed into the air in numerous dense plumes which drifted upwards, their source hidden by the intact structures clustered around the central admin building. The air was cloying and it stank of burning polymers. It caught Duggan in the throat and he coughed. It was tempting to lower his visor and take in the clean air from the suit. He resisted and after a few intakes of the filthy, soot-ridden air, his lungs gave up complaining and he could breathe more easily.

There were fifteen or twenty pool vehicles in the lot, which would have cut the journey time by eighty percent, whilst also significantly increasing the risk factor. The plan was to go on foot and though a few pairs of eyes lingered on a lightly-armoured transport vehicle, no one suggested they give it a try.

This first part of the journey meant crossing the parking lot, which left the squad exposed to anything watching from space. They set off at a run and Duggan felt the muscles in his legs stretching before they even reached the road. The others held back in order to keep pace with him and the thought of it made him angry. He tried harder, only to find he lacked the suppleness necessary to run faster.

The squad reached the far side of the lot without being hit by a space-launched missile. Duggan was panting hard as they spilled through the front double-doors of the research facility. The reception was a smaller, less grand version of that in the main admin building and Duggan hardly noticed it as he followed the soldier in front – a Rank 1 Trooper called Ellena McGraw.

"The rear entrance is through here," said Richards in a loud voice. He crashed through a pair of swinging doors painted in blue and the others followed.

Duggan was a regular visitor to each of the six research buildings on the base and he could visualise the route in his head. A sign overhead said *1 – Propulsion Ignition 2 – Guidance*.

There was a long, straight corridor on the far side of the door. To his disbelief, Duggan saw people working in the offices. A man wearing spectacles and carrying a pile of folders pressed himself to the side wall when he saw the group approach.

"What the hell are you playing at?" Duggan shouted as he ran past. "The damned Vraxar have attacked!"

He didn't wait to find out if his words were effective and he doubted the researcher had any idea who it was berating him. Some things were more important than the micromanagement of his staff and Duggan left the overzealous workers to whatever they were doing.

The corridor branched and they took the left turning. Richards stopped at a pair of alloy-framed metal doors, to which he had no access. Duggan knew what was necessary and he planted his hand on the access panel. The doors slid aside, revealing the archive section of the building.

"In," said Richards, waving the squad through.

The archive room had a high ceiling and many rows of shelves and metal cabinets. This was the place where the researchers dumped their rough hand-drawn sketches or pages of equations relating to projects signed off as complete. The air was carefully regulated and there was a smell of new paper and ink.

They left the archive room. More corridors followed and Duggan was reminded how large this building was. It was a good thing, since each step brought them closer to their destination as well as keeping them hidden from the enemy above.

Their chosen exit was a single door, which led onto another

main street. Once again, Richards held them up and he peered outside. Smoke drifted through the opening.

"Hear that?" Richards asked.

The sound was far away but clear – a cling-cling-cling coming from elsewhere on the base. There were deeper, thumping sounds interwoven.

"Heavy barrels," said Sergeant Karen Demarco. She snapped her fingers, which was something of a feat in a spacesuit. "The OSF wall guns."

Richards nodded, "And the roof emplacements as well, if I'm right."

"Let's hope it's enough to keep the enemy looking elsewhere," said Demarco. "What's out there?"

"It's like we guessed. Most of the buildings outside have been struck in the bombardment. There's rubble and smoke. It might give us an advantage if we don't choke to death first."

"Time for the visors, Lieutenant?" asked McGraw.

Richards was uncertain and he chewed his lip. "Yes, pull your visors down," he said. "Just don't wander out of sight."

Even without their comms, the visors could replicate a human voice and they had earpieces that meant they could pick up sounds easily enough. Given how much everything relied on clear and easy communication, everyone found it hard when they were gone. Duggan smiled inwardly as he remembered how much money the Space Corps poured into making everything robust. Yet here they were, cut off by the Vraxar and having to rely on being in range of each other's voices. He dropped his visor into place and the cool, filtered air tasted sweeter than anything he could remember.

A tiny number in one corner of his HUD gave the oxygen percentage in the surrounding air: 19%. Duggan swore inwardly.

"Come on," he urged.

The squad left the research building and emerged cautiously

onto the street outside. At once, Duggan was struck by the change. The smoke was thick and clung to the ground, making objects indistinct. A few inexplicably abandoned base vehicles were empty on the street, one of them crushed by a slab of concrete. Duggan looked upwards, to find the building opposite was intact. Wherever the rubble had come from it wasn't here.

A few hundred metres to the east – where their destination lay – there was far greater devastation. The walls of the buildings had collapsed, leaving piles of steel and concrete on what was left of the road. One building on the left, unrecognizable from its original form, was almost completely gone, leaving only a single wall leaning outwards at an angle over the road. Through it all, the smoke billowed and Duggan could make out the flickering orange of dying fires in the ruins.

"Keep to the walls," said Richards, his voice given a metallic edge by the visor speaker.

They remained on the left side of the street, keeping a few paces between each squad member. The other side of the street had suffered the greatest damage and there were many large sections of toppled wall which would have presented unwanted obstacles. As well as concrete, dust and grit, there was plenty of glass underfoot. It crunched and scraped beneath their feet and Duggan was grateful it had been designed to shatter into blunt cubes, rather than break into vicious shards. He kept a careful watch for Space Corps personnel. If there was anyone alive here, they weren't showing their faces.

The street opened out into what had once been informally known as the *Lover's Plaza*. The name was a joke – the plaza had originally been little more than a flat square of concrete with a few seats, roads on four sides and surrounded by buildings so drab and unromantic that Duggan had been tempted to have them torn down every time he came through. The Vraxar battleship had stolen that pleasure away from him and the whole area was a ruin.

"They must have dropped a hundred missiles on this place alone," said Richards, hunkering behind an overturned gravity car.

The others waited nearby, hiding in whatever cover they could find. Duggan and Paz were a few metres from Richards, crouched at the side of a mostly-intact flight of steps which led into the husk of an accommodation block. The sound of the OSF guns was louder here and they echoed through the streets, making it difficult to pinpoint their direction.

"It's more open than I remember it," said Demarco. She leaned around the car, trying to find any trace of the Vraxar. "No movement," she said.

"We've got to make this quick," said Richards. "I'd hoped to cut through the barracks, but it looks like that option is denied us. We're going to make a run for the eastern exit road – it's clogged with rubble, so there'll be some climbing to do. Does anyone have a problem with that?"

Duggan knew he was the focus of the question and Richards was trying to be diplomatic. "I've got no problems, Lieutenant."

"The east road takes us as close to the OSF as we're going to get on this mission. Once we're past, it's only a few hundred metres until we reach the entrance to Facility LT3."

The squad knew the way and they gathered themselves. Their faces were covered by the visors and their expressions were hidden. Even so, Duggan knew how to read soldiers. These held no fear and they were impatient to get on with the mission. It was a commendable attitude and one instilled in training.

They moved out, Richards once again on point. He went faster than before, obviously concerned about staying out in the open for too long. Duggan started flagging at once.

"You need to boost," said Richards, looking over his shoulder. "Now."

Duggan knew there was no room for misplaced pride on this mission. He instructed his suit to give him a shot of battlefield adrenaline. A series of microneedles jabbed into various parts of his body, each of them hitting a nerve. He grimaced and then felt the powerful drugs thundering into his body. The adrenaline wasn't meant for people classed as *elderly,* owing to the effects it had on the heart and brain. Duggan didn't care – he rode the wave and his feet ran faster.

A few of the buildings around the plaza burned brightly, whilst others smouldered. The smoke was thicker than before and it added an otherworldly feeling to the sprint. Shapes sprang from the gloom and the sound of footsteps receded, leaving Duggan with the strange impression he was alone in his own dream, or that his version of reality had somehow branched off, taking him to a place separate from everyone else.

The sensor in his visor adjusted slowly to the billowing clouds of smoke and for one moment, it granted him a perfect view of the exit street, only eighty metres away. Somehow, he'd got ahead of most of the squad and, over his shoulder, he saw them trying hard to catch up.

Nearly there.

Without a logical reason for it, Duggan was struck by a sudden, absolute certainty. He looked to the heavens, trying to spot the missile he *knew* was coming.

"Get down!" he shouted, throwing himself to the ground. The plaza was a mess of rubble, but there was nothing which would protect them from a plasma warhead.

The others were trained to respond and they followed Duggan's lead, hurling themselves towards whatever cover they could find.

The missile came, the speed of its flight leaving the sound of its passage far in its wake. Duggan thought he got a sense of it – a blur coming from directly overhead, approaching with incredible, inescapable velocity. The explosion came, ripping apart buildings and throwing countless tonnes of plasma-blackened concrete and metal high into the sky. The sound rumbled on and then it faded, leaving behind the sound of stones clattering down.

Duggan lifted himself from the ground, wondering why he was still alive. He saw. The Vraxar missile had landed a few hundred metres away, somewhere out of sight. Whatever they'd been aiming for, it wasn't the squad.

There's time for that to change, he thought.

Lieutenant Richards was already on his feet, pulling the squad medic Rex Copeland up by his arm. "Move!" he bellowed.

With the impetus of those who'd experienced a recent scrape with death, they ran. Another missile landed before they'd covered more than a few paces. Duggan twisted in his stride, craning to see what the Vraxar were aiming at. It was no use – smoke and the ruins of the Tucson base impeded his sight. As he scrambled over the pile of rubble blocking the eastern exit road, Duggan realised the OSF chainguns had stopped. Far from being reassured, he felt their silence was a sign of the Vraxar's progress within the base.

The squad grouped up and continued on.

CHAPTER ELEVEN

LIEUTENANT ERIC MCKINNEY dashed through the interior of the Obsidiar Storage Facility, a few of his men close behind. The passages were mostly clear, with the guards already at their posts in the fortified areas within the building. Overhead, the ceiling miniguns whined softly on their motors as they turned ominously to track McKinney and the others. Every thirty metres, the men were required to pass one of the heavy security doors. The routine was similar – stop, press the access pad, wait for the door to open, continue through. It was necessary and frustrating in equal measures.

Not everyone within the facility was where they should be.

"Get to your damn post!" McKinney roared at one man, who was dawdling along without a rifle.

It was tempting to pause for the split second required to throttle the man. Instead, McKinney knocked the soldier to one side as he went by and settled for flexing his augmented arm while he thought about the fully-warranted strangulation.

He did stop briefly, at the smaller security station. A man

whose name he couldn't recall was watching the bank of screens, while a group of others shifted nervously.

"What's the latest?" asked McKinney bluntly.

"Small arms, sir. They wound up one of those mobile chainguns for a few seconds and then they stopped. Why haven't they come?"

"They'll come, don't you worry."

"Is it true Sergeant Woods is going to be in charge?"

News within the OSF travelled faster than a fleet warship at maximum lightspeed. McKinney wasn't in the slightest bit surprised they knew.

"Yes. I've been given other orders."

"You're leaving the facility?" pressed the man.

"I have to."

The soldier asked other questions which McKinney had no intention of answering. He exited the security monitoring room, leaving the occupants to discuss the rumours amongst themselves.

The ground-level warehouse area was protected by numerous doors and the men slowed again. Each door required an access code, which it fired off to the OSF processing unit for confirmation. Any area where Obsidiar was handled required high-level approval. Fortunately, McKinney was already approved, but each confirmation took a few seconds to come back.

"Everything's running slowly," he muttered, rapping an access panel with his knuckles.

"How is the timer?" asked Sergeant Li. "I make it ten minutes."

"I've got eleven," said Bannerman.

"So much for precision instruments," said Li, tapping the side of his visor.

"It's going to be tight," said Vega. "Think we can pull it off?"

"Don't ask stupid questions," said Li, saving McKinney the bother of saying the same thing.

The door in front rumbled open, allowing the men access to a wide flight of stairs so pristine it appeared as if they had never seen the underside of a human foot. They started up.

"There's too much that can go wrong," growled McKinney, giving voice to his main worry.

"What in particular, Lieutenant?" asked Jeb Whitlock. "Seems like everything is straightforward to me."

"What planet are you on, Whitlock?"

"Well, the way I see it, we've been through plenty of shit and still come up smelling like a bouquet of flowers you'd be happy to give to the mother-in-law."

It was suddenly clear that Whitlock was actually looking for reassurance and hiding it behind a fake wall of confidence.

"There's always been comms, soldier," McKinney replied. "That's what makes the difference. If something went wrong, or we had to change something, we could manage it. This time?" He thumped the grey wall. "We've been given an instruction and sent on our way. If something goes wrong or there's a forced deviation, we've got no way to recover."

"Even with the comms this would be a crappy job," said Garcia.

"I'm kinda looking forward to it," said Vega.

They reached a landing, with a single exit door and a single access panel. McKinney stepped up to it. The door was three metres high and wide. He pressed his palm against the access plate.

"Haven't you been on one before?" he asked.

"Only in the simulator, Lieutenant. I don't think I've ever seen one in the flesh. What about you?"

"I've not driven one since I got my license." McKinney

grinned. "That was three years ago. They've done a complete overhaul since then."

"You sure you can cope?" asked Bannerman.

"Absolutely."

The door split along an imperceptible seam down the middle and the two parts retracted into the frame. The men crossed the threshold into the OSF warehouse area. In the strictest sense it wasn't exactly a warehouse, though it did contain one object. This was the place where the shaped Obsidiar was brought from the huge storage space deep below. The ceiling wasn't as high as might have been expected if one had seen the OSF from the outside. The reason for this was the thickness of the roof, which was strong enough to withstand a direct strike from a Shimmer missile.

The floor of the warehouse was similarly robust and made from the same material used to lay the base landing strip. As far as construction went, the OSF was as strong as it could be without using a few billion tonnes of hardened Gallenium.

"There it is," said the squad medic Amy Sandoval. "I try to save lives and they build shit like this to take them away."

"You're in the wrong job," said McKinney.

"I think you're right."

The Colossus tank was the Space Corps' deadliest ground-based weapon and as far as McKinney was aware, this was the only example on the Tucson base. Each one cost as much to build as a Crimson class destroyer and it wasn't hard to see why.

This particular model was eighty metres long, twenty-five wide and twenty tall, and it hovered silently one metre above the ground. It was angular and with a long, sloping front made to deflect incoming artillery shells. There wasn't a single word to describe its overall shape, though multi-planed, flat-backed trapezoid would more or less cover it. With a crapload of guns and an Obsidiar core.

There were grey-painted words on the side of the tank, skil-fully added so they were clear whichever angle you looked at them. *Here I Stand.*

"How much heat is that thing packing?" asked Vega in wonder.

The main turret was indistinguishable from the upper section and the thirty-metre barrel poked out like a thick pipe with the power to flatten a city. Behind the turret were two shoulder-mounted plasma launchers that could hit a spaceship in orbit. In addition, there was a massive chaingun set back a few metres from the nose, with its own protective turret. There were two minigun turrets mounted where the flank and the rear angles joined.

"Why are those turrets pointing at us?" asked Whitlock.

Li gave him a push. "It can smell your fear."

"There's a lot more than you can see from the outside," said McKinney.

"Can it fly?" asked Clifton.

"No."

"Pfft," Clifton replied in mock derision. He pointed at the bands of explosives with which he had festooned himself. "Bet I could crack it open."

"Bet you couldn't," said McKinney.

They jogged across the floor of the warehouse. The cover for the central gravity lift was sealed and they crossed over it. The metal was thick and McKinney didn't hear any change in the sound of his footsteps. He felt invigorated by the sight of the Colossus tank and he ran faster, reaching it ahead of the others.

There was a side access door, at the end of a two-metre-deep alcove in the tank's armour, with a twin-rung metal ladder the only assistance to reach it. McKinney pulled himself up and held his hand on the access panel for a long moment. The thrum of the tank's gravity engine through his palm greeted him like an old friend.

"Are you sure you're able to get into this thing, Lieutenant?" asked Munoz.

With a hiss of breaking seals, and backup mechanical locks, the door slid to the left. McKinney turned and smiled at the others.

The inner airlock was red-lit and cramped. The ceiling was low enough that McKinney had to keep his neck bent, though the factory had thoughtfully put a layer of industrial rubber up there to minimise skull damage from the inevitable accidents.

The ten soldiers McKinney had brought with him clambered up one at a time. The human occupants of all Space Corps tanks were apparently of secondary importance to squeezing in as much extra hardware as possible. It was a tight fit and they filled the space before McKinney had got the inner airlock door opened.

"Who's grabbing my balls?" asked Li. "Is it you, Garcia?"

"Piss off."

In the scrum, a gauss rifle went off.

"Who the hell was that?" shouted McKinney, before the concern kicked in. "Anyone hurt?"

By some miracle, the gauss slug had struck the ceiling dead-on and the flattened metal disk had dropped harmlessly to the floor.

"Sorry, Lieutenant," said Roldan. "I think that might have been me."

"Let's have a bit more care."

The inner door opened with the same reassuringly solid noise as the outer one. There was a small ante-chamber beyond, with another low ceiling and a single passage – only just wide enough for two to pass - leading deeper into the tank. The lights were a cold blue, the air smelled of metal and the sound of the engine was rougher here – almost coarse. McKinney set off along the passage.

"Close that door behind you!" His voice was lost in the metal walls, like the words were absorbed by the immense weight of the vehicle.

After a few paces, he reached opposite doors – one leading to the cockpit and the other to the personnel area. Ahead, the passage continued until it reached the entry doorway in the other flank. There were a couple of emergency exits elsewhere and McKinney hoped he wouldn't be using them.

The cockpit door opened onto another short passage and took him into the business end of the tank. There was seating for four, each seat dressed with a cloth covering that appeared to have been pre-torn and stained by special request of the Space Corps, to ensure its soldiers didn't get a liking for nice things. The rest of the room was taken up by screens and a wraparound console that wouldn't have looked out of place in a Fleet Admiral's holiday home.

McKinney got himself comfortable and started bringing everything online. The Colossus tank was intended as a last line of defence for the Obsidiar Storage Facility and it was therefore kept in a state of readiness.

"Are we ready to rock and roll?" asked Li, dredging up another from his lexicon of Old Earth sayings.

"Five minutes."

"How's the control core?"

"Something's dragging it down. It's not stopping the green lights on everything we need."

Li dropped himself into the weapons control seat. Roldan was trained in navigation, Bannerman in both comms and backup navigation.

"Not much for me to do, huh?" Bannerman laughed, putting

his hands behind his head. "What with the comms being dead and all."

"Keep an ear out for Lieutenant Cruz."

"You expecting her to ask you on a date, Lieutenant?" asked Roldan.

It was an open joke amongst the men and McKinney gritted his teeth.

"How about I tie you to the main barrel, Roldan?"

"Hey, I was just asking, you know?"

In reality, there was plenty for Bannerman to do, since he was partly responsible for working the tank's sensors, alongside Roldan.

"We've got everyone seated out the back," said Li.

The tank's main systems booted up into a state of combat readiness. There was a chunk of Obsidiar somewhere in the centre of the hull, large enough to power the whole lot if needed. The only shame was that the scientists hadn't figured out how to miniaturise the energy shield generators enough to fit one of those to the tank. *Can't have it all,* thought McKinney.

At last, the *All Systems Operational: 100%* message came up on McKinney's screen. He lowered his visor and checked how long was left on the timer he'd set.

"We're running late."

"We're always on time," said Li.

"I'm opening the inner door," said McKinney.

The warehouse was protected by an inner and an outer door, each rumoured to be a modified warship armour plate. As far as he was aware, McKinney was the only person currently in the OSF who could open these doors. It didn't stop him sweating while he waited for movement.

"Here we go," he said, breathing out.

The tank's front sensor showed the inner door sliding into the floor. There was a space between the doors which was large enough for the tank - if it went in at an angle - and McKinney took hold of the simple-looking control joysticks. He pushed both forward, expecting a gradual response from the gravity engines. Instead, the walls of the cockpit shook and tank shot forwards.

"Whoa!" McKinney said, pulling quickly back on the sticks.

"Faster than you were expecting?" asked Li.

"It must be all that Obsidiar."

It only took a few moments for McKinney's confidence to return. He brought the tank into the space between the two doors, stopping with the nose a few inches from the outer door. It wasn't intended for both doors to be open at once and the four men waited impatiently while the inner door rose up from the floor. Once it was closed, the outer door descended.

"If there are any Vraxar out there, they're going to get a surprise," said Li.

The door vanished into the floor, revealing the gates for the perimeter wall two hundred metres away. Wherever the Vraxar were, it wasn't here. McKinney gave the briefest look upwards. If Captain Blake was late, early or simply got himself shot down, this was going to be a short trip.

Even without the battleship, we might not cover more than five hundred metres.

With a sense of expectation and trepidation, McKinney prepared for action.

CHAPTER TWELVE

THERE WAS a similar sense of expectation and trepidation amongst the crew of the *ES Lucid*. Captain Blake wasn't known for doubt, yet he could feel it growing within him as each moment of inactivity passed by.

"How long?" he asked.

"Two minutes," said Pointer.

The enemy battleship hadn't moved from its position directly over the Tucson base. The dropship had landed forty minutes ago and continued disgorging its cargo of weapons and half-living soldiers, while *Ix-Gorghal* itself wasn't due back for more than an hour. It was too much to hope that when they stuck their arm into the viper's nest they would only get a single bite.

"Everyone ready?"

"Yes, sir."

The plan was simple enough. At the agreed time, Blake would use the *ES Lucid* to lure the Vraxar battleship away from its stationary orbit. Meanwhile, McKinney would take the opportunity to push through to Fleet Admiral Duggan in the central administration building. Assuming Duggan was both alive and agreeable – and Blake had no idea if he was – then McKinney would do his best to fight his way to the *Ulterior-2*, in order for Duggan to bring the ship out of maintenance mode and inform its core cluster that it was in full service. Somewhere along the way, they'd see if there was any chance of putting *Earth's Fury* to use.

Naturally, there were many things which could go wrong, though ultimately it was better to try than to sit back and await the inevitable. Blake told himself failure wasn't an option.

"Let's do this," he said. "Activate the short-range transition."

He sensed a tiny second of hesitation while the crew came to terms with their future.

"Activating," said Quinn.

The *ES Lucid*'s fission engines threw the heavy cruiser inwards towards New Earth. They cut off almost immediately, leaving the warship a quarter of a million kilometres from the enemy vessel.

"Launching everything we've got," said Hawkins.

She activated the weapons systems, unloading everything they could muster in the direction of the enemy warship. The *Lucid*'s Shimmer missiles raced ahead of the swarming Lambdas and a handful of Shatterer warheads.

"No response from the battleship," said Quinn. "We must be out of beam weapon range."

"Somehow I doubt it," Blake replied.

He pressed a button on his console and felt the sudden surge of acceleration, which he quickly brought under control.

"Forty seconds to Shimmer impact."

The *Lucid* didn't have the firepower to crack open the Vraxar battleship's shield in an open engagement. It wasn't important – this was an exercise in pissing them off.

"Here come the missiles," said Blake. The tactical screen was much smaller than he was used to.

Hawkins struggled to get a final tally. "Only six hundred.

They're faster than our Lambdas and slower than the others."
She scratched her head. "I think they've launched a few at the
surface. I've got no idea what the hell they're aiming those
ones at."

Not all of the Vraxar warships carried missiles, with most of
them relying on beam weapons. Blake guessed the battleship had
been chosen specifically because it was capable of precision
bombing.

"If we take out some of those satellites it'll be a bonus,"
said Quinn.

"The Shimmers are good for it."

"I've initiated our second Lambda launch, sir. Shimmers and
Shatterers still reloading."

At the last moment, the two Shimmer missiles turned sharply
from their course. They split and twisted away from the battleship, hurtling with tremendous speed towards New Earth. Shimmers were the pinnacle of missile technology and they scored
direct hits, each one detonating against a separate Vraxar
satellite.

"Score!" shouted Pointer.

"Two satellites no longer on our sensors, sir."

The remainder of the missiles flew onwards. Blake expected
the enemy warship to be equipped with the same countermeasures as the other larger Vraxar craft. He was right – at the last
moment, the battleship emitted a high-energy pulse which burst
outwards in a huge sphere. The pulse wrecked the guidance
systems of the inbound missiles, rendering them useless.

The Shatterers were far more robust. Four of them crashed
against the enemy's shield, whilst the remaining four curved
away towards the other visible satellites.

"Four more direct hits and four more satellites out of action,"
said Hawkins. "Impact from the enemy missiles is imminent.
Launching shock drones."

On his sensor feed, Blake watched the drones spill out from the *Lucid* in a pre-defined pattern. They sparkled and glittered, reflecting the tiniest particles of light energy and seeming to magnify them in a beautiful pattern of silver confetti.

Three or four hundred – it was difficult to be sure – of the Vraxar warheads detonated amongst the shock drones, creating smears of burning plasma which dwindled to nothingness they crossed the final few thousand kilometres towards the *ES Lucid*. A number of missiles came through the drones and these exploded against the heavy cruiser's shield, the plasma spill making the protective sphere temporarily visible.

"Our shield is holding. Getting ready for our next launch."

"They aren't going to let us get away with that. Hand off to the battle computer."

"Handoff complete."

The Vraxar battleship jumped. It disappeared from its stationary orbit and reappeared thirty thousand kilometres from the *ES Lucid*.

"Stupid bastards," said Quinn with feeling.

The Vraxar tended to keep their distance when they faced an opponent with overcharged particle beams. The captain of this battleship was either too confident or he hadn't been paying attention.

The *Lucid*'s front and rear particle beams whined and thumped. They struck the battleship a thousand metres apart, lighting up a quarter of its hull with instant, incredible heat.

Within a second, the *ES Lucid*'s battle computer dumped another spray of shock drones, emptying its entire stocks in a rapid stream. At the same time, it launched several hundred missiles and once done, it disappeared into a short-range transit of its own.

"Can you see it?" asked Pointer.

"It's right in place," said Blake. "Three hundred thousand klicks towards the New Earth moon."

"Where's *Ix-Gorghal*?" muttered Quinn anxiously. "It's going to show, right?"

"It'll show. It's the battleship I'm worried about for the moment."

Sitting with his crew inside one of the *ES Lucid*'s shuttles, deep within the cluster of shock drones, Blake did his best to ignore the tension which pulled at every muscle in his body. On the shuttle's rudimentary sensor feed, he watched. The *ES Lucid*'s farewell missile salvo detonated ferociously against the battleship's energy shield, engulfing it completely. When the fires faded, the Vraxar battleship was still operational, glowing with retained heat from the particle beams which would take days to disperse. Lumps of molten alloy dropped away from its hull in a stream, hardening and drifting away.

"They aren't leaving," said Hawkins.

"They will. They've got to."

"What if they decide to go back? Or scan through all of these drones?" asked Quinn.

"We don't need to hear the possibilities, Lieutenant!"

The battleship jumped for a second time and Blake held his breath while he waited for the sensors to get a lock on it.

He sighed in relief. "They've gone after the *Lucid*."

"Maybe we didn't need to abandon ship after all," said Hawkins.

Just then, something else appeared, come from the far side of New Earth. *Ix-Gorghal* emerged into local space, less than ten thousand kilometres from the shuttle. Its propulsion systems fired up and it moved towards the tiny craft at the kind of leisurely speed which suggested it wasn't in a hurry for anything.

"Oh crap," said Quinn, his voice hoarse.

Even at this distance and viewed through the shuttle sensors, there was no mistaking the incredible size and menace of the Vraxar capital ship. It approached head on and Blake looked into the wide, wide bore of the front disintegration tube. There was a green light somewhere deep inside, strangely mesmerising to his eyes.

A hush fell upon the crew, as if the outcome could somehow be influenced if only they remained as quiet as possible.

"Have they seen us?" whispered Pointer.

"If they have, we won't live long enough to know it."

Ix-Gorghal turned side-on and sailed past, only five thousand kilometres from the edge of the shock drone cloud. Blake cut the shuttle's engines and shut down the non-critical systems, hoping the reduced power signature would make them less visible. He couldn't tear his eyes from the vast spaceship before him. Its surface was covered in more turrets than he could remember and he was beginning to think many of the outer structures were power housings. *The whole thing might be hollow,* he thought. *Half of the Vraxar race in that one ship.*

Ix-Gorghal came to a halt. It was cold on the shuttle, but sweat dripped from Blake's forehead and ran down his back in a stream.

"Go on, piss off," he said.

"If they wait much longer, we'll miss our chance anyway," said Pointer.

The seconds dragged out and Blake found it hard to keep himself steady. "The *Lucid*'s jumped again," he said, his voice scratchy.

"I always did like that ship," said Pointer. "Better than the *Abyss*."

Just when he was beginning to think luck had deserted him, *Ix-Gorghal* vanished from sensor sight.

"Where did it go?" asked Quinn.

In a way, it was irrelevant. Blake didn't spend time searching for the enemy ship. He pressed a trembling finger onto the activation panel for the shuttle's engines. As soon as he felt them kick into life, he pushed the control joystick forward, giving the tiny vessel full thrust. The engines grumbled and the power readings from the life support system spiked as it struggled to cope with the unexpected burst of acceleration.

"Got it!" said Hawkins, making some adjustments to the console from the shuttle's second seat. "It's gone after the *Lucid*!"

The *Lucid*'s battle computer made another short-range transition and it disappeared from the sensors. *Ix-Gorghal* and the Vraxar battleship vanished a few seconds later.

"Still in pursuit," said Blake.

"Looks like. The *Lucid*'s going to run out of tricks soon."

The *Lucid* had been doomed from the moment the plan was conceived and agreed. There was no way *Ix-Gorghal* was going to stay out of the fight once it started. It could be that the *Lucid*'s battle computer would come up with a way to keep the ship intact for the sixty minutes it was programmed to maintain the engagement. In that case, it would make its escape into a much longer lightspeed jump. If that happened, *Ix-Gorghal* might follow, but Blake was absolutely certain the capital ship would break off and return to New Earth, rather than being led on a wild goose chase.

"Eight minutes until we reach Tucson," said Blake. "That's when it starts getting really interesting. How is everyone holding up back there?"

There were only three seats in the shuttle's cockpit and Pointer was the lucky one standing. She opened the door into the passenger bay and made a cursory look around at the troops crammed inside.

"I can't hear anyone complaining."

"That'll do for the moment."

The shuttle forged on. The fight between the *Lucid* and the

Vraxar ships was far behind and the shuttle wasn't packing a good enough sensor array to keep track of the events. It was unfortunate, since Blake wanted advance warning of the enemy's inevitable return to New Earth. *It doesn't matter much – if they destroy the Lucid and return before we reach Tucson, there's no way we'll be able to slip in without being noticed.* He looked at the distance counter.

"Seven minutes," he said.

"It's going to be the longest seven minutes ever," said Pointer.

Blake tried his best to think of something else. He directed the sensors at New Earth instead, reminding himself how many billions of people were left on the planet, each of them lost and frightened, with no idea what was going to happen. Amongst them was his only grandmother, though he hadn't seen her in months. Life in the Space Corps didn't leave a lot of time for family.

The shuttle continued its journey and Blake wondered what the hell he was going to do once he made it to Tucson.

CHAPTER THIRTEEN

WITH A DEEP BREATH, McKinney brought the Colossus tank out of the main Obsidiar storage building. He sent the command for the door to close behind and waited for the few moments it took to seal the building.

"No point in leaving the door open," said Roldan.

"Absolutely. Is everyone set?"

The Space Corps trained its soldiers to be multi-skilled. If you chose a squad at random from any base throughout the Confederation, you could be sure at least one of them could fly a shuttle, pilot a tank, operate a comms pack or safely blow a hole through a sealed blast door. Those in McKinney's squad were no exception and he was able to call upon men who could do the business in a Space Corps tank, not that many of them had operated a weapon so rare as the Colossus tank before.

"All set," confirmed Li.

"Yep, good to go, Lieutenant," added Bannerman.

"Roldan?"

"Let's do this."

There were so many screens within the cockpit it took a few

seconds for McKinney's brain to settle. When it did, he knew he was going to have some fun - for however long it lasted until the tank got torn apart.

McKinney turned the tank, aiming it along the inner compound to the place the Vraxar had breached the perimeter walls. He pushed the control sticks away from him and with a grumbling roar, the engines overcame the tank's inertia and hurled it forward. McKinney was pressed firmly into his seat and the muscles in his neck struggled to keep his head level. This wasn't the time for a softly-softly approach and he planned to give the enemy a nasty surprise. He got one of his own first.

"That battleship hasn't moved, Lieutenant. I can see it straight overhead," said Bannerman.

McKinney swore and very nearly swung them around. Something inside wouldn't let him. *The die is cast,* he thought.

"Keep me informed."

"Yes, sir," said Bannerman.

Not one of the crew suggested they stop and go back. They'd been cooped up for too long and bringing death to the enemy in this tank was too good an opportunity to miss.

The tank reached a speed of forty kilometres per hour and the outer wall of the main facility building sped by. The east wall was directly ahead, though there was no breach through this section and he was going to have to make a turn.

At the last second, he pulled the sticks to the right. The tank tilted to one side, its left-hand side lifting a few feet higher off the ground. The grumbling in the cockpit became louder and the tank executed the turn with a nimbleness McKinney hadn't expected. It was so agile, he nearly cut the corner too close and the right-hand side of the tank came within a metre of striking the wall of the building. He straightened the tank's course and, on the sensor feed, he saw the wide breach through the inner wall. There were Vraxar soldiers everywhere – in the few minutes since McKinney had left the security monitoring room, the aliens had decided to make their move and hundreds had already poured into the opening.

"Left! Now!" shouted Roldan.

The closest part of the breach was ahead and McKinney pulled the tank towards it. A cluster of Vraxar small-arms fire pattered against the hull, the sound lost before it reached the cockpit. The enemy soldiers were too insignificant for McKinney to change course in order to run them over. He didn't need to – hardly any of the Vraxar tried to get out of the way and they thumped against the tank's nose like flies on a windscreen.

"Plasma rockets incoming," said Bannerman. "Negligible damage."

At the far end of the breach, six or seven Vraxar carried shoulder tubes. They launched a second uneven volley towards the tank. The rockets screamed across the intervening space and burst against the tank's hull.

"Setting chainguns to auto," said Li, making no effort to hide the relish in his voice.

The Colossus tank could track and prioritise several thousand individual targets. Its main processing cores were running far slower than usual, but that didn't stop them from identifying the Vraxar carrying plasma tubes. The front chaingun turret rotated sharply and fired. In the cockpit, the men heard it as a metallic grinding sound. Outside, the barrels spun and heavy gauss slugs poured from the main gun. They punched into the Vraxar, smashing them into an unrecognizable mess of dead flesh and metal. The bullets weren't slowed by the bodies of the aliens and they spent themselves against the broken wall of the compound, throwing shards of stone into the other Vraxar nearby.

With its primary targets eliminated, the gun swept on,

mowing down the enemy soldiers with an effortlessness that made the weakness of flesh all too apparent.

The tank reached the opening with undiminished speed. There were many larger pieces of rubble where the wall had been and they formed a low mound. The tank didn't even slow – it crashed into the three-metre pile of broken wall, casting the pieces in an arc in front and to the sides. Some of the pieces weighed many tonnes, yet the onrushing tank treated them as little more than pebbles on a beach.

"We're past the first wall," said McKinney. "What've we got?"

"Ten thousand Vraxar and a dropship," said Li.

Bannerman added his own shit to the mix. "The battleship doesn't look like it's going anywhere."

Don't let us down, Captain Blake.

Before them was the main body of the Vraxar forces which intended to take the OSF. The eighteen pieces of artillery were in the process of coming through the outer wall, spread in a line and with their gravity engines carrying them easily over the scattering of rubble. Amongst them were the soldiers – there was no way to count the numbers, but there were thousands. Behind it all was the dropship, its flank doors open to release a new wave of artillery and soldiers.

"They're going to flood the whole damn base," said McKinney. "Let's see what we can do to that dropship while we're passing."

"I thought you'd never ask," cackled Li. "Activating main gun and shoulder launchers. I almost feel sorry for the bastards."

There was no doubt the Vraxar were taken by surprise, though even if they'd been aware of what was coming, their casualties would have still been immense. The tank's front chaingun selected the nearest artillery unit and sprayed it with an extended burst. The armoured gun was knocked back and flipped over onto its side, crushing a dozen Vraxar soldiers.

The rest of the artillery was spread and able to fire unimpeded. One of the large-bore guns got a round into the Colossus tank's armour. The projectile deflected somewhere a hundred kilometres into the distance, leaving a deep furrow through the tank's plating. Meanwhile, the Vraxar heavy repeaters opened up, battering the tank with thousands of high-velocity slugs.

The main turret on the tank offered its retort, though not at such small targets as the Vraxar artillery. Its targeting computer took aim at the dropship and fired. Most gauss launchers were designed to have little or zero recoil. The gun on the tank was different and when it fired, the entire hull shook as the forces were carried through the metal. A half-metre ball of metal punched clean through the dropship's side, leaving a wide hole as a sign of its passing.

"If that spaceship is hollow, the shot might have gone out the other side and still be travelling," said Bannerman in wonder.

The words hadn't left Bannerman's mouth, when two missiles from the tank's shoulder launchers exploded on the upper section of the enemy spaceship. Compared to a full-sized, dedicated ground battery, the payload was small. It still gave McKinney a great feeling of satisfaction to watch.

Realising he was being distracted by the results of the tank's barrage, McKinney snapped his attention to his own task. The tank was almost at the outer wall and, in spite of the surprise, the Vraxar had recovered quickly and were directing a considerable amount of firepower towards the vehicle. The sound of heavy repeater fire against the hull reached the cockpit as a thrumming sound, similar to heavy rain on a steel roof. Once or twice, McKinney heard and felt the deep booming sounds of large projectiles colliding against the tank. Afterwards came another sound – this one a deeply-muted rumble and hiss.

"They hit us with two missiles," said Roldan. "They're going to need more than that."

The tank's heavy chaingun chewed up the closest mobile launcher and moved onto the next. The gun had more than enough penetration to wreck the artillery, but it still took a couple of seconds to put each one out of action. The main armament fired a second time, this time throwing its projectile directly through one of the side openings on the dropship. The carnage must have been incredible and not one of the crew cared at all. While the tank continued its headlong flight, the Vraxar kept up their fusillade, their numbers too great to be neutralised quickly by a single opponent.

The breach in the OSF outer wall was huge and there was plenty to aim the tank at. On this occasion, McKinney allowed himself a slight change in course, directing the tank straight at one of the mobile launchers. The tank struck the launcher at the same time as it fired. The plasma explosion ripped the artillery and its crew to pieces and covered the tank's nose in dark flames, which scattered to the sides where they bubbled and spat on the ground.

The Colossus tank climbed up and over a fifteen-metre pile of broken concrete and twisted rebar. It dropped down the other side, the immense gravity drive keeping it above the surface.

"We're clear," said Bannerman.

"Come on!" shouted Roldan.

It wasn't all good news and there were a several alerts on the tank's status readout. "The damage is going to become an issue soon," said McKinney. "We can't take them all out."

His brain reminded him of the eight-thousand-metre battleship watching from forty thousand kilometres above. Each passing second increased the chance the Vraxar warship would lock onto the tank and hammer it with missiles. It felt like an indescribably heavy weight around his neck.

The main gun fired for a third time and the shoulder missiles shrieked off through the rain-laden skies of the Tucson artificial day. McKinney didn't try to guess how many Vraxar died and instead did his best to work out the clearest path to their goal. The OSF was positioned away from most of the base – somewhere between the main population centres, the shipyards and the landing strip. There was a lot of open space and a lot of Vraxar. The crew already had a good idea what the enemy targets were and sure enough, there were many of their soldiers and artillery pieces heading straight for the built-up area of the Tucson base. There were a few maintenance buildings and a warehouse nearby. Other than that, little else.

McKinney got the tank on course and the vehicle sped away from the OSF. The Vraxar at the facility showed no signs of following, while those heading towards the *Ulterior-2* were no longer in sight. That left those heading towards the centre of the Tucson base. These Vraxar aimed everything they had at the Colossus tank.

"Can't you redirect those guns?" asked McKinney. "We're still firing at the dropship and the OSF."

"I'm on it," said Li. "We're acquiring additional targets."

"I've got you a new heading, Lieutenant," said Bannerman, calm and collected.

"Send it to my console."

"You got it. This way cuts left, right, left and then goes straight through the centre, past one of the plazas and on to our destination. It's a little slower than the primary route, but it'll take us away from those Vraxar. It also affords us a bit more cover from above."

McKinney hunched forward. "We're running out of time in more ways than one."

"Yup."

The tank's engines showed no sign of degradation and they

topped out at fifty kilometres per hour. The exchange of fire between the two sides was a brutal one for the Vraxar. With little in the way of shelter, the tank's chainguns cut them to shreds. The slow-firing main armament crunched its way through metal, flesh and the concrete walls of a warehouse without discrimination, whilst the equally-slow firing shoulder rockets dropped amongst the scattered alien forces.

In return, the hull of the Colossus was struck countless times by small arms, heavy repeaters and large-bore gauss projectiles. McKinney glanced at the external view – the tank's armour plating was a mess of dents, scrapes, and ragged holes, many of them several metres deep. In time, it would bring them to a halt and it was a wonder there were no critical alerts yet.

"We're going to look like a tenderised steak," said Li. A moment later, "I hope the replicator is still working."

"This is not a good time to be hungry," said Roldan.

The main built-up area loomed ahead. A pair of slab-sided four-storey buildings – the Psyche Testing Centre and the Alien Languages Research Facility - flanked a wide road. It was fortunate the Tucson base was built with the foresight to expect the transit of heavy loads, since the tank was twenty-five metres wide. It roared between the two buildings, knocking over a tree and smashing a patrol truck into the wall of the Alien Languages Research Facility.

At once, the persistent thumping of enemy fire dropped to nothing and the cockpit fell silent apart from the hum of machinery.

"We made it," said Li.

He spoke too soon.

"Wait!" said Bannerman. "I'm reading a launch from the battleship. Whoa that's a crapload of missiles."

McKinney jerked round in his seat – this was the news he'd been dreading. "Coming for us?"

"I don't think so. They're heading further into space."

"They must have engaged with the ES *Lucid*!" said Li.

McKinney closed his eyes and allowed himself to hope. He was brought quickly down when he heard Bannerman swearing under his breath.

"They've saved six for us," he said. "First three impacts in less than thirty seconds and the remainder ten seconds after that."

"Why'd they need so many for a little old tank like us?" asked Roldan.

Bannerman gave a snorting laugh. "On the plus side, the battleship has left orbit. If we live through these, we'll be home and dry."

The tank had countermeasures in the form of a cut-down Splinter missile system called GLSS. Sergeant Li activated it and six interceptor missiles flew from launch tubes at the rear end of the tank. Their mechanical reloader clunked and boomed through the hull.

"Takes too long," muttered Li, the tension starting to bite.

"The tank wasn't designed to handle this sort of crap," said McKinney.

"Second wave of interceptors on their way."

"Time for a third?" asked Roldan.

"No chance."

It was an uncomfortable, though short, wait for Lieutenant Eric McKinney. It wasn't easy to manoeuvre the tank through the streets of the Tucson base and each of the first two corners scrubbed off most of their forward momentum. With no choice, he left the others to watch the computer-generated dots representing twelve GLSS interceptors as they arced towards the six much larger Vraxar space-launched warheads.

"Only got two of the first three," said Bannerman. "Hold on tight."

The Vraxar missile struck the tank at an angle, which

deflected it the tiny fraction necessary to ensure the occupants' survival. As soon as it detected the deviation in course, the warhead's sophisticated onboard computer decided to initiate detonation on the basis that a proximity blast was better than having the missile ricochet away from the target.

The Vraxar missile exploded in a vast spray of bright plasma. The tank was knocked off course and it collided side-on with the half-collapsed side wall of one of the barrack buildings. Concrete, steel and grey dust showered down upon the brightly-burning vehicle, tonnes of rubble crashing against the heat-softened alloy plating.

The explosion roiled through the streets, setting fire to everything it touched. The sound of the explosion receded and the tank's huge Obsidiar-backed gravity engines howled with the incredible stresses of the power being forced into them. The tank shot out from the dying plasma flames, black smoke pouring off, while the hull glowed a mixture of oranges and whites.

Inside, the soldiers struggled to keep it together. The tank wasn't responding well and McKinney struggled with the controls. The cocoon of screens around him each proclaimed their own tale of woe and there were more red status lights than any other colour, with amber a distant second.

"One left," said Bannerman.

McKinney's eye caught sight of the missile at the same time as Bannerman uttered the words. There was a lone dot on the tactical screen and it was going to hit them in approximately two seconds.

Sergeant Li mashed the launch button for the GLSS. "Come on you piece of shit!"

McKinney had faced death many times and he was undecided as to whether it got easier with each new confrontation. He didn't want to die and he swore with helpless anger at the enemy missile.

On the surface of the tank, the two remaining operational GLSS tubes swung open and jettisoned their contents. The first interceptor missed by a wide margin and was lost to the skies. The second interceptor struck the Vraxar missile less than two hundred metres from impact. Unfortunately, it only took out the propulsion section. Once again, the computer embedded in the enemy warhead decided to detonate.

This second explosion was in mid-air, directly above the tank. At this distance, the force of the blast was greatly diminished and it wasn't enough to move the tank. The expanding sphere of plasma threw fiery liquid in all directions, once again engulfing the vehicle.

Deep within the hull, McKinney saw the white light through the remaining two operational sensor arrays. The control joysticks were already as far forward as he could make them go, but he pushed harder anyway, hoping to eke something extra from the engines.

And then they were through. The tank was badly damaged – its two shoulder launchers were out of action, along with the three chainguns. One weapon remained, miraculously showing the only green status alert anywhere in the tank with the exception of the replicator.

"The main turret," whispered McKinney with a feeling of awe. "Whoever built this stubborn bastard of a tank deserves a medal."

While Bannerman used the internal comms to let the men out back know they were in the clear, McKinney continued shaking his head in wonderment that they'd somehow lived through an attack from a Vraxar battleship. He didn't release his grip on the control joysticks and made the final turn. A third of the tank's engines had burned out and it was only the Obsidiar core keeping them ticking. It made the vehicle clumsy and

McKinney clipped the corner of an intact building, knocking out a huge section of wall.

He worked out how to compensate and got them heading straight. Whenever he attempted to increase their speed beyond thirty-five kilometres per hour, the entire vehicle shook violently. He took the hint and guided them carefully down the long, final street towards their destination.

It had been a short journey in terms of time, but an exceptionally long one in terms of incident and McKinney grinned to the others when he parked up near to the central administration building.

"Well folks, we made it."

"Now we've just got to kidnap the admiral of the fleet and cart him back to the *Ulterior-2*. In *this* tank." said Li.

"We getting out," said McKinney. "I've got no idea how long we're going to be inside and even less idea when the battleship will come back."

"*If* the battleship comes back." Roldan saw the looks he was getting. "The *Lucid* might have blown it up."

"I'm not counting on it."

One of the tank's external doors – the one closest to the first missile blast – was melted shut and refused to budge. The opposite door slid open without a problem and McKinney leapt out quickly in case the lingering heat damaged his suit. The others came after him and he pointed them towards the main doors for the administration building.

"Wait inside and take cover."

As McKinney followed them, he couldn't resist a look over his shoulder at the tank. It was still recognizable through the shimmering air which surrounded it and the steam which rose from the raindrops falling on its hull. The metal was blackened nearly everywhere and there were patches of sullen red where the heat remained. Hardly a place was free of ballistic damage, most of it caused by the Vraxar artillery around the Obsidiar Storage Facility.

Through the grime, McKinney saw the words, still proud and unbowed in their proclamation of defiance against whatever might come.

Here I Stand.

With a smile, he turned away and entered the building.

The interior of the central admin building was only partially familiar to McKinney and he lowered his visor to check out the internal layout on his HUD. Before he could study it, he caught sight of the atmospheric oxygen reading as it ticked down from 19% to 18%. Time was running out.

He found what he was looking for on the map and broke into a run. "Stay here," he shouted to Sergeant Li.

McKinney wasn't at all surprised to find he was excluded from the group with authorisation to enter the underground command and control bunker. He was, however, able to enter one of the rooms near to the access lifts, and this room had a hard comms link to the personnel below.

He connected and found himself talking to a patient comms lieutenant called Priscilla Montgomery. What she told him wasn't what he wanted to hear and he didn't accept her words with good grace.

"What the hell do you mean he's gone to Facility LT3? Why is he needed there?"

"I don't know the reason he left, Lieutenant. If you're thinking of going to speak with him, I must warn you it's a restricted area. On the off-chance you *do* find him, please let him know we've received a most peculiar message from an officer who claims to be on the *Ulterior-2*."

McKinney thanked Lieutenant Montgomery and hurried back to his squad. They caught his mood immediately.

"Not good?" asked Li.

"We missed Fleet Admiral Duggan and he didn't get Captain Blake's message. He's gone elsewhere on the base."

"Damn."

"What are we going to do, Lieutenant?" asked Munoz.

"We haven't got a choice. If we fail, then everything else fails with it. Everyone back to the tank - we've got to get this done before the battleship returns."

As they climbed into the tank they'd so recently left, McKinney was left with the impression it was already too late. He was a soldier first and foremost, and a man with a sense of duty. McKinney didn't consider giving up and he readied himself to climb the next peak, hoping this summit would be easier to reach than the last.

CHAPTER FOURTEEN

THE EAST ROAD was like something from a mad artist's night-mare. To either side, the damaged, smoking ruins leaned inwards as if to peer down upon the soldiers passing beneath. The smoke billowed and swirled, whilst fires raged. In many places, the emitters which created the artificial daylight had stopped working, creating pools of street-level darkness. To Duggan, it felt as if the war between the darkness and humanity's attempts to vanquish it was somehow allegorical with the fight against the Vraxar.

Through it all, rain fell in a fine mist which clung to the soldiers' protective suits and made the footing amongst the rubble treacherous. For the first time, Duggan realised how much he hated the rain and how much it dictated his life here on New Earth. It was a little early to plan moving his office to somewhere warmer and drier.

The soldiers advanced with a slowness borne of caution. After the recent missile strike, Lieutenant Richards had taken to walking closer to Duggan, leaving Sergeant Demarco on point. Duggan could see the reason for it in the set of Richards' face –

the man was determined to see this through, no matter what it took.

Richards cleared his throat. "It's another four hundred metres along here and then we cut through Barracks Block 12. After that, we should see our destination."

"As easy as that," smiled Duggan.

"Yes, sir, as easy as that."

There was plenty of cover available – most it was abandoned vehicles, parked up at their destinations. As he travelled, Duggan did his best to peer into the buildings to see if there was any sign of life or activity. There were underground bunkers more or less everywhere throughout the base and he hoped the personnel were safe inside, waiting for the all-clear.

His hopes were dashed when R1T Billy Wheeler checked out the insides of a building he was passing.

"Oh shit," said Wheeler.

Richards called a halt and went over to look. Duggan wasn't a man to stand patiently waiting and he followed through a doorway in the concrete wall. There was no door and the frame was twisted out of place.

Through the doorway was a large, open area, with corridors leading in several directions. There were metal desks and furniture thrown everywhere, most of it twisted and crushed. Much of the roof was gone, but it was easy to see the path taken by the missile – right down the middle of the building.

"They must have guessed we'd be underground," said Duggan, standing on the edge of an uneven hole in the floor and looking into the darkness. "They used armour-piercing warheads to achieve maximum casualties."

The hole went down and down. Duggan used the image intensifiers in his visor and saw the sharp ends of broken reinforcement bars protruding from the sides. At the bottom, he could make out an open space – part of the bunker network in this area of the base. The detonation of a warhead in the confined area below would have incinerated everyone. If this was replicated in other areas of the base it would explain why the main command and control bunker had received so little contact.

Lieutenant Paz arrived and she stood to one side, sharing his pain.

"Perhaps the Vraxar are on to something," Duggan said bitterly.

"Sir?"

"If you hope for a peaceful life on a planet somewhere, you're nothing more than an easy target for whichever alien species happens by. The Vraxar never stop moving – every conflict is of their own choosing. They hit and move without suffering the vulnerabilities of other species."

"The Estral nearly beat them. Perhaps the Antaron will go one better."

"A fifty-year war with the Estral doesn't seem to have left the Vraxar weakened."

"If they fought an extended war, they'll be down on resources, sir. There could be no other outcome. Any commander who brags about his numbers is doing so for a reason."

"It would give me some hope to think so – that we might be facing an enemy desperate for a quick result against the Confederation."

"They've made plenty of mistakes so far. They lost a lot of spaceships to the Inferno Sphere."

Duggan turned away from the crater. "Let's see if we can make New Earth their biggest mistake yet."

There was movement in the doorway and Alene Krause threw herself through, closely followed by Kenny Steele.

"Mobile repeater," shouted Krause, getting herself out of sight.

Richards swore and sprinted towards the doorway. He peered out. "Where?"

"Coming in from the right-hand intersection a couple of hundred metres along."

"Did they see you?"

"I don't know, Lieutenant."

Duggan's instincts kicked in and he joined Richards, keeping to the opposite side of the doorway. The remainder of the squad were in positions of cover outside, either behind gravity cars or crouching in the shadows of fallen masonry. Sergeant Demarco was in a doorway on the other side of the street, looking along the barrel of her gauss rifle. She lifted one hand briefly to show she was aware of Richards' presence.

Richards leaned further out, to get a view along the street. He ducked back quickly.

"Mobile repeater," he confirmed. "A big one."

Duggan had to see. He dropped into a crouch, mentally thanking the battlefield adrenaline for keeping his stiffness and aches at bay. It was hard to miss the Vraxar repeater – its front protective shielding was a three-metre metal square, through which the barrels protruded. The rest of the artillery piece was made from a long frame with a gravity engine supporting the barrel. It was the sort of device which could keep a thousand soldiers pinned down indefinitely and it was on the street outside. There was a large crew of Vraxar with the gun, many of them standing on the housing, whilst others milled around nearby. Duggan was sure he detected uncertainty – like the enemy troops had got ahead of their forces and weren't sure what to do next.

"Where's Lopez?" asked Duggan, taking command automatically. He bit his tongue – this wasn't his squad. "Apologies, Lieutenant."

Richards took Duggan's place in the doorway. "He's fifty metres east, behind a truck. He's not looking this way."

"It's going to take more than a single rocket to take out that repeater."

"Yes, it is, sir, and I count upwards of forty Vraxar with it. They're not moving."

"We're stuck here whether they move or not."

Duggan crawled back into the doorway and Richards obligingly moved aside once more.

"This is terrible luck for us, Lieutenant. Five minutes sooner and we'd have been past the intersection."

"We'll have to sit it out and see what they do."

The situation was as bad as it appeared. Since there was no comms, it was impossible to coordinate an attack or a retreat without alerting the enemy to their presence. The soldiers were trained in a basic language using hand gestures, but Lopez – the furthest advanced of the squad - still wasn't looking.

"I never did like a stalemate," said Duggan softly.

This particular stalemate was quickly ended. Lopez, the man with the plasma tube, decided to act. He took a cursory look around and entirely failed to spot Duggan in the doorway fifty metres away. Duggan closed his eyes when he saw Lopez spin the plasma tube onto his shoulder. The blue charge-up light was like a tiny, clear pinpoint through the smoke and rain. Lopez jumped out from the edge of the boxy, utilitarian transport truck and into sight. With perfect timing, the rocket burst free from the plasma tube and flew in a straight line along the street. Quick as a flash, Lopez threw himself back behind the truck.

The Vraxar had little time to react and the rocket exploded against the front plate of the heavy repeater, the flames showing through the smoke as a muddy grey-brown. The rocket wasn't enough to shut the gun down and it opened fire immediately. The cling-cling-cling of the metal was accompanied by the high-pitched whine of its power source. Even from this distance, the sound was clear and crisp.

The truck was the main target of the attack. The vehicle was heavy, but the upper section wasn't solid. The repeater slugs ripped through it like it was no more than cloth. Lopez crouched low, his shoulders hunched and the plasma tube forgotten at his feet. Duggan recognized the look – the soldier had spent everything plucking up the courage to fire and now he was lost in the aftermath.

"He's losing it," said Duggan. "Damnit!"

Huge figures moved through the smoke as the Vraxar spread out away from the gun. They hid behind cars and moved into shattered buildings. Duggan found his gauss rifle at his shoulder, while his eye tracked the orange shapes highlighted by the movement sensor in his visor. He put a bullet through the head of a converted Estral and did the same with a second. Across the road, he dimly sensed Sergeant Demarco firing her own rifle. The other soldiers joined in, keeping low and leaning out to shoot in controlled bursts.

The control computer in the Vraxar heavy repeater registered the presence of multiple targets and it began raking left and right across the street, whilst the soldiers supporting it crept forward outside its firing arc.

A couple of slugs pinged off the wall near the doorway, sending shards of concrete rattling off Duggan's suit. He knew when it was time to back off and he pushed himself out of sight.

Lieutenant Richards didn't wait idly by for his squad to be wiped out.

"Wheeler, Krause, find a way upstairs," he ordered. "I want someone shooting from above. Steele, see if you can find a way out of this building. If we need to get the Fleet Admiral to safety I want to know where the exits are."

"Lopez needs to get his shit together, sir," said Steele, running after the others.

"No kidding," muttered Richards. The failure of Lopez reflected badly on them all.

The heavy repeater followed a fairly predictable pattern of sweep left, sweep right, followed by a short burst of suppressing fire against four areas of cover which sheltered the squad. Duggan took advantage and sent another couple of shots towards the advancing Vraxar. It quickly became apparent their vision wasn't enhanced and their return fire was badly aimed.

He heard voices nearby.

"Sir, you should stay out of the firing line," said Richards.

Paz didn't sound happy either. "He's right, sir."

As Duggan backed away for the second time, his eyes locked onto those of Lopez. For that split second, time slowed to a standstill and there was only the two of them. Through the noise, the smoke and the falling rain, the soldier's face was frozen in an expression of terror – that of a man whose inaction meant he faced certain death, yet who couldn't overcome his fear in order to take control of his own destiny. *Only you can make the choice,* said Duggan's gaze.

The moment passed and Duggan pressed himself against the interior wall of the building. "The artillery is damaged from that first rocket," he said. "The enemy are advancing along both sides of the street – we'll be overrun if we can't take out the repeater."

"Maybe even if we do," smiled Richards grimly. His voice hardened. "Sir, you will stay out of danger."

There was something Duggan was driven to see, even if it cost him his life. The repeater strafed away towards the centre of the street.

"Lopez..." he said. "He can't do it alone."

Duggan returned to his position in the doorway. He was in time to watch R1T Bernie Stein rise from his crouch behind an uneven chunk of stone, with the barrel of his plasma repeater in hand. The weapon roared and spewed out a brightly-glowing stream of hot slugs. Too late, Stein attempted to drop back out of sight. The Vraxar heavy repeater shifted target and three or four of its bullets smashed through the soldier's upper body. One round would have been enough, but the mobile repeaters were a brutal method of waging war and this one reduced Stein's body to a bloody paste.

With a lightning bolt of certainty Duggan, knew what was coming. His gaze jumped to where Lopez huddled. The soldier watched his comrade die and the expression of fear vanished like it had been wiped away with a cloth. Lopez' face become a mask of anger and he grabbed his plasma tube like it was the throat of a man he despised. *His own throat,* thought Duggan.

With an incoherent shout of fury, Lopez charged up the plasma tube and darted from cover. He'd barely covered two paces before one of the Vraxar hit him in the leg with a bullet from one of their hand cannons.

"He's trying to shoot around the front plating," said Duggan.

Lopez managed another three limping paces before the next rounds hit him. Duggan saw blood fountain from the soldier's back and then, suddenly, he was missing the lower half of his left arm.

Lopez fell and the rocket launched. It whooshed through the clouds of smoke, leaving a pattern of steam through the rain. In a blossoming sphere of cleansing light, it exploded against the main section of the Vraxar heavy repeater, behind the protective front plate. The gun was strong, but the plasma rockets packed a real punch. When the fire receded, Duggan could make out the extensive damage to the artillery barrel housing. The protruding barrels spun slowly once or twice more and then abruptly stopped. The bodies of the repeater crew had been thrown far away and he could see several of them burning fiercely.

Incredibly, Lopez was still alive. His head was at an angle and his right cheek pressed hard against the stone-littered pavement. The man's eyes were glazed and Duggan stared into their depths, seeing the hope of forgiveness. Duggan raised a thumb. *You did good, soldier.*

The man's eyes closed for the last time and the fighting continued. Duggan fired another few rounds, scoring one certain kill and another maybe. Lieutenant Richards was angry now, but not so much that he dared manhandle the Space Corps' most senior officer.

"Sir, come away from the doorway!"

The fault was Duggan's and he knew it. *I'm putting everything at risk!* With that thought, he scrambled into cover behind the wall. A bullet ricocheted from the place he'd been only two seconds before and clattered against a pile of metal furniture across the room.

The relief on the faces of Paz and Richards was evident and Duggan knew he'd gone too far.

"My apologies," he said numbly.

"He's a stubborn bastard," said Paz with satisfaction.

Richards' eyes went wide at the familiarity and he clearly had no idea how to respond. "That's no problem, sir," he said in the end. "Please let my squad keep you safe."

"I will do exactly that."

Richards took over the position in the doorway and with a far greater caution than that exhibited by Duggan. He kept up a commentary on the events outside.

"McGraw's a good shot. She's taken out two there. They're advancing too fast. Wheeler and Krause must have found a place upstairs. Those shots aren't coming from ground level."

"How many left?" asked Duggan.

"Twenty at a guess."

"More than I'd hoped."

"They aren't well-trained, sir. A rookie could see it."

Richards was right – the Vraxar weren't especially good

when it came to ground combat. Duggan had a couple of guesses as to why that might be – the chief one was a lack of motivation. The second reason was because the Vraxar likely didn't resolve many important engagements by means of ground combat. Everything they did was based on the deployment of overwhelming force from space.

"We're running out of time, Lieutenant. They only need a couple hunkered down to make it hard for us to get by."

Kenny Steele returned from his scouting mission. "It's not going to be easy to get out of here, Lieutenant."

"How come?"

"I found one entrance totally blocked by rubble. There's another exit in the eastern wall, but it leads back onto this main street. We could probably pick our way over a pile of rubble to the west..." Steele tailed off to indicate he'd already decided it wasn't a good idea.

"Can we get behind the enemy if we leave by the east exit?" asked Richards. Stone chips flew and he ducked.

"I don't think so, sir. That street comes out sixty or seventy metres further along this main route."

Richards looked outside once more. "They've got ten or twelve enemy soldiers still at one-fifty metres." He swore. "Movement. There's another bunch of these aliens coming from that intersection. They're moving fast."

"They must have got word from this first group. How many?"

"They're still coming. Maybe two hundred."

"Not good."

With an angry sigh, Richards announced the next piece of bad news. "There's a large-bore gun with them."

The enemy reinforcements were enough to decide the outcome and the gun was just a cherry on top of the cake.

Duggan turned his head left and right, looking for a way out of this. The only exits would take them closer to the approaching enemy and besides, he didn't want to abandon the soldiers still out in the street. With a grunt, he ran to the missile crater in the floor. His memory wasn't wrong – there was no way in hell they were going to make their escape to the bunker beneath. Maybe one or two would survive the fall - it wasn't an acceptable outcome.

There was a rattle of incoming projectiles and Duggan spun in time to see Richards crawling away from the doorway, clutching his chest.

"Damnit, hit," he gasped.

Paz got there and did her best to check the wound. "Your suit has sealed it up. You need a medic."

She wasn't given the chance to say anything else. The wall exploded inwards, showering the four of them with pieces of concrete. Duggan turned instinctively, too slowly, and felt something heavy smash into his ribs. Other, smaller pieces struck him in numerous places and he was knocked to the floor. The pain was immense and his suit injected him with one of its remedies.

The painkiller kicked in and Duggan got to his hands and knees. The second Vraxar artillery gun had put a slug through the wall, knocking a huge hole in it. The projectile had continued onwards and made another hole on its way out.

Duggan crawled over to where Paz and Richards lay, half-buried beneath the remains of the wall. They stirred and he pulled at some of the larger chunks. He wondered where Trooper Steele had got himself to, and then he remembered the soldier had been standing right in the place where the slug had come through. There was nothing left to find.

Glancing through the gap, Duggan got an excellent view of a gravity car being thrown along the street by another shot from the heavy gauss gun. The vehicle wasn't merely knocked a few yards – it was hammered away with contemptuous ease and Duggan heard it skitter and scrape somewhere far out of his sight. All that remained of the squad medic Rex Copeland, who'd been crouched behind it, was a wide smear of vivid scarlet along the centre of the road.

"The medic's gone. We've got to get away," said Duggan. "On your feet!"

Richards was more badly hurt than it appeared and he struggled to get up. Paz was dazed and Duggan noticed a crack across the middle of her visor where she'd been hit by flying debris.

The gun fired again and this time, rubble fell from the upper floors of the building. Wheeler and Krause were still up there and Duggan hoped they hadn't been standing too close together when the slug hit. In his head, he tried to work out how many were left of the squad. Numbers had always been important to him and this one eluded him. He heard the gun fire again, and this time the target was the doorway where Sergeant Demarco was concealed. It seemed as though half of the building collapsed with the power of the shot.

The sound of footsteps from outside reached him. He saw the hulking figures of converted Estral as they approached, emboldened by the arrival of the artillery piece. It was game over and Duggan knew it. He looked at the rifle in his hand and took comfort from this oldest of friends. He lifted the gun to his shoulder and readied himself for the end.

CHAPTER FIFTEEN

ON THE BRIDGE of the *ES Ulterior-2*, Lieutenant Maria Cruz watched the sensor feed in horror. From its position in the trench, the battleship didn't have a commanding view of the entire Tucson base, however its arrays were still able to see the enemy dropship near to the Obsidiar Storage Facility. The sensors also afforded her an excellent view of the thousands of enemy troops and artillery flooding across the landing strip towards the spaceship.

The battleship's advanced comms were capable of making a direct connection to the soldiers standing guard outside, but the traffic would be one-way only. Fortunately, there was a speaker system for the boarding ramp area.

"Corporal Baker, are you there?"

The response didn't take long. "Yes, Lieutenant."

"You won't be able to see them from where you're standing, so I'll give you a friendly warning. You've got about fifty thousand Vraxar coming your way."

"You're shitting me?"

Cruz didn't know how to respond to such a stupid question.

"No, Corporal. I am not shitting you. Have you seen Lieutenant Griffin? We need to get this spaceship sealed."

"No, ma'am. I have not seen Lieutenant Griffin."

Baker's voice wavered with stress and Cruz pounced on it.

"What on earth is going on with this Lieutenant Griffin? Is he some kind of a special officer who comes and goes as he pleases, leaving the most valuable warship in the Space Corps wide open during an enemy attack?"

The wavering turned into near panic.

"I don't know, Lieutenant."

"You damned well do know, Corporal! We are being attacked by Vraxar and you're covering something up!"

The answer came out in a rush.

"He went for a nap, ma'am."

There it was. An entire battleship put at risk because one man wanted to go for an on-duty snooze.

"It was his birthday yesterday," said Baker, as if this explained everything. "He was late back."

Cruz put her head in her hands and took a series of deep breaths to calm herself. "I'm sure nobody has to know. Tell me where he is."

Baker sounded like a sinner in the confession box and she relieved herself of the burden. "He's on the *Ulterior-2*. In the captain's quarters."

"Get your squad onboard, Corporal. Stay in the airlock and if you see any Vraxar, shoot them. Is that something you can understand?"

"Yes, Lieutenant. Hold the airlock. Kill aliens."

"Once I find Lieutenant Griffin, I'll get him to seal the ship. Until then, don't move."

Cruz didn't wait for a response and she cut the connection. Were the situation not so serious, she'd have spent time shaking her head in disbelief. As it was, she ran from the bridge, questioning the intelligence of her fellow humans.

"How did he think he would get away with it?" she wondered.

The answer was only too apparent – if you had someone willing to cover for you, it was possible to get away with all sorts of indiscretions. If the base hadn't been put on alert, no one would have ever learned about Lieutenant Griffin's unscheduled post-birthday nap. The only wonder was how he'd managed to stay asleep through the noise of the alarms. Then she noticed for the first time that they weren't sounding on the *Ulterior-2*. *Maybe they haven't installed them yet, or maybe someone shut them off.*

She didn't pursue the subject further. The crew's quarters weren't far from the bridge and they comprised a single corridor with a few rooms leading off. With the warship in maintenance mode, the interior security wasn't fully operational and she pressed her hand against the access panel for the captain's suite of two rooms. The door slid open and she went inside.

The room stank of stale alcohol. Lieutenant Todd Griffin lay snoring on the white sheets of the single bed, with a half-finished tray of curling fries and drying slices of pizza at his side. He was a middle-aged, grey-haired man, with the pinched, nasty face of someone who enjoyed belittling anyone of a more junior rank. Cruz hated him at once and prepared to give him a vicious nudge with the toe of her boot. Then, she had a better idea. His security tablet was on the table a few feet away. Cruz picked it up and accessed the relevant screen. She didn't have the clearance to order the ship sealed, so she lifted Griffin's hand and pressed it to the tablet, hoping the ship's core wouldn't notice his comatose state.

Cruz held Griffin's palm in place for a few seconds and let it drop. The man snuffled but showed no sign of waking up. She checked the tablet.

"Yes!" she said quietly.

Cruz exited the captain's room and sprinted towards the bridge. Once there, she checked the sensor feeds to be sure. To her vast relief, the *Ulterior-2*'s boarding ramp was closed. Cruz wasn't in the mood for socialising with Corporal Baker and, in fact, she was furious about the entire Griffin situation.

"She can stay in the airlock for all I care."

With the *Ulterior-2* sealed against unauthorised entry, Lieutenant Maria Cruz took her place at the comms console again. Outside, the Vraxar advanced and she hoped they didn't have any special tricks which would allow them entry. Not for the first time, she tried to activate the battleship's defence systems. Once again, the *Ulterior-2*'s computer rebuffed her efforts. With little else to do, she sat back to wait.

———

FATE HAD other plans for Fleet Admiral John Duggan, the man who had defied the odds more times than he could remember.

He stood with his gauss rifle jammed against his shoulder and waited for the first of the Vraxar to show themselves. A noise reached his ears – it was a harsh, rough-edged grumbling sound. Part of his mind recognized it for what it was, though it was so unexpected he couldn't quite fit its existence into the reality of what was happening around him. He heard a gun firing – it wasn't the Vraxar artillery, this was something larger and far more devastating.

Before he could make sense of it, a huge, angular object hurtled along the street, heading towards the Vraxar rather than away. The Colossus tank crumpled cars and rubble as if they weren't even worth notice.

Duggan didn't delay. He ran to the opening and outside. In terms of width, the tank was almost a perfect fit for the street but it wasn't tracking straight and it clipped the walls on both sides. As it rumbled on, it spread the Vraxar against the side walls like butter. Here and there, one of the alien soldiers managed to drop prone and the tank went harmlessly over their heads. Duggan shot them one at a time, calmly adjusting his aim to fire bullet after bullet through their skulls.

About a hundred metres away, the tank slowed and then came to a stop. The main gun fired again, the booming echo dislodging precariously-balanced debris from the walls overhead. Duggan lifted his arm and waved vigorously.

Slowly, the tank reversed, doing further damage to the walls as it travelled. There were plenty of Vraxar ahead of it and Duggan heard their bullets ping off the tank's impervious hull. The rear emergency hatch was a plate of metal two feet square. It dropped open and a man got out. He dashed through the smoke towards Lopez' plasma tube. Meanwhile, a second man struggled free of the emergency hatch. He walked to keep pace with the reversing tank and reached inside, pulling out his own plasma tube.

"Here!" shouted Duggan.

One of the soldiers, his features hidden behind his visor, lifted a hand in acknowledgement. He didn't come closer – instead, he activated the retractable ladders on the rear of the tank. Previously-concealed rungs slid out from several places along the tank's rear.

"Up!" said the soldier loudly, beginning an awkward climb with his plasma tube.

Another face showed itself at the emergency exit hatch and a third man climbed free. Trooper McGraw broke cover. She jumped out of a half-buried doorway and ran like a hare towards the tank. Duggan stopped gawping and fixed his attention on Paz and Richards.

"We've got to move," he said.

ANTHONY JAMES

Paz was pulling herself together and she gave a mock salute. "The cavalry has arrived."

The third man sprinted from the tank towards the three of them. "We're looking for Fleet Admiral Duggan."

Duggan lifted his visor and then replaced it. "I'm Duggan."

"R1T Munoz, sir. Get onto the tank." The man hesitated, wondering if he'd been too abrupt. "If you please."

Duggan was relieved, but there was business to take care of. "I want someone to check the upper floors. We had two up there."

Munoz didn't like it and struggled to deal with the conflict. "I was told to get you to the tank."

Duggan made his mind up. "Let's go."

Munoz helped Lieutenant Richards, while Duggan and Paz did their best to run. Meanwhile, others had come from the tank. They lay flat and fired through the gap underneath. The two soldiers with plasma tubes were perched high up on the rear ladders and one of them fired a rocket to the east. The second man disappeared over the top.

The main gun boomed for a third time and the tank drifted back with the recoil. Its gravity engine complained loudly as it fought to stabilise the vehicle. Duggan reached it first and gave Paz a boost into the emergency hatch. Either he was stronger than he remembered or they'd improved the battlefield adrenaline since last time – Paz flew through the hole with an exclamation of surprise, and crawled inside.

Munoz arrived, walking awkwardly with Richards leaning heavily against him.

"Is there a medic onboard?" asked Duggan, helping push Richards onto the tank.

"Sandoval," Munoz grunted through his effort.

Lieutenant Richards wasn't in a good way, but his suit was keeping him going. There was someone waiting and Duggan saw

164

hands pull the soldier deeper inside. He took one last look around at the blood, the smoke and the interminable rain. Two plasma rockets shrieked in quick succession, detonating close by with percussive thumps. Through it all, the gauss coils of the soldiers' rifles whined.

As he climbed inside, he heard footsteps receding. It was Munoz, sprinting away to check the upper storeys for Wheeler and Krause. This single act of loyalty reinforced what Duggan already knew – he was in safe hands.

The insides of the tank were as cramped as Duggan remembered them. He crouch-walked through a low room, where Sandoval was hunched over Richards, with her med-box wired up to his chest.

There was no time to stop and talk. "How's he doing?" he asked in passing.

"He might live."

It wasn't the perfect answer but it was better than *he'll definitely die.*

Duggan located the cockpit. The pilot turned and raised his visor. "Good evening, sir."

"This is a useful habit you have, Lieutenant McKinney."

"Thank you, sir." McKinney got on with the task of bringing Duggan up to speed. "We counted more than two hundred enemy soldiers with two artillery guns."

"Two? They must have sent up second gun."

"They didn't last long. Everything's out of action on this tank except the main turret and that's not much use against a spread force. The targeting's out too and Sergeant Li here is having to do it the old way."

"Manual aiming," said Li.

Duggan leaned in close to the display showing the front sensor feed. "Not many Vraxar left now."

"I'm sure there are plenty on their way."

Two more plasma rockets exploded in the street, near to the intersection and it was clear there wasn't much opposition left anymore. McKinney spoke into his mouthpiece, using the tank's speaker system to get the message through.

"Webb, Vega, get back onboard."

"Has Munoz returned?" asked Duggan.

McKinney pressed a hand to his earpiece and listened intently for a few seconds.

"He's inside the hatch."

"Did he find...?"

"Munoz, please report." McKinney listened again and relayed the soldier's response. "Negative. There was nothing left of the upper floors. He says we've got a Sergeant Demarco with us."

Duggan shook his head in a mixture of sorrow at the dead and wonder at Demarco's survival – he thought she'd been buried under ten thousand tonnes of rubble. "How the hell did she get out of that?"

"Sealing the rear hatch," said McKinney. He spoke the next words quickly. "We need to get you to the *Ulterior-2* and the *Earth's Fury*, sir. Captain Blake has done his best to draw away the Vraxar warships and is inbound on a shuttle. If you can bring those ships into a live state, he is hopeful we can gain something from this situation."

"Such as what?" Duggan asked. It wasn't a fair question.

"I don't know, sir. I'm just doing what I can."

Have I lost the fighting spirit? Duggan asked, hating that he still couldn't see a way out of this. *Has it leaked away with each passing year?*

He tried to weigh up the options, aware there wasn't time for thinking. Looking back, everything seemed much simpler when he was on a spaceship with only his crew and a few soldiers. Here he was, potentially holding the lives of four hundred billion men and women in his hands, with no clear idea what to do.

Someone touched him on the shoulder and he found Lieutenant Paz there. "We can't let *Ix-Gorghal* reach our other worlds. Whatever it costs us here."

"There's still *Ix-Gastiol*," he replied softly.

"What is it you keep saying to me? One step at a time, sir. If we destroy *Ix-Gorghal*, we give the Confederation a fighting chance."

It was a terrible decision but in reality, nothing had changed since he set out with Lieutenant Richards and the squad.

"There's a change of orders, Lieutenant McKinney. Facility LT3 is along this road and we're going there first."

McKinney couldn't hide his disappointment, as if he'd just discovered the legendary Fleet Admiral Duggan was nothing more than a scared old man. "Yes, sir."

Duggan's eyes gleamed dangerously and his face took on an expression few living people would have seen before. "Don't worry, Lieutenant. I won't be staying at Facility LT3. As soon as I'm done, we'll go to the *Ulterior-2* and the *Earth's Fury*. Captain Blake will have his ship."

McKinney grinned. "Yes, sir!"

It was an infectious look and Duggan couldn't help but return one of his own.

McKinney took the control joysticks and fed power through the tank's engines. The noise climbed, until it reverberated throughout the cockpit. There was something primal about the sound – the tank was clearly badly damaged, yet Duggan felt its indomitable anger pouring through the walls. It was something he hadn't felt since his days on the *ES Detriment* or perhaps the *ESS Crimson*. His eyes misted and he blinked them clear.

The Colossus tank thundered onwards, along the eastern road towards Facility LT3.

CHAPTER SIXTEEN

THE *ES LUCID'S* shuttle entered the New Earth upper atmosphere, still travelling at near-maximum velocity. The hull temperature climbed rapidly and Blake slowed the vessel in order to stop them burning up. It had been a difficult journey for everyone onboard.

"I think I hate the anticipation most of all," said Hawkins. "I don't mind the actual fighting itself, but when it comes to the waiting for the fighting, I'd rather be asleep."

"Or drunk," said Quinn.

The shuttle bumped and shook as it was gripped by turbulence. Blake held tightly onto the controls and studied the ground far below.

"That dropship must hold a million soldiers," he said. "They're everywhere."

"Plenty of them going for the *Ulterior-2* and the *Earth's Fury*."

"I hope they got them shut tight," said Pointer.

"They should be sealed," said Blake. "It's standard procedure to lock the doors once the base alarm goes off."

"I don't think we'll be getting in through the lower boarding ramps," mused Hawkins. "There are thousands of Vraxar and I can see approximately thirty artillery units on the landing strip, with more on the shipyard area. They've positioned missile launchers amongst the construction machinery. If they're anything like our artillery, they'll be able to target us long before we land."

It wasn't going exactly as Blake hoped. Ideally, he intended setting the shuttle down next to the *Ulterior-2*, open up the nearest boarding ramp using his captain's clearance to override any lockdown, and then stroll onboard. Once safely within, he planned to take stock of the situation and await the arrival of Fleet Admiral Duggan. With the Vraxar closing in, it was going to be a little trickier to manage.

"How is the Fleet Admiral going to get to us?" said Hawkins, asking the question Blake had been purposely ignoring.

"We might be able to activate some of the Hadron's counter-measures to clear a path."

"Won't that increase the chance the Vraxar battleship will decide to blow the *Ulterior-2* to pieces, sir?"

"Stop asking difficult questions, Lieutenant Hawkins. This was never meant to be a carefully-planned mission. We take it as it comes."

"Whatever you say, sir."

"Thank you. Now, in light of the enemy presence around the docking trench, I'm going to set us down on the roof."

"I didn't know there was a way in from the top," said Quinn.

"There are at least four upper access shafts on every fleet warship. They're only meant to be used during maintenance."

"I really did not know that."

With so many Vraxar guns to contend with, Blake brought the shuttle in a wide arc around the base, intending to fly it in low. It added time to the journey, which was infinitely better than being knocked from the sky by a dozen heavy repeaters. Once they were far enough from the base, Blake levelled the shuttle at an altitude of one thousand metres and aimed directly for the Tucson base.

"Ladies and gentlemen, you will shortly be able to see the magnificent spires of Frontsberg below us."

"It was a shithole last time I visited it," said Quinn. "The air stinks of rotten eggs."

Frontsberg was one of New Earth's industrial capitals and it extended for dozens of kilometres in every direction – a sprawling mess of component factories, smelters and furnaces. It was founded hundreds of years before and was, for many people, the perfect example of dystopia. Oddly enough, the citizens living there seemed to enjoy the two hundred days of average annual rainfall and the happiness ratings for the city were amongst the highest in the Confederation, along with worker efficiency and industrial output.

With the speed of the shuttle, Frontsberg was soon far behind and Blake prepared for the final approach to the base. It was going to take quick reactions to achieve what he intended.

"Set the nose gun to track and respond."

"Track and respond activated."

"Let's hope the plating on this shuttle is up to the task."

At fifteen kilometres out, the first of the Vraxar heavy repeaters began firing. Hard slugs of metal pounded the nose of the shuttle, filling the cockpit with a clattering din. The front end of the shuttle was built the strongest, owing to the stresses of atmospheric entry, and the repeater fire glanced away. The first gun was joined by a second and then a third.

"Ten klicks," said Blake. "I'm taking us lower."

He pointed the shuttle's nose down until they were at five hundred metres. The ground was undulating and at the speed they were travelling he was reluctant to go much lower. The autopilot wouldn't activate for such a dangerous manoeuvre and Blake was forced to do the hard work himself.

"They got the rockets going," said Hawkins. "Crap," she spat.

The shuttle's rudimentary tactical display showed eight dots to represent the enemy missiles. They raced across the screen with terrifying speed. The shuttle's nose cannon started up, the sound like an industrial drill going through a block of solid granite. The dots vanished.

Hawkins wiped sweat from her brow. "Got them."

"Five klicks."

At that moment, the shuttle was struck by something with enormous force. It shook the entire vessel and Pointer stumbled into the bulkhead wall. A red light filled the cabin as the warning alarm started up.

"That was a big gun," said Hawkins. "You've got to go lower, sir."

"Don't I know it, Lieutenant."

With his teeth gritted, Blake took the shuttle as low as two hundred metres. The ground still wasn't level and he was required to make constant small adjustments to keep from crashing. Tucson lay ahead, yet every second was a battle against defeat and death.

"More missiles," said Hawkins.

Once again, the nose cannon grated, throwing out thousands of rounds in an impossibly short time. It failed to shoot down the final two missiles and they plunged towards the shuttle. Blake reacted instinctively and dragged the craft to one side. The missiles detonated against the ground underneath, the explosions vanishing quickly behind.

"We're coming in," said Blake.

The outskirts of the Tucson base were visible to the naked eye and Blake did his best to keep the few perimeter buildings between the shuttle and the Vraxar artillery. The heavy repeater fire on the hull lessened and he expelled the air he'd been holding in his lungs.

The lull was a short one. The shuttle flashed over the tops of the perimeter buildings and the drumming against the hull began anew. Another large-bore slug smashed against them and the impact produced a visible deformation in the cockpit floor.

"Is everyone in the personnel bay aware of what they need to do?" said Blake.

"Yes, sir," said Pointer. "They need to get the hell off this shuttle as soon as the doors open."

"Get back there, then. Lieutenant Quinn, you can join them."

The two officers got a move on and joined the ES *Lucid*'s complement of soldiers in the rear bay. Blake ignored the commotion and focused on getting the shuttle exactly where he wanted it.

"There's the *Ulterior-2*," said Hawkins. "Looks even more impressive from here."

"Set the nose gun to full auto."

"Yes, sir."

The nose cannon spun and sprayed its projectiles indiscriminately into the Vraxar on the landing strip. Blake watched a couple of artillery units broken to pieces and the shuttle was close enough for its sensor to register the shards of concrete thrown up by the bullets ripping through the enemy soldiers and into the ground. It was satisfying to watch, but in reality, it was little more than a drop in the ocean.

A third heavy round struck the shuttle's nose. Blake heard the shriek of tearing metal and felt air rushing through a breach somewhere by his feet. A fourth round hit them shortly afterwards and suddenly, Blake found himself able to see the ground through a hole in the cockpit floor to the right of his seat. He attempted to buy some time by banking sharply left and using the

Ulterior-2 as a shield. The heavy repeater fire lessened and no more large-bore projectiles hit the shuttle.

"Five hundred metres. This is going to be tight."

The upper section of the Hadron was a mixture of flat armour, rounded beam domes and the four vast, awe-inspiring Havoc turrets. Near the back, there was an area of exposed Gallenium engine where the shipyard hadn't managed to get the last of the armour plating in place. Other than that, the battleship looked finished.

At the last possible moment, Blake slowed the shuttle. The life support units were damaged and he felt the braking forces pushing him towards the console. He kept tight hold on the control sticks, his muscles straining.

With just a few metres until the shuttle was atop the *Ulterior*-2, Hawkins gave the announcement Blake had feared.

"Missiles."

Blake's heart fell.

One of the Vraxar missile launchers was positioned close to the side of the *Ulterior*-2 and hidden from sight by a huge mobile crane. It fired a salvo of eight at what was effectively point-blank range.

On this day, luck was smiling on Blake and the occupants of the shuttle. The craft entered cover at the top of the battleship and the eight inbound missiles exploded against one of the Havoc turrets.

"Down we go," Blake said.

The landing wasn't gentle, but in the circumstances, it was one he was extremely proud to accomplish. He heard the exit doors drop open and the sound of people running down the ramps.

"Nice work, sir."

He climbed from his seat, his eyes drawn to the wide split in the cockpit floor. "I'm glad it's over."

"Me too."

Blake and Hawkins exited the cockpit, to find the passenger bay already close to empty. They joined the back of the pack and were soon outside. There was no need to repeat the instruction to move away from the shuttle and the soldiers ran hard for the cover offered by the nearest Havoc turret. It was windy up here; the gusts buffeted them and soaked them with sheets of rain.

"Where's the nearest hatch, sir?" asked Hawkins, running alongside Blake.

He wiped the rain from his forehead. "Damned if I know."

"Oh."

The front portside Havoc turret was enormous and showed no sign of damage from the eight Vraxar missile strikes, apart from a slight smouldering. By the time Blake reached it, there were more than one hundred and twenty people hiding behind it, with plenty of room to spare.

"Damn, this thing is big," said Quinn.

"What now, sir?" asked Lieutenant Evie Wilder, the commanding officer of the *Lucid*'s soldiers.

"We hunker down until we see if they've got anything which can hit the top of this battleship."

"How long will that take?"

Blake turned his gaze towards the battered shuttle. It was a crumpled mess of impact damage and looked far worse than he'd imagined when he was in the cockpit. No further Vraxar missiles landed on it. Beyond the shuttle, his eyes were drawn to the pall of smoke which hung over most of the Tucson base. If they ever got out of this, it was going to take a lot of rebuilding.

"I think we're already in the clear, Lieutenant. Tell your squads to spread out and find an access hatch."

Wilder was admirably short of pointless questions. She spun on her heel and bellowed at the troops. "We need to find an access hatch into this spaceship." She raised her voice further. "Why are you still standing here?"

Driven by the desire to avoid death at the hands of either the Vraxar or their commanding officer, the soldiers ran. Blake joined them in the hunt, sprinting through the wind and rain in the hope it wouldn't take long to find what he was searching for.

The upper area of the *Ulterior-2* was extensive and with the utter smoothness which only unlimited funding could afford. Blake looked for a blemish of some kind, which might indicate the presence of a hatch.

"The internal area isn't huge, so the hatches must be somewhere towards the centre," he said to the troops nearby.

His logical thought was no match for random chance.

"Here!" shouted one of the soldiers from sixty or seventy metres away.

Blake was one of the first to reach him, along with Lieutenant Pointer.

"Good work," he said to the soldier, clapping him on the back. "Move aside, please."

"Yes, sir."

As it turned out, the hatch was flush to the hull and its seam was nearly invisible. There was an access panel next to it, again flush to the alloy plating. Blake knelt next to it and punched in his code. The effect was immediate – a two-metre, square section of the hull dropped downwards with a hiss. It descended a metre and then stopped.

"It's a lift, sir," said Pointer, nudging him with her elbow. "I can see a lift control pad."

She was right and Blake jumped onto the top of the plate. "You, come with me," he said, singling out his crew.

"What about us?" asked Wilder.

"I'll send the lift back up. If it needs access codes, I'll override them as soon as we reach the bridge."

A soldier's lot was to accept vagaries of fortune such as this one and Wilder stoically accepted. "Yes, sir."

Blake activated the lift and it slid deeper into the inside of the *Ulterior-2*. At some point, the lighting kicked in, filling the shaft with the usual white-blue. The lift ride was not suitable for the claustrophobic and fortunately none of the crew were afflicted. After a gradual descent which lasted sixty seconds the lift stopped, level with a narrow passage leading towards the middle of the ship.

Blake led the way. "Send the lift back up," he called over his shoulder.

The maintenance corridor was long and straight, with few side-turnings. There were consoles in the walls at regular intervals and Blake marvelled at the engineering work involved in building something as massive as a fleet warship. He had a passing interest in the construction, but usually only saw the finished product. These hidden passages were where the technicians worked long, hard hours, installing and checking the hundreds of systems of which a spaceship was comprised. It was an eye-opening experience.

The passage ended at a blank wall. An access pad gave the game away and Blake once again punched in his authorisation code. The wall slid aside and he stepped into a more familiar part of the warship. While he waited for the others to emerge, he poked at a console on the wall next to the opening – it was the same type of console that was dotted through every warship. Eventually, you just stopped noticing them.

"This is how you reach the passage from the main personnel area," he told the others.

"Yeah."

It wasn't important and they didn't dwell.

Blake set off at once. "The bridge has got to be this way." He heard the others running after.

His instinct didn't fail him. His feet guided him along the wide corridor, through a mess hall, along another two corridors and up some steps. The bridge door opened at his approach and he stepped through.

"Hello, sir," said Lieutenant Cruz.

"Well met, Lieutenant. How are things here?"

"Quiet."

"All right for some. What have we got?"

"Very little. No weapons, offline engines and an extremely suspicious main core. Most importantly, no enemy battleship."

"Good and bad in equal measures." He took his seat. "Let's see what I can do. First things first..." he muttered, remembering his promise to set the upper maintenance lift to free access. It was easily done and he turned his attention to the next step of his semi-formed plan, which was to stealthily bring a few of the Hadron's engine modules online and keep them running at a whisper to avoid detection.

The other crew members didn't take long to sort themselves out and find seats at the appropriate stations.

"Lieutenant Quinn, I would like you to see if the fission suppression modules can be used in order to conceal the build-up in our engines."

"I can't do much at the moment, sir," said Quinn. "You should be able to assign a higher-level access to our consoles and then we can begin helping you out."

"I'm on it."

Something was wrong and Pointer was the first to notice the frustrated set of Blake's shoulders.

"What is it, sir?"

"This isn't right. Even when the ship's in maintenance mode I should be able to bring the engines up and order a limited test firing of the weapons systems."

"My console is still pretty much locked down," said Hawkins.

"I'm denied access," said Blake, tapping repeatedly at one of his screens.

"How come?"

A terrible realisation came and Blake made some additional checks. It was as if he had the same level of access as any random civilian who somehow found themselves on the bridge of a fleet warship and decided to see what happened if they pressed a few buttons. He checked the personnel files and discovered he had access to only one – his own.

"Admiral Morey went and did it," he said. "Shit."

"What is it, sir?"

"I'm not, *sir* any longer, Lieutenant Pointer. Admiral Morey managed to get me dishonourably discharged from the Space Corps less than five minutes ago. Now I'm just plain old Charlie Blake and our chances of salvaging anything at all from this mess have just fallen to effectively zero."

"How did the ship know?" asked Hawkins. "There are no comms, so its databanks shouldn't have received the update."

"No comms, except on *this* warship," said Cruz.

"Oh, of course."

It was a terrible development and Blake felt numbness spreading throughout his body. He leaned back in his chair and closed his eyes.

CHAPTER SEVENTEEN

FACILITY LT3 WAS A PLAIN, six-storey square building, without windows and with only two ways inside. A high wall surrounded the central building and there was no need for a road, since the facility was built on an area of the Tucson base which was already concreted over. It wasn't a huge distance from the closest building, yet it was somehow quite clearly aloof. There were no signs advertising the purpose of the facility – it was simply there, an anonymous block with vague notices warning against unauthorised attempts to access.

Most of Facility LT3 was intentionally designed to operate without personnel and the many security systems were fully automated. There was a guardhouse outside the wall, still occupied by twenty-five soldiers who didn't have any idea what they were guarding. The tank came to a stop outside, whilst the guards did their best to come to terms with this unexpected arrival.

"Still at their station," said Sergeant Li.

"Can't blame them for that," said McKinney.

"They're not wearing their visors and we're down to 17%

oxygen," said Roldan. "I bet they've been wondering why they get out of breath taking a crap."

"Any sign of the Vraxar on the rear sensor?" asked Duggan.

"No, sir. If that was an advance force, we wiped them out."

"I'll need to hurry. Tell those soldiers outside I'm coming."

"I'll organise my men to assist you."

"I don't need a guard. It'll just be me and Lieutenant Paz."

"Negative, sir. You will have an escort. I will come, along with four others."

Duggan saw from McKinney's face that he wouldn't be dissuaded. Lieutenant Richards tried to be as forceful, he just didn't have the depths of confidence which came from experience.

"Who will pilot the tank?"

"Sergeant Li knows enough to get by, sir. It doesn't matter that he's only trained in light tanks, since this one won't be going anywhere until we return. Isn't that right, Sergeant?"

"We'll be glued to this spot, Lieutenant. Who's in charge of the gun?"

"I'll send Clifton up."

"Are you sure that's safe?"

"I'll rely on you to keep an eye on him."

With that, it was sorted.

"Fine, let's go," said Duggan.

He ducked out of the cockpit, with McKinney and Paz following. Behind, he could hear Li changing seats, while Corporal Bannerman gave the anxious guards outside a heads up about who was coming.

"That side," said McKinney, indicating one of the passages. "The opposite one got melted shut."

"The battleship?" It was the first chance Duggan had been offered to ask about the extensive damage.

"One missile hit and a second near-miss."

"We're still moving."

"This tank is going to do whatever we need it to do, sir." McKinney leaned into the passage leading to the personnel bay. "Vega, Webb, Garcia, Whitlock! Get your guns, you're coming with me."

Two minutes later, Duggan and his escort were outside the tank. The facility guards didn't have much idea what was going on, since they were effectively cut off from the rest of the Tucson base by the lack of comms and the requirement to stay at their post. Duggan didn't want to spend time explaining, so he simply told the man in charge to put on his visor and shoot any Vraxar who came near.

Facility LT3 possessed a brooding menace which only became apparent from close up. It put Duggan in mind of an Old Earth castle from millennia ago, perched high on a hill and looking down on the villages below.

There was a metal gate through the outer wall, which was wide enough to allow the transit of several specific objects, with a few inches to spare on either side. The gate was closed, though there was a secondary gate nearby meant for those on foot.

"What is this place?" said Vega, more to himself than anyone else.

"That's classified," said Paz.

The personnel gate was a featureless block of alloy, sheltered by an overhanging slab of concrete. A weatherproof access panel was fixed to the wall next to it. Duggan walked towards it, glancing up at the two miniguns hidden underneath the roof of the shelter. The soldiers didn't fail to notice the weapons and he heard them muttering amongst themselves.

Duggan planted his hand onto the panel. "Command Code: Duggan. Six guests with my approval."

The access panel stayed red for a long few seconds while the facility computer performed a multitude of checks. It abruptly changed green and the door slid open, revealing a fifteen-metre tunnel through the wall, with a second door at the end.

"It'll only remain open for ten seconds," said Duggan. "Get in quickly."

It was the sort of command the men could understand and they hurried through. Duggan marched ahead to the next door, ignoring the four additional miniguns inside which tracked his movements. He pressed the panel and repeated his command code. Once again, the door opened and the group passed beyond.

The inner compound was a hundred metres across and with an illumination which was intentionally much lower than the rest of the base. The two doors into the main building were identical to those on the outer walls. Dozens of camouflaged ground-level repeater emplacements aimed their multiple barrels at the group. A couple of the soldiers swore quietly and they stuck close to Duggan, worried they might be torn to pieces if they got too far away. They were right to be concerned, though they had a bit more leeway than they realised.

When they reached the central building, Duggan repeated the procedure of opening first an outer door and then an inner one. They emerged into one end of a long, narrow room which went from the centre of the building, along the inner wall to the left of the main cargo door.

"A window," said Whitlock, walking towards the viewing panel which ran much of the room's length.

"A replicator," said Webb, pointing at the latest-model device embedded into the wall near the door.

"It's not time to eat," growled McKinney.

Duggan beckoned them onwards and strode along the room. He looked through the window into the big open space inside the facility. It was brightly lit, affording an excellent view of the flat, cuboid Obsidiar-powered gravity winch on the ceiling. Directly below was a cargo lift, also powered by Obsidiar.

"Maybe they should wait here, sir," whispered Paz.

"They can come," said Duggan.

There were two hidden airlifts at the end of the room, their doors indistinguishable from the walls.

"Command Code: Duggan. Nine-nine-five-gamma," he said.

Both airlifts opened. They were large enough to fit a dozen inside and the group followed Duggan into the left-hand lift. Inside, it looked like any other airlift and Duggan pressed the single destination button.

"Is there something down here that is going to defeat the Vraxar, sir?" asked Whitlock.

"Kind of. There's something important I need to do and then we can go back."

The airlift took a few seconds to reach the bottom of the shaft, indicative of how far it had travelled. The door whooshed open and Duggan stepped out into a large, square room with a pair of multi-purpose consoles, a few chairs and a table. There was another door leading out of the room, as thick and strong as every other door in Facility LT3.

"This place is deserted," said Garcia.

"You sound spooked," said Vega.

"I don't like it."

"Sheesh, you've run through the centre of a Neutraliser and you let a couple of empty rooms on a Space Corps base get to you?"

"Shut up, man! I can't explain it."

Duggan walked to one of the consoles and checked the audit reports for the facility. There were no ingress requests since the delivery team a few hours ago. He navigated his way to a secondary menu and found what he was looking for.

>>> Benediction: Assembly Complete.

Paz leaned over. "Was there any doubt?"

"No. Putting the final pieces together was straightforward."

McKinney was getting edgy. "Sir, we don't have long."

"I know, Lieutenant. I need to do this next part alone. There are no Vraxar in here."

"Want me to come?" asked Paz.

"This needs a witness."

With that, Duggan used the console to activate the access panel on the far door. He stepped away and then paused in thought. He looked at McKinney and found the other man looking back at him, carefully studying. Duggan had read plenty of reports on the soldier's combat performance and his instincts told him that McKinney was as trustworthy as they came.

"Do you want to see what's at stake, Lieutenant?"

McKinney knew, or at least he'd guessed close.

"I'm not sure that I do, sir."

"There are some things you can't close your eyes to, soldier."

"That's the truth. I'll come." McKinney gave the order for the others to stay put and then he followed Duggan.

Without hesitation, Duggan opened the door. It glided into its recess, revealing a red-lit corridor.

"There are a series of explosives throughout this facility," said Duggan. "If we ever get the comms back or install a hard link, I could seal it from anywhere in the Confederation. You'll soon see why that might be necessary."

The corridor was less than twenty metres long, yet Duggan found each stride along it became progressively harder. In a way, he was thankful he'd got this far before the enormity of his intentions became such a burden. At the second door, Duggan took a deep breath when he reached for the access panel. He shook his head clear and opened the door.

The storage room for Benediction lay beyond. It was a large space, several thousand metres below the surface. The walls were smooth alloy and there were several overlapping gravity winches on the ceiling, set around the central gravity lift. A huge automated crane stood idle to one side, its work complete.

"Benediction," whispered Paz, following Duggan inside. McKinney hesitated and then came after, his eyes moving to take in every detail.

The bomb was a dull grey cuboid with rounded corners and edges. It was sixty metres at its longest, with a height and width of forty metres. For various technical and strategic reasons, it had been brought here in pieces for final assembly by the crane and winches above. The seams where the pieces joined were clearly visible and they formed a cross on the facing side.

"Come," said Duggan.

He strode over the smooth floor, his footsteps producing no echo at all. It was far colder than he expected and he was glad for the insulation of his spacesuit. As he came closer to the bomb, he smelled the sharp tang of its metal shell and heard the faintest of humming noises from deep within the casing.

The activation panel was exactly where it was meant to be – at head height near to one corner. The name plate was fixed next to it and he read the details.

No. 000041. *Benediction.*

There were other words stamped beneath

Let me be the greatest and the last.

"Amen to that," said Duggan.

"This will kill...everyone?" asked McKinney, his voice hushed.

"After the detonation, there'll be nothing left of New Earth, or anything within approximately six million klicks."

"The price is high, sir."

"There's no guarantee we'll have to pay it."

"What are you going to do?"

McKinney deserved answers, since he was letting someone else decide his fate.

"I'll set the timer for six hours. By that point, atmospheric oxygen levels will be at approximately 6% and everyone on New Earth who isn't in a bunker will be dead."

"Why not twenty-four hours, sir?"

"I don't want to risk the enemy leaving before detonation. *Ix-Gorghal* is the prize and we can't let it slip through our fingers."

"I hope to hell we can pull something off so we don't have to be responsible for this."

"You won't be responsible, Lieutenant. This is on my shoulders alone."

"I am responsible now, sir. You made me responsible the moment you invited me into this room."

"How come?"

"If I wanted, I could shoot you dead, sir, and then there'd be no one to start the timer. The fact that I choose *not* to kill you makes me complicit."

"We're all a part of it," said Paz.

"You don't need to be."

"It's too much ask of you alone, sir."

McKinney looked tired. "Do it, sir. Set the timer away so we can be out of here and on to a place where everything makes sense. Even if that *sense* comes in the form of a hundred thousand alien soldiers."

Without another word, Duggan activated the timer on the bomb. It wasn't an involved process – he entered a series of access codes and then tapped in the number of minutes using a pad of mechanical switches.

"Done," he said.

000:000:05:59:50

"We'd better set a corresponding timer in the visor computers as well," said Paz. "I'd hate to be late back."

"Couldn't you have done this from the *Ulterior-2*?" asked McKinney, scratching his head as the question came to him.

"Well spotted, Lieutenant. Yes, I could have used the Hadron's comms system to accomplish the same thing."

"Why didn't you, sir? We could be onboard the ship already."

"Or we could be dead on the landing strip, or the *Ulterior-2* destroyed from orbit. Coming direct to the facility gave us the greatest chance of success."

McKinney would have likely said more had Duggan been of a lower rank. As it was, he kept his mouth shut and shrugged his acceptance.

With the bomb activated, Duggan led the others from the room. In the two minutes it took to return to the other soldiers, he had time to reflect upon his feelings. Strangely, he felt better now the die was cast. He'd made the decision for good or ill and it forced him into a position where he had to do his utmost to stave off a seemingly unavoidable outcome.

I always did fight better with my back to the wall.

The other four men were right where they were meant to be. They milled about nervously and made wisecracks to disguise their anxiety. Their curiosity was plain, though not one of them dared ask a question and there was no mistaking the relief when Duggan told them to get into the airlift.

The return journey to the tank was completed with a greater urgency than the way in. Five minutes later, the squad emerged through the outer wall of Facility LT3, to find the tank exactly where they'd left it. Moments later, they were inside and heading for their seats.

CHAPTER EIGHTEEN

FLEET ADMIRAL DUGGAN leaned against the cockpit wall inside the damaged Colossus tank, watching the very brief preparations to depart. Clifton left for the passenger bay, while McKinney swapped with Li and got into the driver's seat.

"Show me the quickest course to the *Ulterior-2*," said McKinney. "Captain Blake said he'd draw the enemy battleship away for as long as he could, but for some reason I think our time is running out. It's been over thirty minutes now."

"Closer to forty," said Bannerman.

"No," said Duggan.

"What's that, sir?"

"We've got our insurance policy in place and now we're in this to win, Lieutenant – no half measures. Set a course for the Obsidiar Storage Facility - the outer gate."

"It's swarming with Vraxar, sir."

"And it's the place we keep the ammunition for the *Earth's Fury* main gun."

The two men locked eyes and McKinney grinned broadly. "Yes, sir!"

Lieutenant Paz jabbed Duggan in his bruised ribs. He looked at her and she raised an eyebrow.

"There's no going back now, Lieutenant."

Sergeant Li was the first to question the assumed method. "How are we going to get in?"

"We aren't," said Duggan.

"Then...?"

"Too many questions, Sergeant. We could be halfway there by now."

McKinney didn't wait for a reconfirmation of the order. The moment Bannerman provided details of an efficient route, he got the tank moving.

"We're going to keep amongst these buildings here, sir. So it's back into the built-up area and then cut right towards the OSF," said Bannerman when he saw Duggan's interest in how they were getting to the facility. "Even if the buildings don't prevent the battleship seeing us, they should provide some protective cover."

"We might get lucky, Corporal. Assuming the enemy ship returns, their comms team are more likely to be concentrating on their own troops. It gives us a chance. Once we arrive at the OSF, we'll be close to the Vraxar activity and that's when we need to worry."

Li was irrepressible, even when confronted by a Fleet Admiral. "So how *are* we intending to pick up this ammunition, then? I assume it's too heavy to carry on our shoulders."

Duggan didn't approve of secrecy just for the sake of it. "From what Lieutenant McKinney has told me, the Vraxar have breached the east wall, so there may be little in the way of resistance at the main gates. There's a hard link from there to the central facility. I can order the crawler carrying the ammunition to exit the OSF."

"After that, we escort the crawler to its destination?" said Roldan with a bemused look on his face. "Those things are slow."

"Not if you hitch them to the back of a tank," said McKinney, catching on.

Duggan nodded. "Exactly. There's a gravity winch on the back of every tank. The Colossus tanks could likely tow a destroyer if they needed to."

"I thought I was meant to be the crazy one," said Li.

Roldan couldn't resist. "You're thinking of Clifton. You're the dumb one."

"Did you hear that, sir?" asked Li. "That was a breach of military discipline right there."

Duggan remembered the days and laughed. "Put it in your report, Sergeant. I'll read it after our victory."

"I'm only a sergeant. I don't write reports."

The tank lumbered on, entering a wide main street which joined one side of the Tucson base to the other. This route to the OSF was intended to avoid known areas of Vraxar activity and was slightly longer than going direct. Duggan watched the sensor feeds and felt his simmering anger bubbling away at the sight of the devastation. Entire blocks had been hit by missiles, without apparent need. There again, the Vraxar weren't anything like humans and they acted on their own obscure motivations.

"I don't suppose there are any more of these Colossus tanks on the base, sir?" asked McKinney. He knew the answer already, but maybe they kept a few locked up somewhere classified.

"I'm afraid this is the only one, Lieutenant. We've got three undergoing assembly in one of the workshops and there are a dozen Gunthers parked in various strategic places around the base."

"Is it worth trying to find one?"

"I'd feel safer in this," said Duggan. "Even beat up as much as it is."

McKinney did his best to keep the tank close to its maximum speed. It was a difficult task, since the vehicle had developed a tendency to pull strongly to the side after the missile strike. As a consequence, he needed to keep the control joysticks slightly to the side in order to compensate. It made steering hard and the rear of the tank kept catching on solid objects.

"Sorry about the damage, sir," he said, watching a previously-intact two-storey building collapse on the rear sensor.

"We'll blame it on the Vraxar when the Confederation Council enquire about the extent of the repair costs, eh?" said Duggan.

"That works for me."

"Less than a thousand metres to the OSF perimeter gate," said Bannerman. "One more left-right and it'll be dead ahead."

McKinney managed the left turn, by drifting the tank sideways and then accelerating through the corner. The right-hand turn was straight after and he was slightly late bringing the tank's nose around. It crunched through a series of walls, overturned a truck and knocked three parked cars into a wall.

"Damn those Vraxar," said Sergeant Li.

Bannerman chuckled. "Yes, damn them."

"Business now," said McKinney. He called loudly into the internal comms. "Rear bay personnel, get into position on the flank exit hatch."

The banter stopped and the soldiers prepared themselves for whatever might lie ahead. The early indications were promising – the outer gate was intact and there was only moderate damage to the walls around it. The biggest sign something was amiss was the smoke coming from within the compound.

"They took out the gate guns," said McKinney. "And left the gates."

"We're not planning to be here long," said Roldan.

"Just as well."

The tank emerged from the protective cover of the buildings and entered the open area around the Obsidiar Storage Facility.

"Bring me as close as you can to the gatehouse," said Duggan, pointing his finger at a small stone-built structure set a short distance from the wall.

"That dropship is still there," said Bannerman. "I wonder if they managed to empty it yet."

"We've got Vraxar to the left," said Roldan. "One artillery gun and crew, looking the other way."

"On it," said Li.

Li had a knack. It took him about two seconds to target the main gun and fire, scoring a direct hit. One moment, the artillery gun was in place, the next it vanished as though it had never existed.

"Rear bay personnel, prepare to exit the tank," said McKinney on the internal comms. "Protect the Admiral." He brought the tank around and placed it between the gatehouse and the likely direction of a Vraxar attack. "Go, go, go!" he shouted.

Duggan grabbed his gun, ducked through the cockpit door and hurried along the passage leading to the exit hatch air lock. He could see light coming from outside, partially obscured by the group of men and women clambering through. He went after them, impatiently resisting the urge to push the soldier in front.

His turn came and he jumped free of the tank. There were eight soldiers out here with him, including McGraw and Demarco from Lieutenant Richards' squad. His eyes swept the area – the tank was to his left, with its nose aimed at the OSF main gate. To his right was the single-storey gatehouse, an ugly lump of concrete which took each of the Space Corps' worst architectural design ideas and magnified them tenfold. There was a single metal door and the kind of small, reinforced windows they fitted to maximum security prisons.

A series of booms rolled upwards and outwards from the

central compound area and Duggan ran as quickly as he could to the gatehouse. The door responded to his palm print and slid open. He stepped aside and let Garcia and Vega check out the interior.

"Clear!"

Duggan entered, to find the place deserted. A table with cups was the only sign of prior occupation. On normal days there would have been ten guards inside. Now, it was empty and Duggan recalled hearing Lieutenant McKinney say how he'd brought everyone within the compound walls.

"What is this crap?" asked Garcia, nudging a tray of something no longer edible with the butt of his rifle.

Duggan ignored him and approached the gatehouse console. It was online, operational and responded sluggishly to his access codes.

"Let's see," he said to himself.

Garcia and Vega were suddenly agitated. "Someone's shooting outside," said Vega.

"Sir?"

"I heard you."

Duggan located the approval screen and authorised the release of Obsidiar from the storage facility. Immediately, the comms speaker on the console crackled into life and he could hear a number of panicked voices at the other end.

"This is OSF Technician Amy Horvath, who's there?" came a voice.

"Fleet Admiral John Duggan. I've ordered the Obsidiar crawler to the surface."

"We're being overrun here, sir! I don't know how many are left alive, but we've been pushed right back. Are you able to send reinforcements? We don't have long!"

There were times when all you could do was accept a lost cause, no matter how painful it might be. It never got easier.

"There will be no reinforcements, Technician Horvath. We have none to spare."

"You can't leave us here, sir! They're going to kill us!"

There was nothing he could say and he didn't try. He closed the channel, turning sorrow into fury, directing his anger towards the Vraxar instead of at his own helplessness.

"How long?" asked Garcia from the window. "It's getting busy outside."

Duggan played through the crawler's route in his mind – up the lift, into the central warehouse. From there, through the two main doors, over the compound, then two more doors until it was finally out of the OSF.

"Eight minutes, give or take."

Garcia swore. "It's going to be tight, sir. Can we take cover in the tank?"

Ideally, the squad would remain in the tank while the crawler made its journey. Unfortunately, the highly-secure nature of the OSF meant that each outbound Obsidiar shipment was carefully managed. The crawler would stop at each gate and Duggan would be required to open them, one-by-one.

"Negative. I need to stay here, otherwise everything stops."

"I thought you might say something like that."

Duggan joined Garcia at the window. The squad were no longer on the ground and had climbed onto the tank's hull, from where they were able to fire into whatever enemy forces approached. Duggan recognized Dexter Webb only because of the plasma tube on his shoulder. The soldier launched a rocket from his place on the rear section of the vehicle and then dropped prone to avoid return fire.

Try as he might, Duggan couldn't get a clear view beyond the tank in order to judge what was arrayed against them. The tank's main turret rotated and the gun thumped, the recoil sending the tank a few feet towards the gatehouse.

Vega leaned outside and shouted. "Yo, Whitlock! How many are there?"

The response drifted in faintly through the door. "Shitloads and they've brought their extended families."

Vega turned towards Duggan and lifted his visor, as though he felt it a necessary courtesy. "Trooper Whitlock advises me there are a considerable number of opponents."

"I believe I heard the word *shitloads*."

"That's the technical term, sir."

"We're going to be overrun."

"There is a strong likelihood of that, sir."

"We don't have eight minutes," added Garcia.

"In that case, we'd better speed things up."

"How?"

Vega was closest to the door and therefore the chosen candidate for what Duggan intended.

"Go to Lieutenant McKinney. I would like him to turn the main armament onto the facility doors. After that, come back here."

Vega lowered his visor and went. Through the side window, Duggan saw him cover ten rapid steps to the tank and throw himself bodily into the access hatch. Across the room, the gatehouse console beeped, advising him that the crawler had reached the top of the gravity lift. Duggan sent his approval for it to proceed towards the inner door. This part of the crawler's journey was short and the console beeped again a few seconds later.

"First inner door opening," he said.

Duggan's instruction reached the tank crew. The Colossus tank fired its gun once more, the force of it making the tray on the gatehouse table vibrate. The OSF doors were designed to repel an anticipated assault from light-to-medium weaponry, along with the occasional heavier-duty attack. What they were not designed to be proof against was the main gun on the Space Corps' most advanced tank. The projectile smashed into the outer gate with terrifying force. The alloy slab crumpled and buckled, but stayed in place.

"Going to need a couple more shots," said Garcia.

Vega returned. "Did you see that?" he asked in excitement. "We're about to break into the place we were assigned to protect!"

The irony wasn't lost on Duggan and though he felt the return of his old battle lust, he couldn't take any joy from the destruction of Space Corps property, in spite of his light words to McKinney earlier in the tank.

The first inner door opened and Duggan sent the command for the crawler to move into the space between outer and inner doors. Then, he approved the closing of the inner door and waited impatiently for it to complete.

The tank fired again, striking the damaged facility door for a second time. The noise was tremendous and Duggan was glad he wasn't any closer. A huge split appeared in the door and rubble fell from the facility walls nearby.

"How's the crawler coming along, sir?" asked Vega. He lay prone on the floor inside the gatehouse door, doing his best to look underneath the tank at whatever was coming.

"Slowly."

"That's why they call it a crawler, huh? There's a lot of pressure out there now."

The inner door closed, allowing Duggan to open the outer one. He heard another noise – a clunk of two solid metallic objects colliding at speed. Garcia peered through the window.

"I think they've got a mobile gun trained on the tank," he said. "Webb's just taken a shot at it."

"One isn't enough."

The third shot from the tank knocked the outer facility door clean out of its support frame. It fell to the ground, went up on one side and then crashed down again. There was just about enough angle for the tank to hit the inner perimeter door.

"If it takes another three shots for the next, it'll be quicker to wait," said Duggan.

"Waiting isn't good," said Vega. "The enemy are spreading out around us. If it takes much longer, they'll be able to take shots at us when we run for the tank."

McKinney evidently thought the same and he moved Colossus tank sideways, bringing it a few metres closer to the gatehouse building. It took another ringing blow from the Vraxar artillery gun and the soldiers arrayed about the hull pressed themselves tighter against it.

"Steady, Lieutenant," said Garcia under his breath.

Duggan made his mind up. "Vega, get into the tank and order Lieutenant McKinney to hold fire on the gate. If he hits it again, it might jam and we'll end up waiting longer."

"On it."

Vega was off again and vanished once more into the side hatch of the tank. The order was sent too late and the main armament fired a few seconds later. The inner perimeter door bent across the middle, but didn't fall.

"Damnit!" said Duggan.

The second of the facility's main building doors closed behind the crawler and Duggan sent the command for the remaining perimeter gate to open. For a moment, it looked as if it was operational. It slid a short distance into the ground and then stopped. The gatehouse console reported a blockage on the door. Duggan swore again.

"That's torn it, huh?" asked Garcia.

"We need to get back into the tank," said Duggan. "Now!"

There was nothing more he could do from here, so Duggan

ran from the gatehouse, just in time to see Vega emerging from the tank.

"Get back in!" shouted Duggan. "Everyone inside!"

The men and women crawled towards the access ladders in the Colossus tank's flanks. It was a good distance up and there was a lot of climbing for those at the highest level. Duggan urged them to hurry.

He saw movement to his left – a small group of Vraxar came into sight a hundred metres away, trying to flank the soldiers clinging to the tank's hull. Duggan aimed and fired. His shot went through the closest Vraxar, knocking it backwards. Garcia fired three rapid bursts, killing two more. The rest scattered or dropped prone.

Once again, the tank's gun fired, the recoil bringing it within three metres of the gatehouse wall. The final door was bent out of shape, held in place by its frame.

"Best get onboard, sir," said Garcia. He saw Duggan's hesitation. "None of this works without you."

Duggan got himself inside and through the passage until he reached the cockpit. The crew were grim-faced and focused.

"They've got a big gun around the far end of the facility wall," said McKinney. "They move it out, hit us and then move it back."

"Shoot it next time it comes out," growled Duggan.

"With pleasure, sir," said Li.

"The squad are still coming onboard," said Roldan. "Waiting on Munoz, Clifton and Webb."

The soldiers were well-trained and motivated. They piled into the tank and closed the outer hatch. Just when the tank was finally sealed, the Vraxar artillery gun floated out from behind the corner of the facility wall a little over two hundred metres away. It didn't get a chance to fire and the Colossus tank blew it to pieces in a split second.

"Buh-bye," said Sergeant Li.

McKinney was an intelligent man and knew exactly what his next orders would be. He sent power through the tank's engines and the cockpit shook. "The gate?"

"Take it down, Lieutenant."

The tank accelerated through an increasing quantity of Vraxar small-arms fire. The absence of the outer door left a gap easily wide enough for the tank to go through and McKinney didn't let up once they were past.

"Uh, Lieutenant, we're still waiting on reload."

"Let's keep some ammunition for later, Sergeant. Hold on tight."

The tank smashed into the outer gate, racketing it backwards and tearing it free from its alloy frame. At the moment of impact, McKinney dragged the control sticks towards him and the tank slowed rapidly, ending up within the compound and hovering over what remained of the door. Inside, the crew were shaken, but the tank's life support kept them shielded from the worst effects of the collision.

"There's the crawler," said Duggan.

"I see it."

The flatbed gravity crawler was fractionally narrower than the gates through which it was required to travel and the vehicle itself was little more sophisticated than a floating platform with a rear-mounted crane and a navigation computer. The crawler waited mid-way across the inner compound, with a grey cuboid Obsidiar magazine on top.

"Pick it up," said Duggan.

McKinney rotated the tank on the spot and reversed towards the crawler, watching his progress on the single rear sensor feed.

"There's movement," said Bannerman. "I can see Vraxar foot soldiers to the east. No artillery yet."

McKinney didn't answer and he brought the tank steadily

closer to the crawler. "Activating winch." He huffed out his breath. "We have a successful pickup."

"Get us out of here, Lieutenant. *Now* we can go to the *Ulterior-2*."

"Shouldn't we take this crawler to the *Earth's Fury*?" asked Li in puzzlement.

"In good time, Sergeant."

There was a lower, deeper note to the tank's engines when McKinney guided it towards the gates. "They can feel the weight."

"Eyes front, Lieutenant," admonished Li. "I estimate about fifty centimetres of clearance to each side."

"It's a little less," said Duggan.

It wasn't the easiest way to exit and McKinney took it slowly. Even so, he managed to knock chunks out of both inner and outer walls. Meanwhile, the Vraxar continued their endless small-arms attack on the Colossus tank. After a tense two minutes, the vehicle emerged from the Obsidiar Storage Facility, towing its prize. Duggan thumped his fist against the bulkhead wall behind him.

"We made it," he said, hardly able to believe.

"We haven't won yet, sir," said Roldan.

"You need many small wins on the road to final victory, soldier."

"One step at a time," he means, said Lieutenant Paz, sitting on the floor in the corner.

Any satisfaction at this minor success was soon taken away. The squad medic, Amy Sandoval leaned into the cockpit. "Sir? I thought you might like to know – Lieutenant Richards has just passed away."

Duggan's face hardened. "Thank you for letting me know."

"Shit news always comes in twos," said Sergeant Li prophetically.

The words were hardly out of Li's mouth when Bannerman confirmed the prediction. "I'm picking up an eight-klick object establishing a stationary orbit directly above our heads, at an altitude of ten thousand klicks."

"The Vraxar battleship."

"One and the same, sir. That trip to the *Ulterior-2* is about to get a whole lot harder."

Rather than crumbling under this barrage of ill-fortune, Duggan forced a smile to his face. "I swore to myself that whatever happened, I'd do everything to beat these bastards. I don't care what they send – we're going to the *Ulterior-2*."

The words were brave and the men were buoyed by them. Deep in his heart, Duggan knew their luck had finally run dry.

CHAPTER NINETEEN

CHARLIE BLAKE COULDN'T REMEMBER EVER FEELING quite as low as he did at this point in time. He'd been on the bridge of the *Ulterior-2* for almost thirty minutes and it felt closer to a lifetime. His expulsion from the Space Corps had been a given from the moment he told Admiral Morey what she could do with her orders. Still, he blamed himself for the timing of it. *If I'd kept up the pretence I was following orders for a little longer, maybe I could have kept the act going.*

It probably didn't matter – there was no sign of Fleet Admiral Duggan, and without his signoff, the *Ulterior-2* wasn't likely to offer much threat to the Vraxar battleship. And then there was *Ix-Gorghal*. It would surely take twenty or more Hadrons to put a dent in that spacecraft's shield, let alone shoot it to pieces.

When Blake first conceived the idea of using the *ES Lucid* to lure away the Vraxar spaceships, he'd been confident that *something* would happen which he could capitalise upon as events progressed. In his mind's eye, he thought there would be a way to get *Earth's Fury* loaded and after that land a few shots on *Ix-*

Gorghal – give the thing a bloody nose or drive it away. The harder he looked back on it, the more foolish it appeared.

Now, he was stuck in the middle of a neutered battleship, whilst the enemy troops outside used some kind of device to try and circumvent the security locks keeping the boarding ramps sealed. Once they succeeded, they'd pour inside and no doubt murder anyone they found, before carting the bodies off to *Ix-Gorghal* for conversion.

Even worse, *Earth's Fury* was left unsealed because of Lieutenant Griffin's reckless disregard for his duty and that vessel was no doubt full of crumbling Vraxar animated corpses. This same Lieutenant Griffin was now locked inside the *Ulterior-2*'s brig, in spite of his loud, foul-breathed protestations of innocence.

"The Vraxar battleship is back," said Pointer glumly. "At a lower altitude this time."

"The *Lucid* did better than I expected," said Blake. "How long did we get out if it?"

"Fifty minutes," said Quinn promptly. "Maybe it decided on an extended jump and still has *Ix-Gorghal* following it."

"It doesn't really make a difference," said Blake. "If nothing changes, we're totally screwed."

"You probably don't want to hear that a six-hundred-kilometre object just skimmed off the upper edges of New Earth's atmosphere, do you?" asked Lieutenant Cruz.

"Heading?"

"Same vector as before – looks like it's settling in for another long, slow orbit of the planet."

"There you have it," said Blake bitterly. "Business as usual for them, as if there's nothing to worry about."

"That's good news, isn't it?" asked Hawkins. "It means they're not expecting anything."

Blake threw up his hands. "That's because we haven't got anything left to surprise them with. We're prisoners here until the Vraxar outside manage to crack open the boarding ramp and then they'll kill us."

"Their battleship is moving again," said Pointer.

Something in her tone made Blake look over, though without much interest. "What are they doing?"

"Coming lower and doing it fast. Nine thousand klicks, eight, five, slowing, three, two thousand, one thousand, slowing again, five hundred klicks."

"Strange," said Hawkins.

"Entering the upper reaches of the New Earth atmosphere," continued Pointer. "Still descending."

The Vraxar battleship came lower and lower. Each time the crew thought it was going to stop, it kept on going. Eventually, it *did* stop.

"Three thousand, one hundred metres," said Pointer. "Directly over this base."

"Atmospheric oxygen levels have just fallen to 16%," said Quinn. "They're getting ready for the next stage."

"That'll be the harvesting of our corpses, Lieutenant. Then the drilling of holes into our backs so they can prop us up against a metal pillar for a ten-year flight to find the Antaron."

"I thought you didn't approve of pessimism, sir," said Hawkins. Like the others, she refused to address him as a civilian.

Blake sighed. "I don't." He stood and winced at the knots in his muscles. "I'm going up top for some air."

"They'll be able to see you from that battleship," said Pointer.

"I doubt it matters – they've already demonstrated how they hope to capture the *Ulterior-2*. I'll be surprised if they send down a missile for one man."

Blake left the bridge and retraced the route to the upper access shaft. He called down the lift and waited for it to arrive.

"Need some company?" asked Pointer from behind.

"Sure."

The lift arrived and they climbed onboard. It ascended through the shaft at its own pace, until it reached the top, where it became part of the hull. On a peaceful, sunny day, the view would have been magnificent. On this day, the wind-blown rain spattered their spacesuits, and ran in rivulets down the surface of their visors. Far from suppressing the appearance of devastation on the Tucson base, the rain increased the volume of the smoke, which rose into the still-dark skies above.

Blake dropped to his haunches and looked up. The artificial light from the base generators was failing. Even at its usual intensity, it wouldn't have illuminated the Vraxar spaceship three kilometres above. He used the image intensifiers in his visor to look at what they faced. The enemy battleship hung, motionless, like a black-bladed sword waiting to swing down upon them.

"Looks kind of old, don't you think?" asked Pointer. She sat next to him on the *Ulterior-2*'s plating and pulled her knees up.

"I know what you mean. As if they stole it five hundred years before and keep it running out of sympathy."

"You have a funny way of looking at things."

"I don't hate that ship," he said, his voice distant. "The way I see it, that thing up there is a record of what the Vraxar did to the species who built it. Maybe they'll reduce it to parts once they're done with us and before they move on to the Antaron."

"And then it'll be forever lost."

Blake settled down next to her, unmindful of the rainwater covering the metal. "Us with it. Four hundred billion souls gone and forgotten."

"Fleet Admiral Duggan is a man who comes through."

"I was beginning to think I was too. Look at me – look at all of us – now."

They sat together for a time – mere seconds or minutes, Blake wasn't sure how long. He closed his eyes to block out the sights and found it strangely peaceful, with only a near-imperceptible hum of something deep within the *Ulterior-2* to break the silence. He didn't mind. If you were born to fly spaceships, that was all you wanted – the sound, the sights and that *feeling* of being part of something able to defy nature and physics.

"Maybe if we get out of this, we should go on that date," said Pointer.

"You picked an odd time to change your mind."

"I can see you need the motivation." He turned his head and saw her expression was serious. "I mean it," she said.

He didn't answer and they sat together without speaking. He put his arm around her and she didn't pull away.

"We need something to happen," he said. "It can't end like this."

They were interrupted by a disembodied voice, come seemingly from thin air. "Sir?"

It was Lieutenant Cruz, using the speaker system integrated into the maintenance shaft access panel.

"What is it, Lieutenant?"

"You aren't going to believe this."

He opened his mouth to ask the question. Just at that moment, the sky itself seemed to explode and the Vraxar battleship was engulfed in the plasma fires of what must have been a thousand missiles. The sound came a moment later and with such force Blake felt as if his insides would disintegrate with the resonation.

"Urgh," said Pointer, leaning in closer and putting her hands to her head.

The heat and flame roared down and around with a punishing fury which promised agonising incineration for any living thing caught within. The HUD inside Blake's helmet peaked at five hundred degrees and remained there, while he held onto Lieutenant Pointer, hoping they would somehow live through this storm of fire.

Blake got a sense of something and he looked up, trying to make out the details through the sun-bright plasma. The sensor in his visor snapped into sudden focus, revealing a new shape in the sky.

"The *Sciontrar*," he breathed. "They shouldn't be here for hours."

The Ghast Oblivion was at an even lower altitude than the Vraxar battleship and Blake guessed it was hardly more than two kilometres above the Tucson base. At close to six thousand metres long, the *Sciontrar* was the smaller of the two spaceships, yet the Ghasts somehow managed to cram in more deadly technology than either the Space Corps or the Vraxar could manage. The Oblivion launched another salvo of missiles – Shatterers which moved with such speed they defied the human eye. This time, the explosions were fewer, though individually the blast spheres were monumental in size.

A new sound reached them. It began as a whine, which built rapidly into a shrieking howl. The air vibrated and Blake groaned with the pain in his head. He squinted at the *Sciontrar* and saw a blue glow near the front of the vessel.

"They're warming up their Particle Disruptor," he shouted.

"It'll kill everything on this base!" Pointer yelled back.

"Quick – back to the lift!"

Before they could regain their feet, the howling stopped abruptly and the rumbling aftereffects of the missile blasts came once more to the fore. The *Sciontrar* accelerated towards the south. The Ghast spaceship weighed in excess of thirty billion tonnes, yet its speed rose with crushing inevitability and it raced towards the horizon.

The Vraxar battleship followed, flying sideways at first, before it began rotating in flight to aim its nose towards the disappearing Ghast vessel. The first of the sonic booms reached Blake and Pointer. A series of them followed, the sound like a hundred joined-up peals of thunder. The *Sciontrar* vanished from sight, with the Vraxar chasing after.

The Ghasts had one more gift to bestow. Eight rear Shatterer tubes fired at a distance of a thousand kilometres. It took the missiles only a single second to accelerate and reach their target. They crashed into the Vraxar dropship, their armour-piercing warheads ripping through its protective plating. The explosion was huge and it tore the dropship apart, hurling millions of tonnes of metal and carbonized bodies in every direction.

From the top of the *Ulterior-2* Blake couldn't see the blasts directly, but he knew exactly where the Shatterers had struck. The plumes of white fire went upwards for more than a thousand metres, carrying red-glowing pieces of the dropship's hull high into the air.

The noise faded and the fires receded. The temperature reading inside his HUD showed two hundred degrees and continued to fall. With the immediate danger over, Blake stopped on the edge of the lift hatch, tempted to run to the other side of the *Ulterior-2*, so he could look down onto the shipyard and landing strip. The battleship was wide and it was a long sprint to get there.

The nearby speaker came to life.

"Sir? Are you there?" asked Cruz.

"Still here, Lieutenant. I assume you saw that."

"Clear as day, sir. Wow."

"That about sums it up," he replied, not yet certain what the ramifications were of the *Sciontrar*'s arrival. One thing was certain – the appearance of the Ghast battleship was exactly what he'd been wishing for.

"We'd best get inside," said Pointer.

Before Blake could respond, a shadow fell over the hull of the *Ulterior-2*. He jerked around, fearful of what he would find.

Ix-Gorghal was above, travelling at a height of five or six thousand metres in the direction of the *Sciontrar*. It was difficult to guess its altitude or its speed since it was so enormous it gave off none of the usual visual cues to make the judgement. Over the base it swept, on and on, until it blocked out much of the sky. The hundreds of underside turrets rotated constantly, following targets known only to the Vraxar crew.

"Don't fire," whispered Pointer.

Blake held his breath, willing the huge spaceship to keep going and leave the Tucson base alone. With a sense of infinite relief, he watched *Ix-Gorghal* continue on the same course. It felt as if it took an age for the vessel to pass overhead. It was travelling much faster than it appeared and soon, the rear section of it went by, leaving Blake and Pointer staring with unashamed awe.

Then, it was gone. In its wake, a strong wind swept across the Tucson base. It picked up the rain and flung it hard against the two figures crouched on top of the *Ulterior-2*.

"I've seen enough," said Blake.

He activated the lift and it descended a short distance into the battleship's plating. The two of them jumped onto it and Blake pressed the button to take them down. Within seconds, the shielding effects of the shaft blocked out the wind and much of the rain.

The lift descended, whilst above, the gale brought by *Ix-Gorghal* continued to howl.

CHAPTER TWENTY

IN YEARS GONE BY, the Ghasts had been humanity's mortal enemy. The two sides had spent decades fighting for reasons which were still debated amongst scholars of war. When the conflict was at its most terrible, entire planets of both humans and Ghasts had been destroyed, killing billions.

Here and now, Duggan knew he couldn't want more fearsome or dedicated allies.

For a short period after *Ix-Gorghal* disappeared out of the Colossus tank's sensor arc, the occupants of the cockpit shared something – the togetherness of those who'd found death, only to be hauled from the brink by the most unexpected of miracles.

"That was..." said Lieutenant Paz, tailing off to silence.

"Yeah," said Roldan.

"Definitely."

Duggan was the most experienced of all, yet even he was mesmerised by the appearance of the *Sciontrar* and the events which followed. He snapped out of it the quickest, shaking his head clear.

"Ladies and gentlemen, this is our moment. If we live

through it, we'll raise a glass to Tarjos Nil-Tras and his crew. We haven't earned the right to celebrate yet."

"No, sir!" said McKinney, his voice crisp and his eyes clear. He had the look of a man born anew, who was going to grasp the opportunity with both hands and never forget what gave him this chance.

"Take us to the *Ulterior-2*, Lieutenant!" said Duggan with vigour. His body ached from age and the battering it had taken from the earlier engagement on the eastern road, but his voice was strong. "We don't know how much time we have, so let's treat every second as if it's precious."

Even the tank seemed somehow eager. The coarse vibration from its engines was muted and there was an underlying smoothness which had been lacking only minutes before. Duggan made his way to the front of the cockpit so he could better see the front sensor feed. He clapped McKinney on the shoulder in a show of camaraderie.

"Here we go, sir."

McKinney slammed the control sticks to their furthest extent. The tank ignored the unimportant facts of inertia and accelerated hard, dragging thousands of tonnes of gravity crawler and Obsidiar ammunition behind.

Roldan aimed the rear sensor array at the wreckage of the dropship. The Ghasts hadn't held back and there was nothing recognizable as a spaceship amongst the burning, glowing mound of melted alloy.

"I hope there was a million of those bastards still inside," he said.

"The Ghasts did them a favour," Paz replied.

As the tank moved out, Bannerman worked hard plotting the best course for them to take to their destination. The tank crew were blessed with a new energy, but they hadn't lost sight of the overwhelming numbers of Vraxar they'd witnessed spilling out of the now-destroyed dropship and onto the Tucson base.

"The enemy exited the dropship here," Bannerman said, poking at the map on one of his screens. "They fanned out here and here, with others into the OSF. We're coming around the opposite side of the facility, between what's left of these warehouses then out onto the landing strip. A few thousand metres after that we reach Trench One and the *Ulterior-2*."

"We'll be exposed, but this should minimise the amount," said Roldan.

Duggan nodded. "Once we reach the shipyard there should be plenty of cover amongst the cranes and there was a big gravity crawler near to the *Ulterior-2* when I visited yesterday."

Only yesterday, he thought. *Or was it today? It feels like forever.*

McKinney guided the tank away from the OSF and into another of the wide streets. This near to the shipyard, the roads were built to allow the transit of the largest crawlers and there was plenty of room for the tank to travel without hitting the adjacent buildings.

There were component warehouses on both sides, filled with everything required for spares and repairs. Gun barrels, launch tubes, engine blocks, life support modules and even spare landing gear were packed within these buildings. There was extensive damage, though the warehouses had got off more lightly than the occupied areas of the base.

"Here we go," said McKinney, turning at the intersection. "Any second now we should be able to see what we're dealing with."

The street was cluttered with abandoned vehicles, including a seemingly undamaged light tank which was at an angle across the road.

"Don't stop," said Duggan.

The Colossus tank ploughed into the much smaller Grant Mk4, pushing it first to one side and then tipping it completely onto its side. Within the cockpit, the crew felt the impact but the Colossus didn't slow.

"We should build more of these things, sir," said Sergeant Li.

"This one is certainly coming through its live test with flying colours," Duggan agreed.

"There we are," said McKinney. "The landing strip."

The tank was still within cover of the warehouses; however, the front sensor was already able to get a good viewing arc onto the landing strip ahead and beyond it, the shipyard.

The rows of spaceships which had been parked here only hours before were gone, destroyed by *Ix-Gorghal* a short time after its arrival from lightspeed. Now there were Vraxar foot soldiers and a few pieces of artillery.

"Most of them must have reached the shipyard," said McKinney. "These look like stragglers."

"The last ones off the dropship before the Ghasts took it apart," said Roldan.

There was no delineation between the landing strip and the shipyard. One area simply ended and the other began. The tank's sensors picked up the many work vehicles close to Trench One. The visible upper section of the *Ulterior-2* dwarfed everything, making the heavy plant appear tiny and insignificant.

"The shipyard was busy when I set off the base alarm," said Duggan. "Procedure is to abandon everything in place and get to safety."

"Cranes, crawlers, bots, haulers," said Li. "Plenty of everything."

"Plenty of Vraxar too," said Bannerman.

The enemy soldiers were visible in huge numbers. They moved in amongst the machinery like ants coming back to their nest. Duggan saw many artillery guns, most of them stationary and aimed at the *Ulterior-2*, as if they had any hope of even scratching the battleship, let alone putting a hole in its side.

"How do you plan to get inside, sir?" asked Li.

Duggan's eyes found what they'd been hunting for. "There!" he said, pointing at an elongated cuboid with a squared back and something which vaguely resembled a nose. "Lifting shuttle."

The lifting shuttle was more than two hundred metres in length and forty tall. If you weren't paying attention, it could be easily mistaken for a fixed building. It was mostly gravity drive and designed to haul pretty much anything into the skies above a half-built spaceship hull and drop it into place.

"That thing?" asked Roldan doubtfully. "It looks kinda slow."

"It is, but it's solid engine and not much else. You're going to help me get onboard."

The shuttle was parked a short distance from the main clusters of plant and about five hundred metres from the *Ulterior-2*. Duggan saw McKinney's eyes narrow as the soldier sized up the task before him.

"There are lots of Vraxar, sir."

"Bring the tank in close and I'll take it from there."

"You'll require an escort."

"Of course."

"What about us, sir?" asked Li. "How are we going to get this ammo to the *Earth's Fury*?"

Duggan gave him a broad smile. "Sit tight in the tank and you'll find out."

Li caught on immediately. "I never did like heights."

"You're a lying shit, Sergeant," laughed Roldan. "You're not scared of anything."

By the time the short conversation was over, the Colossus tank was a quarter of the way across the landing strip. McKinney altered course slightly, aiming for the lifting shuttle, while Roldan called through to the passenger bay and told the soldiers to prepare for deployment.

"Thirty-eight klicks per hour," said McKinney. "Come on you beautiful, stubborn bastard!"

For a time, the tank's approach went unseen by the enemy and the vehicle came ever closer to the shuttle. Inevitably, the good luck ended. A number of Vraxar near the *Ulterior-2* noticed the approaching tank and a few of them took pot shots with their hand cannons. It was a waste of ammunition and the slugs plinked harmlessly off the tank's thick plating. The enemy got a heavy repeater turned and it started up. A dozen glowing lines traced through the patches of light and darkness to betray the path of the bullets.

"Big gun," said Li, identifying one of the larger artillery pieces a few hundred metres away. "There - near that gravity crane."

"What are you waiting for?" asked McKinney.

Li wasn't waiting for anything. He lined up the crosshairs on his targeting screen and fired. The Vraxar gun was struck with tremendous force and it flipped over several times before coming to rest on its side.

It was getting hotter. A second heavy repeater joined the first and was soon followed by a third. Within the cabin it was uncomfortably loud and Duggan lowered his visor to block out some of the sound. Two much larger projectiles clanged away from the tank's nose in rapid succession and Duggan felt the bulkhead wall he was leaning against shake with the impacts.

"If you would like to pass on a suggestion to the design teams, sir, maybe you could ask them to work on the reload interval for the main gun," said Li.

"I'll be sure to pass the message on," said Duggan drily.

At the front of the cockpit, McKinney said little. Each time a new target was identified, he altered their course to try and bring pieces of construction machinery between the artillery and the tank. It was only partially successful and each time he cut off the firing angle for one gun, it seemed as if another took its place.

"They definitely know we're here," said Roldan.

Li fired the main gun again. Against single targets, the weapon was tremendous. Faced with so many smaller enemies, it was of limited use. Even so, this second shot smashed into a heavy repeater and carried straight through into a second artillery unit directly behind. Both guns were destroyed, along with a dozen of their crew.

"Did you like that?" snarled Li, the first unrestrained expression of anger Duggan could remember seeing from the man.

"Here comes the shuttle," said McKinney. "I'm going to try and drift us in sideways."

"Get ready to jump," said Roldan to the rest of the squad waiting near the exit hatch. "There's a lifting shuttle, which Fleet Admiral Duggan hopes to inspect. Keep him safe guys and gals."

McKinney made a final change of direction and aimed directly for the flank of the shuttle. The craft was nearly parallel to the *Ulterior-2* and from this close, it cut off much of the incoming fire.

"You're coming in fast, Lieutenant," said Bannerman.

"I've got this."

McKinney left it late. He pulled back on the left control stick and used the thumb switches to apply the brakes on one side. The tank shook and its rear came around until the vehicle was in a controlled sideways drift. Duggan had been out of action for too long and he gritted his teeth in anticipation of the collision. It didn't come.

"Perfect," said McKinney, wiping sweat from his brow.

If not exactly perfect, it was near as damnit.

"Squad, exit the vehicle!" shouted Roldan on the comms. "Move it, move it!"

Duggan picked up his rifle, beckoned to Lieutenant Paz and dashed into the passage outside. The rest of the soldiers were in the process of jumping through the exit hatch and Duggan went hot on their heels.

It was windy outside and there was no let-up in the rain. The artificial lighting had failed nearby and this area of the ship-yard was gloomy like dusk on a winter's day. Before him, Duggan saw the slab side of the lifting shuttle, hardly ten metres away. The squad of soldiers were already spread out defensively and they kept their gauss rifles ready in case there was enemy movement.

The door to the shuttle was thirty metres away, towards the craft's blunt nose. Duggan spotted it and waved the squad in that direction.

"There's the door," he said.

It wasn't the right time for caution and the group ran towards the shuttle entrance. It was a struggle for Duggan to keep up and he gratefully accepted Garcia's assistance. Together, they got there and Duggan experienced relief when he saw the access panel ahead.

The tank's main gun thundered and the vehicle rocked back.

"We've got to move," said Whitlock, glancing behind. He spun and fired a series of shots from his rifle. The coils on the gun whined and he kept it up, round after round.

"Shit," said Munoz, firing his own rifle.

Duggan crossed the last few paces to the access panel and slammed his palm against it. The red light turned green and the door slid open to reveal a flight of steep, narrow, brightly-lit steps leading into the depths of the shuttle. As the earlier dose of battlefield adrenaline and painkillers gradually wore off, the aching pains were becoming an impediment and Duggan groaned inwardly at the climb before him.

He went in first, forcing one weary leg in front of the other.

The cockpit on these shuttles was near the top and it felt as if the climb was closer to three hundred metres rather than thirty.

"A little further, sir," said Lieutenant Paz from directly behind.

Ricky Vega was next and he called up the stairwell. "You need to boost, sir."

The soldier was right and Duggan requested another injection of adrenaline. The spacesuit micro-computer evaluated his physical state and considered his age. To Duggan's chagrin, it refused his request. He cursed and overrode the software. Needles jabbed into him and a fresh dose of adrenaline roared through his bloodstream. He felt his heart give the familiar kick. It missed two beats and the visor computer sent numerous warnings to his HUD. Duggan's brain viewed the situation dispassionately and without panic. His heart started up again, the aches faded and his strength returned.

A few paces from the top he could see the tiny antechamber leading into the cockpit. He surged up the remaining steps, just as a shout came from the shuttle entrance.

"Man down! Man down!"

"Get him, quickly!"

The voice of Medic Sandoval was added to the chorus. "Get him onboard!"

Any delay would jeopardise everything and Duggan left the soldiers to seal the shuttle and get the injured man up the steps. He reached the landing and activated the cockpit door. It opened and inside was space enough for one to sit and four or five to stand shoulder to shoulder. It was years since he'd flown anything like this and time hadn't improved the comfort offered. The lifting shuttles were meant to be directly controlled by the shipyard computer and as such, they were only fitted with the most basic pilot consoles. It would have to do.

Duggan threw himself into the foam seat, his hands and eyes

already preparing themselves. The shuttle's engines were running at idle, which was good news since he wouldn't need to waste time bringing them out of sleep.

"Is everyone in?" he asked.

He sensed Lieutenant Paz at the open cockpit door. "Yes, sir."

Duggan activated the 360-degree sensors and turned off the autopilot. The security software requested confirmation, which he provided by briefly touching a biological reader between two of the feed screens. His hands fell onto the control bars and instinct took over. He drew the controls back and the shuttle's engines hummed smoothly, lifting the craft off the ground.

As soon as the shuttle lifted off, the Vraxar realised what was happening. They began firing at both the shuttle and the now-exposed Colossus tank. The lifter wasn't specifically made to take a beating, yet it was near-solid Gallenium and untroubled by repeater slugs, large or small.

The shuttle climbed rapidly and as soon it reached an altitude of one hundred metres, Duggan targeted the gravity chains onto both the Colossus tank and the crawler it was towing. It wasn't a complicated system – the chains locked on, a light went green and that was it.

"Here we go," said Duggan. "Nice and easy."

The tank and crawler were heavy. Even so, the lifter was made to carry far, far greater weights. Its engine note changed slightly with the added load, the difference hardly noticeable. The shuttle climbed, the tank and crawler coming with it.

Lieutenant Paz put her hand on his shoulder and bent forward to watch the sensors. "Where are those missile launchers?" she asked.

"They're down there somewhere."

This was just one immensely risky episode amongst many. Duggan had no idea how many ground-launched missile strikes the shuttle could survive, if any, and he had a distinct preference to remain ignorant. He didn't waste time trying to point the lifter's nose towards the *Ulterior-2*. Instead, he flew it at an angle, pushing the engines to maximum. The shuttle had vast wells of power, but it wasn't designed to use them for speed. Even so, it wasn't as slow as Duggan had initially feared and it rose quickly, following a direct line from its landing place towards the top of the *Ulterior-2*.

The ground below was covered in a writhing swarm of Vraxar. The shuttle's sensors picked them out easily enough – the majority were Estral, their grey faces a mask for the anguish of whatever lay within.

"There must be fifty thousand," breathed Paz.

"More," said Duggan. "Look at the *Earth's Fury*."

The second ship was also surrounded by the alien troops. There weren't so many as there were near the *Ulterior-2*, yet there were still thousands of them on the edges of the docking trench.

The lifter wasn't fitted with missile detection systems and at this short range it wouldn't have made a difference. One of the ground multi-launchers fired upwards. It was difficult to miss and several plasma explosions struck the Colossus tank. The vehicle was sent rocking by the force, but the gravity chains held it tight and it stabilised.

A second volley came, this time hitting the crawler. Like the shuttle, the crawler was little more than a block of metal. The blasts sent it wobbling and from above it looked almost unscathed. Duggan was sure looks were deceiving and he hoped it would stay together since it was acting as a shield for the magazine of Obsidiar ammunition.

A third series of missiles crashed into the crawler and the heat seeped through to the top plate, giving it a dark red glow. The magazine remained fixed in place, held by the gravity load bed. To Duggan, it felt as though the Vraxar had chosen to piss him off by shooting at something which was, to all appearances, the lowest-priority target, instead of trying to knock out the shuttle.

"What are they playing at?" said Paz angrily.

"They're just doing what they do."

"The crawler doesn't look as if it can take much more punishment."

"It can't."

"What happens to the magazine...?"

"I don't think we should test it out."

The next round of missile launches saw one warhead explode off the rear of the lifter, with the remainder striking the crawler. The metal of the vehicle burned and the crawler sagged across the middle. It was still held tightly by the shuttle, but the heat was spilling into the Obsidiar magazine.

With a prescience which had served him well in the past, Duggan's mind knew what was coming. He glanced at the sensor feed and saw one of the mobile launchers completing its final adjustments. The lifter was nearly at the *Ulterior-2. Not close enough,* he thought.

With a rapid movement, Duggan banged the side of his hand onto the purge mechanism for the gravity chains. The tank, the crawler and the magazine of ammunition dropped away.

"What?" said Paz.

Without a word, Duggan, retargeted the tank and the magazine with the chains. The tank jerked to an immediate halt and swung, scraping into the side of the *Ulterior-2.* The second chain latched successfully onto the magazine. The weight of the crawler ripped it away from its cargo and it continued downwards. A fraction of a second later, the missile launcher fired and the crawler was engulfed in flames. If the magazine had been in place, it would have likely been ruptured or warped out of shape by the heat.

The top section of the *Ulterior-2* filled the underside view feed and the lifter shuttle made it to safety. Duggan let the tank fall from ten or fifteen metres, relying on its engines to cushion the blow for the occupants. He spent a few seconds longer with the Obsidiar magazine and made absolutely certain it was treated to the softest of landings. Once the magazine was released, he landed the shuttle on top of the battleship, eschewing finesse and dumping it down hard.

"Time to move," he said urgently.

"Let the Fleet Admiral exit first!" bellowed Sergeant Demarco.

Duggan worked his way through the press of soldiers in the antechamber. Clifton was full-length on the floor with his eyes closed, and Sandoval crouched nearby. It made the tight space even more uncomfortable. The medic met Duggan's eyes.

"Induced coma. I think he'll make it."

It was enough and Duggan set off on the stairs, with Paz following and the rest of the squad preparing to get Clifton down the stairwell. Outside, the closest Havoc turret loomed high above their heads and its long, long barrel pointed into the sky. It nearly had sufficient bore to fire the entire Colossus tank that was currently heading across the armour plating towards them.

"Which way?" asked Paz, her eyes seeking an entrance.

"Here," said Duggan. He marched confidently towards the location of an entrance hatch.

"How did you know?" asked Paz, watching as he pressed the access panel.

"You do realise I approve the design of these things?" he asked mildly. "Do you think I just write my name on the signoff sheet and not bother checking what's going to come out of the shipyard at the end of it all?"

"I am slandered by the accusation, sir," Paz replied, glimpses of her usual good humour showing through.

They got onto the lift and it descended through the armour and into the depths of the *Ulterior-2*. Duggan breathed deeply, taking in the scent of pure Gallenium and the far more ephemeral sensation of raw, unadulterated power which came with every Hadron in the Space Corps fleet. There was something extra with the *Ulterior-2* – it felt new and different. It felt special.

CHAPTER TWENTY-ONE

IT WAS good to step onto the bridge of the *Ulterior-2*. The people onboard – faces Duggan knew well – were already standing and they saluted his arrival.

"Captain Blake," smiled Duggan. "Good to see you got here in time."

"Good evening, sir. Do I need to bring you up to speed with anything?"

"Soon. Firstly, I need to send the final authorisation codes into the *Ulterior-2*'s core cluster and then take this ship out of maintenance mode. After that, she's all yours. I assume you have a plan?"

Blake faltered. "I have been discharged from the Space Corps, sir, and am therefore unable to fly the *Ulterior-2*."

"What is this nonsense?" asked Duggan, looking for signs that Blake was making an inappropriate joke.

"Sir, please bring the *Ulterior-2* online," Blake insisted, ushering Duggan towards the captain's seat.

Duggan sat, wondering what the hell was going on. It could wait for a couple of minutes. He tuned out everything around him and logged into the main console. There were several layers of security to work through in order to sign a fleet warship off for duty and a new Hadron had several layers more than anything else.

The *Ulterior-2* offered up some unexpected resistance.

"Missing, presumed *dead*?" said Duggan, when he saw why his first attempts were denied. "I am very much not dead, nor am I missing."

The core cluster took some persuading. Finally, a combination of biological data, in conjunction with several command codes, convinced the battleship that reports of Duggan's death were likely the result of human error.

Immediately the sign off was complete, numerous additional options appeared on the crew's console screens and several previously-empty menus filled up with an array of options.

"Lots of stuff still offline," said Lieutenant Hawkins.

"Wait," said Duggan. He sent one final command and the ship came out of maintenance mode.

"That's more like it." Hawkins' eyes gleamed. "The Havoc cannons will be ready to fire in less than two minutes."

"Activating fission suppression systems," said Quinn.

"You're trying to conceal the engine warmup?" asked Duggan.

"That's the hope, sir."

"Good plan. We don't know when *Ix-Gorghal* will return and we need to keep its crew in the dark."

"What next, sir?" asked Blake.

"What's next is you tell me how you got yourself discharged."

Blake told him and Duggan was less than pleased about Admiral Morey's conduct.

"I won't accept cowardice amongst my junior officers, let alone my second in command!" Duggan roared. He was absolutely livid. "How dare she! The total, unmitigated gall of it! We are the Confederation and we do *not* abandon entire planets to our enemies!"

"Can you reinstate him, sir?" asked Pointer, her soft tones cutting through Duggan's anger.

"Of course, I can reinstate him!" he said, his anger directed at Morey rather than Pointer. "Except it'll take twenty-four hours before his rank becomes active again."

"With no way to move things along?" asked Hawkins.

Duggan calmed himself. "Yes, I can do that. I'll need to sign into each of the new personnel records and give them an approval stamp. Then, I'll need to manually re-approve each and every one of his training entries before the *Ulterior-2* will accept his competence."

"Will that take long?" asked Cruz.

"At least an hour. More likely two."

Blake jumped up from one of the spare seats. "We don't have one hour, let alone two!"

"Then what do you propose?" asked Duggan.

"Activate the *Earth's Fury*, sir. Bring it into service, the same way you did for this one," he said with sudden enthusiasm. "With the comms lockdown, it won't have received the updated personnel records from the Space Corps databases."

Duggan nodded in approval. "It won't know you've been discharged. What then?"

"I've seen the design plans for the *Earth's Fury*, sir. I know how to load the gun. If I take that lifter shuttle off the *Ulterior-2*'s roof I can drop the magazine into the loading chamber. After that, I'll go onboard and shoot it at *Ix-Gorghal*."

Duggan was familiar with such makeshift plans as this one, having come up with more than a few himself in the past. He therefore felt uniquely positioned to spot the inherent flaws.

"I don't know if *Earth's Fury* is ready to fly and it doesn't have life support."

"It might not even need to fly, sir!" said Blake, warming to his idea. "As soon as *Ix-Gorghal* returns, we'll shoot at it from the ground. The worst that can happen is it destroys the ship."

"No, Captain Blake. There are worse possibilities than that."

"Like what, sir?"

"If by some stroke of luck you force *Ix-Gorghal* into a position where its commanding officer feels the requirement for an overwhelming response, there will be unintended consequences."

Blake had a mind capable of making huge logical leaps. "You've activated Benediction?"

"I have. It'll explode in less than six hours. If we accidentally push the Vraxar into destroying New Earth before then, the bomb will be destroyed with it."

"We have to take this chance!" said Blake with fervour.

"No, Captain Blake, we don't."

"What if I promise to hold fire until *Earth's Fury* is far enough away from New Earth that it'll be the sole target of reprisals?"

"If that is what you promise, then that is what I will accept."

It was a long shot, but Duggan attempted remote activation of *Earth's Fury*. To his surprise, the *Ulterior-2*'s comms systems were able to make the link.

"The weakness of our comms systems has been a concern for some time," he said. "If this battleship is anything to go by, we may be close to overcoming those problems."

"You're able to sign off the *Earth's Fury*?" asked Blake.

"I'll tell you shortly."

It took far less time to activate the second warship. The *Ulterior-2*'s AI clusters already trusted Duggan's position as Fleet Admiral and the *Earth's Fury* was set to trust other fleet warships. Therefore, the process was finished in moments.

"Is it done?" asked Blake.

Duggan sat back and pushed his fingertips through his short

hair. "It's done. I don't know for certain how much of the *Earth's Fury* is operational. I'm sure you'll find out once you get over there. One thing I do know - the gun definitely works."

"Whatever the problems, we'll deal with them, sir."

"That's what I like to hear." Events were moving on and Duggan was keen to bring himself up to speed with the remaining details. "What of the *Sciontrar*?" he asked. "Is it still fighting the enemy?"

The high-spirits faded. "We don't know, sir," said Lieutenant Pointer. "They've entered lightspeed several times since the beginning of their engagement with the Vraxar battleship. This latest time has been longer than the others."

"We'll keep our fingers crossed Nil-Tras comes out of it in one piece. Until then, we'll assume the *Sciontrar* is missing or destroyed and act accordingly."

"There might be another problem, sir," said Cruz.

"Lieutenant, if there's a lesson for you to learn, it is to never use the word *might* when what you really mean is *definitely*."

"Sorry, sir. The *Earth's Fury* wasn't sealed after the base alarm. It is *definitely* filled with Vraxar."

"Failure upon failure," muttered Duggan. He flexed his hands, which were powerful even now. "I wonder what it would feel like to..."

"We have the officer responsible locked in the brig," said Pointer helpfully. "I'm sure we can keep a secret."

"That won't be necessary, Lieutenant." He put it from his mind for the time being, conscious that base-wide failures were his responsibility as well. Instead, he focused on those matters he could influence in the immediate future. "Did I see soldiers in the corridors leading to the *Ulterior-2*'s bridge, Captain Blake?"

"Yes, sir, you did. Those are the *ES Lucid*'s complement."

"I assume from that you've lost a second heavy cruiser?"

"In a good cause, sir."

"You'll need those troops on the *Earth's Fury*. It is equipped with internal countermeasures which should have activated the second I brought the ship into active duty. Those countermeasures may not clear out a strong enemy presence, particularly if they've been disabling the ceiling guns on the way."

"I hope the corridors are filled with the chewed up remains of Vraxar soldiers," said Blake with relish.

"The only way you'll find out is by getting over there. I've remote-activated the seals, so whatever Vraxar remain inside should be the last."

Blake took the hint. "The *Ulterior-2* is already secure, so I'll take most of the soldiers with me. I'll leave enough to guard the bridge."

"That will be fine."

There was an unspoken question hanging in the air which couldn't be put off any longer.

"Does this mean you're going to fly the *Ulterior-2*, sir?" asked Blake.

"I don't see an alternative."

"It'll be good to have you back in action."

"This isn't what I wanted – I'm old and slow."

"We'll see."

Duggan waved off the compliment. "I'll need to keep some of your crew."

"I can probably handle the *Earth's Fury* alone, sir. It's just a flying gun."

"You'll need additional expertise to get it up in the air, Captain, and a dedicated officer for the main armament." Duggan cast his eyes around the room. "Take Lieutenants Pointer, Quinn and Hawkins."

That left ensigns Toby Park and Charlotte Bailey in control of several major systems on a Space Corps battleship. Their thoughts on the subject were plain on their faces, yet neither hid behind excuses.

"I'll do my best, sir," said Bailey.

Park nodded in agreement. "You can count on me, too."

"That's it settled," said Blake.

"Not quite, Captain. The targeting software for the Havoc cannons is based on the same systems built into the Colossus tank we recently dropped onto the roof of this battleship. Send Sergeant Li up here – he seems to have an aptitude for it."

"I'm sure he will be delighted, sir."

"Go. The lack of comms between our two ships will make things difficult. If you get far enough from New Earth, they may become available again. This will require more than teamwork. I'm trusting you with everything, Captain Blake."

"We won't let you down."

"I know. As soon as I see you on the roof, I'll turn on the *Ulterior-2*'s countermeasures to knock out the enemy missile launchers. And everything else, for that matter." Duggan smiled without humour. "It isn't a healthy time to be a Vraxar on the Tucson landing strip."

Blake and the others made haste through the bridge exit door and Lieutenant Paz sat herself in the corner out of the way. Her areas of expertise didn't encompass bridge duties. A little while later, Sergeant Li sauntered in with the confident air of a man who'd been asked to show someone how to turn on a television.

"Sergeant Li, please take a seat next to Ensign Park. You're in sole charge of the Havoc cannons. We'll be lifting off soon, so if you have questions, now is the time to ask them."

Li didn't sound perturbed and poked at the targeting console. "Four upper guns, two lower and one each near the nose and tail. It'll be like controlling eight tanks at the same time."

"You're aware there'll be no time for pissing around, Sergeant?"

"I might talk, but I always get the job done, sir."

"That's what I wanted to hear."

It would take Blake a few minutes to reach the shuttle and Duggan spent the time familiarising himself with the *Ulterior-2*'s onboard systems. In truth, there was little change in the interfaces since he'd last flown in anger and he also was part of the team which approved major software changes. The comms were updated, but Lieutenant Cruz seemed to be on top of things. His hands moved of their own volition, without conscious thought. *The body has aged, but it still remembers.*

"Ensign Bailey, update me on the engines."

"Lieutenant Quinn managed to get the fission suppression set to cover their warmup, sir. We could get off the ground right now if you wanted to."

"How long until we reach a state of full readiness?"

"Ten minutes."

"That's faster than I was expecting. What about our other critical systems?"

"Both Obsidiar cores are at 100%. The energy shield is fully charged and awaiting activation. Stealth systems online and available. Eight dedicated Short-Range Transit cores running within expected parameters."

"Lieutenant Cruz, any response from the *Sciontrar*?"

"They're silent on the comms, sir."

"Watch out for Captain Blake and tell me when you see him on the roof."

"The maintenance lift has just reached the outer hull. The *Earth's Fury* crew are running for the shuttle."

"Ensign Park, please activate the *Ulterior-2*'s external countermeasures. Set them to fire indiscriminately until there's nothing left."

"Yes, sir!" said Park. "Countermeasures activated."

"Keep your eye on the sensor feed and remember this is payback for what they've done."

"Projecting our external feeds onto the main viewscreen," said Cruz.

It began at once. The *Ulterior-2* was equipped with 184 Bulwark cannons, which could shoot down incoming missiles at two hundred thousand kilometres. This wasn't their only use - they were versatile weapons and could be instructed to target more or less anything.

The Bulwarks sprang from their hidden compartments on the battleship. They appeared tiny against the might of its hull, yet Duggan knew exactly what they were capable of. At precisely the same moment, every gun which could identify a target started firing. Slugs poured into the tens of thousands of Vraxar gathered around the *Ulterior-2*.

The crew watched the bulkhead screen in silence. Bulwark projectiles tore through the massed ranks of alien troops, reducing them to unrecognizable pieces and leaving greasy liquid upon the concrete. The artillery fared no better – where the slugs struck them, they were knocked backwards, deformed and then broken into pieces.

Still the onslaught continued. Once the final artillery gun was destroyed, the *Ulterior-2*'s battle computer directed the Bulwarks to strafe the landing strip and shipyard. The underside cannons ripped through the troops at the bottom of the docking trench. The Vraxar were scythed down like wheat.

Many of the enemy were hidden from sight by the shipyard machinery. It didn't save them. The *indiscriminate* firing mode on the guns directed them to keep shooting until every identified target was eliminated. The Bulwarks pounded the cranes, crawlers, robots, reducing them to scrap. Here and there, a cane toppled, crushing the Vraxar behind. In other places, the sustained Bulwark fusillade went clean through the solid machinery and maintained fire until there was nothing left to shoot.

Once the numbers surrounding the *Ulterior-2* thinned, the battle computer took aim at the clusters of troops around the *Earth's Fury*. This new carnage was accomplished with similar efficiency. There were thousands of Vraxar hidden from sight around the far side of *Earth's Fury* and since Duggan couldn't remote active the second spaceship's Bulwarks, those remaining would have to wait for later.

One-by-one, the Bulwarks ran out of targets and stopped firing. The statistics for the short engagement appeared on the tactical display, as though the battle computer had a sense of pride in its achievement.

> Targets Identified: 88,300. Targets Eliminated: 88,299. Time Elapsed: 72 seconds. Estimated Targets Untracked: 12,093.

"Twelve thousand remaining?" asked Park.

"Out of sight, behind the *Earth's Fury*," said Duggan.

"What about this single enemy left from the identified targets?" asked Li indignantly, as though it was an affront for a single Vraxar to have escaped.

"If you chase perfection, you'll spend your life in frustration, Sergeant."

"Captain Blake is on his way," said Lieutenant Cruz. "The shuttle is up in the air and it's a short trip."

"Is he carrying the Obsidiar magazine?"

"Yes, sir. No signs of additional damage to either the lifter or its cargo."

"We might get something out of this yet," said Duggan.

He checked through the *Ulterior-2*'s onboard status displays. It would take another few minutes to reach 100% on every system. All things considered, the battleship was about as ready as it would ever be. It wasn't a moment too soon.

"Sir, there are two incoming spaceships, travelling fast and low. They're heading our way."

"The *Sciontrar*?"

"With the battleship coming after."

A familiar calm descended upon Duggan. The excitement of battle – a joy he couldn't resist – gripped him. His skin went cold, his pupils widened and he prepared for the fight.

CHAPTER TWENTY-TWO

THE *SCIONTRAR* APPEARED on the horizon as a fast-moving meteor of flame and burning anger. It flew over the Tucson base so fast it was a wonder it didn't burn up from atmospheric friction. The Ghost battleship followed, hot with its own fires and hardly two thousand metres above the surface of New Earth. In its wake, it shook buildings and heat spilled into the rain-heavy air, turning it into thick clouds of steam.

And then, the two ships were gone, heading towards the horizon.

"Sergeant Li, target and fire as soon as you're able."

"Yes, sir. Let's see what a real big bastard of a gun can do."

Duggan took the control bars of the *Ulterior-2*, as smooth and cold as he remembered. They ran with precision through their runners and he pulled them towards him. The Hadron's gravity engines were beautifully smooth and they gave no sign of stress at the lift-off. The *Ulterior-2* rose from its trench, thirty-seven billion tonnes of engines, weapons and armour climbing into the darkness of the New Earth skies as if the battleship weighed no more than a feather.

There was no time for subtlety and a trail of sonic booms followed the immense craft's vertical climb, rattling windows and shaking the damaged buildings all across the base.

"Activate stealth modules and our energy shield."

"Stealth modules and shield online."

"I have locked onto the enemy spaceship," said Li. "The horizon won't save them from this..."

Sergeant Li fired two of the upper Havoc cannons. Duggan knew the design difficulties only too well and he was expecting the result. The guns fired and a pair of twenty-metre, hardened Gallenium slugs, each weighing 146,000 tonnes were propelled from zero to 200,000 kilometres per second in the blinking of an eye.

The sound and the recoil were tremendous. The Havoc cannons gave off a whining boom which reverberated through the entire ship, shaking the walls and the equipment. The projectiles struck the rear section of the Vraxar battleship. Its energy shield was already gone and the slugs plunged through a thousand metres of armour plating and engines, leaving two enormous holes as evidence of their passing.

"Whoa," said Li.

The Hadron was far too heavy to be thrown off course by the recoil, but Duggan felt movement in the control rods and he kept a tight hold. He fed a surge of power into the engines and turned the nose at the same time. As the spaceship tilted around and gathered speed, the Colossus tank on the upper section slid off the back, plummeting towards the ground. Duggan couldn't afford sentimentality and put it from his mind.

"It wasn't enough to finish them. Let's have another go," he said.

The *Ulterior-2* responded well to the controls and its speed climbed rapidly. Soon, the Tucson base was far behind and a few seconds later the Hadron crossed over the coastline of the Postern

Ocean. Duggan took the spaceship higher and higher, trying to open up a firing angle onto the Vraxar battleship. Below, the white-capped waves merged together until it seemed as though a carpet of cold grey-blue rolled away in every direction.

"The Vraxar energy shields have failed," said Ensign Bailey. "Doesn't that suggest the Ghasts have the upper hand?"

"It does."

"Why is Tarjos Nil-Tras still running, then?"

"You don't think he's running from the battleship, do you?" asked Duggan.

"In that case..."

"*Ix-Gorghal* could be anywhere."

"Why isn't it still following?"

"Only a fool gets dragged into a low-altitude pursuit, Lieutenant. *Ix-Gorghal*'s captain likely broke it off some time ago and will be waiting for the *Sciontrar* to come to him. In the meantime, the Ghasts will keep running and hope to evade *Ix-Gorghal* – they're buying time and nothing more."

Another thought came to Duggan and it worried him. *What if Ix-Gorghal is already following with its stealth modules activated? It could be ten klicks away, ignorant of our location, but close enough to hit us as soon as we reveal our presence.*

"Hold fire for the moment," he said. "There's something about this situation I don't like. Lieutenant Cruz, try contacting the *Sciontrar* again."

"There's no comms response, sir," said Cruz. "Whatever is keeping New Earth quiet is working on the Ghasts now they've come close enough. I can talk to them, but they can't answer back."

"Let them know we're following close by and are evaluating."

"Two of the Vraxar satellites are in view, sir," said Park. "I can hit them with Shimmers, which might allow comms in this area."

"Hold fire, I said! It's important the enemy think the New Earth prize is still theirs for the taking. I don't want to push them into a position where it's more convenient to simply blow the whole planet to pieces and move on to the next one. And a weapon launch will give our position away if *Ix-Gorghal* is close."

"Oxygen levels at 15%," said Cruz. "Not a good time to be living at altitude."

Even with the *Ulterior-2* operational and up in the air, the situation was a poor one. Havoc cannons or not, the Hadron wasn't going to worry *Ix-Gorghal* for long and a confrontation was inevitable.

"There's only one thing with a chance of hurting that bastard," said Duggan under his breath.

"What's that, sir?"

"The *Ulterior-2* isn't made to beat *Ix-Gorghal*, Lieutenant Cruz. Our sole purpose should be to keep the enemy ship away from the *Earth's Fury* and give Captain Blake an opportunity to test out that gun. The Vraxar battleship is a variable I don't want in play – we'll have to take it out without making ourselves vulnerable to a surprise attack from *Ix-Gorghal*."

"Won't that give the Vraxar an excuse to blow up New Earth?"

"It might, so we'll need to engage *Ix-Gorghal* quickly, keep it occupied and hope the distraction is enough."

Sergeant Li was sharper than his easy-going manner suggested. "The enemy spaceship will leave a pretty big hole in New Earth if we shoot it down from here, sir."

"It's not travelling with anything close to sufficient velocity to escape New Earth's gravitational pull if we destroy it on its current vector," confirmed Ensign Bailey. "However, it is definitely travelling with enough speed to kill half of the population and wreck several million square klicks of the surface."

"Let's see what we can do to draw them away," said Duggan.

The Ghast and Vraxar warships were four thousand kilometres ahead and one thousand below, each of them leaving a thick trail of grey smoke which extended for twenty thousand kilometres or more. They traded blows, with the Vraxar spaceship unloading everything it had, whilst the Ghasts launched missiles in smaller, staggered clusters of four or five.

Duggan increased the *Ulterior-2*'s speed. The Hadron was built to withstand repeated particle beam strikes and an unintended consequence of its heat-dispersal technology was an ability to fly at greater speed through a dense atmosphere than any other ship in the fleet.

The gap closed steadily and the nose of the *Ulterior-2* started warming up.

"Sir?" It was Lieutenant Cruz and she sounded worried.

"Tell me."

"There's an anomaly two thousand klicks behind us and slightly to one side. A large object is displacing the positrons we're leaking from our uncovered engines."

It was a good spot. The *Ulterior-2*'s gravity drive was partially exposed and the shielding applied in the shipyard was only a temporary measure until it could be properly covered up by the outer plates. The Hadron was likely spilling a handful of particles through the air as it travelled. There was only thing big enough to have a measurable effect.

"*Ix-Gorghal.* So, they *are* here. Are there any clues as to whether its seen us?"

"Gut instinct tells me we'd be dead by now. I've seen first-hand what it can do and I wouldn't expect it to be long before it finds us."

"Seems like we were lucky just getting off the ground," said Duggan. "We must have activated the stealth modules with moments to spare."

It was going to require a fine balancing act to destroy the

Vraxar battleship whilst also allowing the *Sciontrar* and the *Ulterior-2* an opportunity to stay ahead of *Ix-Gorghal*. Nil-Tras was a wily captain and he was somehow managing to keep the cusp of New Earth between himself and *Ix-Gorghal*, whilst at the same time holding the Vraxar's interest by leaving his stealth modules switched off.

The Ghast was also lucky. At any point, the capital ship could fly higher in order to get a firing angle, or it could simply adopt a high, stationary orbit and wait for the *Sciontrar* to pass underneath.

At which point Nil-Tras would enter lightspeed again, thought Duggan with a smile of admiration.

He increased the *Ulterior-2*'s speed further and the battleship skimmed effortlessly above New Earth, coming closer to the enemy spaceship with each passing second.

"One thousand klicks," said Cruz. "Five hundred. Two hundred. I am no longer able to pinpoint *Ix-Gorghal*."

"Descending to three thousand metres."

Duggan pushed forward on the control sticks and the *Ulterior-2* plummeted towards the ocean below. The spaceship's altitude dropped rapidly and he hauled it level at exactly three thousand metres. Pieces of ice floated amongst the waves and the water looked as cold and uninviting as anywhere out in space.

"Pray that Tarjos Nil-Tras is in a listening mood," said Duggan. "Lieutenant Cruz, contact the Ghasts and ask them to climb directly away from New Earth."

Cruz hurriedly passed on the message. "Done."

"The Vraxar haven't stopped firing their missiles at the Ghasts, sir," said Ensign Bailey. "I think the *Sciontrar*'s energy shield is on the brink of failure."

"In which case they'll be glad when they find out what we're going to do."

Even though Duggan knew it was coming, the steepness of

the Oblivion's climb caught him unawares. The *Sciontrar* hurtled towards the edges of space, leaving the Vraxar battleship far below.

"They're not following, sir."

"They will," said Duggan through gritted teeth. *They've got to.*

The Vraxar could be predictable on occasion and now was one of those times. The larger Vraxar ship gave chase and Duggan detected something ponderous about it – a hint which only an experienced eye could detect.

"It's old and damaged," he said.

The enemy ship gathered speed. The higher it went, the less friction it encountered from the atmosphere. Duggan followed, doing his best to keep the *Ulterior-2* on a parallel course.

"We've cleared the outer edges of the atmosphere," said Cruz.

"The Vraxar spacecraft will no longer crater on New Earth," said Bailey.

It was all Duggan needed to hear.

"Sergeant Li, Ensign Park. Target the enemy with everything we have and blow them into pieces."

"Yes, sir!"

The *Ulterior-2* was every bit as tightly-packed with weapons as a Ghast Oblivion and Duggan was delighted to put it to the test.

"Targeting Havoc cannons," said Li.

Park fumbled with the controls. "I am attempting to lock on with Shimmers. Particle beams are coming."

The Havoc cannons fired – the two uppers, one lower and the nose gun fired at the same time. The enemy ship was only a few hundred kilometres away, its front quarter softened by heat. The Havoc projectiles crashed through the plating, causing terrible damage. The *Ulterior-2* shook and one of the automated alarms kicked in, blaring loudly. Duggan turned it off without thinking.

"Awaiting reload of Havoc cannons."

"Ensign Park?" asked Duggan quietly.

"On it, sir. Firing front overcharged particle beams. No angle for the rears."

Two of the *Ulterior-2*'s high-intensity energy beams raked through the structure of the enemy warship, sending the already-hot metal way past melting point. A thousand cubic metres or more of the Vraxar battleship's flank exploded outwards, filling the void with a million tiny new stars, their lives measured in fleeting minutes.

Ensign Park's struggles would not be helped by bad tempers and raised voices. Duggan had already locked the Shimmers onto the enemy craft and his finger hovered over the launch button.

"Got them!" shouted Park.

The Hadron was packing thirty-six Shimmer launchers, not all of which could target an enemy as close as the Vraxar battle-ship. Twenty of the enormously rapid and hugely expensive armour-piercing missiles flew from their launch tubes, armed themselves and collided with the enemy warship in less than half a second. The results were catastrophic and the huge craft was torn asunder right across its midsection.

The Havoc cannons finished their reload and Li fired again, a sheen of sweat on his forehead the only sign of the stress he was under. The thunder of the guns was accompanied by a different sound – that of overstressed metal tearing.

"What the hell?" asked Li, immediately out of his depth.

"Our front underside Havoc cannon is gone," said Ensign Park. "I don't think we took a hit from anywhere."

"We didn't," said Duggan. He swore. "The force of the shot tore it away from the hull."

The Havoc cannons had done enough. The front piece of the

enemy vessel was twisted and mangled, smashed out of shape. Before Duggan was able to decide if the battleship was completely out of action, the sensor feed turned entirely white. When it cleared, there was nothing which could be readily identified as the warship which had hung over the Tucson base for these past hours.

"That was the *Sciontrar*," said Cruz. "The Ghasts launched eleven hundred missiles."

"They like fireworks, Lieutenant. They always have."

"Oh crap."

Duggan jerked around in his chair. "Lieutenant Cruz?"

"A projectile just hit the *Sciontrar*'s shield. A second one went through."

The main bulkhead screen showed the details. A huge gauss slug had crunched into the rear section of the Ghast battleship, crumpling the metal and leaving a thousand metres of it misshapen. A third projectile hit and then a fourth. The *Sciontrar* was spun around by the force of it and twisted sections of armour plate tumbled away. All of a sudden, the Oblivion winked out of existence, leaving the *Ulterior-2* alone to face the might of *Ix-Gorghal*.

CHAPTER TWENTY-THREE

VIEWED FROM UP CLOSE, the *Earth's Fury* made Captain Blake shiver with a peculiar mix of fear and wonder. The space-ship looked like something designed by a child – straight edges, flat sides and with a slight tapering being the only indication it had a nose. The gun, however, was something else. The main barrel was a fifteen hundred metres long and slender enough to break from a single missile strike. It didn't matter – there was something overtly threatening about the complicated array of beams, cylinders and connecting tubes. It seemed ancient, yet also like something from a thousand years in the future; a weapon to either save humanity or to amuse the capricious whims of a supremely powerful, unknown race who watched the Confedera-tion's struggles from afar.

The lifter shuttle hung in the air above the rear of *Earth's Fury*. In normal circumstances, it would have been easy enough to lower the Obsidiar magazine dangling from the gravity chains into the loading slot for the Shield Breaker gun. Once the maga-zine was lowered into this slot, gravity clamps would drag it into the chamber deep inside the spaceship.

"Those repeaters are pissing me off," said Blake.

Shots from the ground clattered against the shuttle and the magazine. The *Ulterior-2* had been exceptionally effective in clearing the area, but wasn't able to kill the Vraxar who remained out of sight behind the *Earth's Fury*. The enemy had no missile launchers with them and were targeting the shuttle with three heavy repeaters and a single wide-bore gun. The repeaters were no problem – it was the wide-bore which would cause the damage. Consequently, Blake had spent the last few minutes moving the shuttle this way and that across the upper section of the *Earth's Fury*, whilst the Vraxar tried their best to get a clear shot with the big gun.

It was a stalemate and Blake was conscious of the passing time. Before he could figure out a solution, several additional distractions arrived, one after the other.

"That's the *Sciontrar!*" he said, watching the sensor feed.

"That thing is hot and travelling fast," said Hawkins. "Where's the battleship?"

The answer wasn't long in coming and the Vraxar spaceship rumbled across the base in a direct line after the Oblivion.

"Come on, Nil-Tras," said Quinn. "Get those bastards."

Before Blake was able to resume his efforts at loading the Shield Breaker, the *Ulterior-2* took off with such suddenness it would have been easy to miss were he not already watching the sensor screen. One minute it was in its trench, the next it was rising vertically at speed.

"Battle is joined," he said.

"That means we need to move this along, sir," said Pointer, patting him on the shoulder.

Her words brought him back to the unfinished task. "I need thirty seconds clear above the load slot. I'm not getting anything like that much time before the gun gets us in its sights."

"They should have fitted these lifter shuttles with nose cannons, huh?" said Quinn.

The words were an expression of frustration; nevertheless, they gave Blake an idea.

"Lieutenant McKinney!" he shouted.

"Sir?"

The tiny inner space of the shuttle was packed with soldiers – one hundred men and women somehow squeezed onto the steps, the antechamber and into the cockpit. It was cramped and uncomfortable for everyone.

"How's about the soldiers near the exit door open it up and start dropping grenades?"

"Yes, sir, I'll get on with it." There was a moment in which McKinney drew in his breath, before he bellowed down the stairs. "Who's at the bottom?"

Blake didn't hear the answer and didn't need to. McKinney shouted again.

"Webb, if you can knock out that wide-bore I'll make sure Garcia buys you a drink next time we're off duty."

"I'm hard up, sir," called Garcia.

A few of the others jeered and McKinney demanded silence. A warning light informed Blake the lifter's outer door was open.

"He's ready when you are, sir."

"I'll move us into position."

Blake piloted the shuttle out from the cover provided by the *Earth's Fury*. He knew Webb was on top of his game and didn't give him much time. A plasma rocket shrieked just as Blake took the shuttle out of sight once again.

"Well?" called McKinney. "Right, I'll let him know."

"Is it done?" asked Blake.

"He reckons he scored a direct hit, sir. One more for luck."

"One more it is."

He took the shuttle sideways and the sound of a repositioned heavy repeater began again. Blake cursed it under his breath. Webb fired a second rocket and Blake took the shuttle into cover.

"Webb?" yelled McKinney. "Right, I'll let him now."

"What about this time?" asked Blake.

"One wide-bore out of action, sir. Three mobile repeaters remaining."

"Screw the repeaters," said Blake. "Tell him to close the door."

The outer door closed and Blake took the lifter shuttle straight into position. The Obsidiar magazine hung below, suspended by the invisible forces of the gravity chains. He ignored the repeater fire and brought the craft carefully lower, making fine adjustments to the length of the chains. With a grunt of relief, Blake got the magazine into place and allowed the *Earth's Fury* to take over the loading. The chamber mechanism severed the chains and the magazine disappeared into the depths of the ship. A protective plate slid across the opening.

"Done. Now we can get on with business."

There was plenty of space amongst the support beams and cross-braces of the Shield Breaker. Blake set the shuttle down a quarter of the way in from the edge and next to a cylinder which had a diameter of five hundred metres and was half as much tall. It was part of the gun's power source, though he couldn't remember how it worked.

"Time to get out," said Blake. He tried to stand and realised how tight it was in the cockpit. One of the soldiers was pressed against the back of the pilot's seat, making it hard for Blake to get up.

"Sorry, sir."

The soldiers tumbled from the shuttle, glad to be outside in the rain, if only for a brief spell. By the time Blake and the crew exited, the squad was already muttering about how much better it was to be dry.

McKinney was nearby.

"We're equidistant from two of the maintenance shafts," he said. "I don't know which is closest to the bridge."

"The central one," said Blake. "That takes us to within a couple of hundred metres of the bridge entrance door."

"What if they got onto the bridge and trashed it?"

"The door should only open to maintenance personnel. I doubt they've had time to blow it." Blake shrugged. "This is either going to work or it isn't."

There were five squads of twenty, already organised by McKinney. Without comms, there were more confusion than usual and it took additional seconds until everyone was ready. They kept their suit visors on top of their heads and a hundred pairs of eyes watched Blake and McKinney.

"Let's get moving!" shouted McKinney.

The central maintenance shaft was on the far side of the power cylinder. Blake and McKinney set off in the lead and the others followed. Something inside the cylinder squealed softly. The sound wormed its way into Blake's chest and stomach, and made him feel queasy within a few seconds. He stepped away from it and heard the men behind him also backing off.

"This gun is going to shoot down *Ix-Gorghal* is it?" asked McKinney. He tipped his head back and his eyes followed the twisting metal tubes and criss-crossed beams.

"It's the only chance we've got," said Blake.

"I know about the Obsidiar bomb, sir."

"That isn't a chance, Lieutenant, it's an admission that we failed." He joined McKinney in staring upwards. "The Shield Breaker doesn't look like much until you get amongst it. Now I can see it from close up, I'm..." He paused. "Hopeful isn't the word. Maybe I can see a pinpoint of light through the keyhole."

"It's something to aim for."

The gun towered above them and it was tilted at a thirty-degree angle. It was fitted to a movable plate, allowing it to rotate in a limited arc. The loading end joined with an enormous square housing in which the Obsidiar slugs were fed into the barrel. Wherever the original designs had sprung from, this gun had clearly been heavily-modified to get it onto a spaceship.

The central maintenance shaft was directly below the barrel, and it operated in the same way as the maintenance shafts on the *Ulterior-2*. Blake held his breath when he entered his access codes. To his profound relief, the *Earth's Fury* security system accepted the codes.

"I'm still part of the Space Corps on New Earth," he said under his breath.

The lift came and McKinney got onboard, along with a dozen others from his squad.

"You're coming on the third trip, sir?" he asked.

Blake confirmed what they'd previously agreed. "Yes, Lieutenant. The crew comes after the next group. Don't get yourself killed."

"That'll only happen if Webb here gets trigger happy and fires a plasma rocket at our feet."

Webb wasn't at all bothered by the suggestion. "I resent that accusation, sir," he said mildly.

The lift descended with an exasperating lack of speed. The troops left on top were arrayed in whatever positions of cover they could find and most of them glanced regularly towards the shaft to see what was going on. For many, this was their first potential engagement with a real enemy and their nervousness was plain to see.

"The lift is coming back up," said Sergeant Demarco. "Get ready."

The second group sank slowly into the shaft. Blake leaned over and watched their gradual progress towards the exit tunnel at the bottom. The lift stopped and the squad vanished from sight.

"We're next," said Blake.

The lift arrived and the crew jumped onto it, along with a few of the soldiers who could fit. Blake poked the destination button with one finger and tried to remain calm while the lift finished its journey. After what seemed like hours staring at the grey walls of the maintenance shaft and the top of Lieutenant Hawkins' head, Blake was relieved when the lift stopped.

"Let's go."

Blake stepped off the lift platform and into the maintenance tunnel. The passage was wide enough for two to pass but the ceiling was low, forcing him to keep his knees bent. He listened for the sounds of combat as he walked and heard nothing except the crew and soldiers following him. It was too early to take it as a good sign – the walls of a spaceship were thick and unreflective. The metal did funny things with sound; there could be a full-scale war just ahead and he might not know about it.

A side passage led off at a right-angle and a soldier waited patiently at the junction. The man raised an arm and pointed in the direction the others had taken.

"That way."

"Any resistance?"

"No."

There was something in the soldier's eyes which suggested there was more to it than he was letting on. Blake didn't stop to question him and pressed on along the original corridor. There was another soldier in the distance - perhaps a group of them - and Blake hurried towards them.

He reached the end of the passage, where it entered the main area of *Earth's Fury*. There were, in fact, three soldiers here and they waved him out. It was immediately apparent what had disturbed the man in the maintenance tunnel. Blake gagged at the smell and swore quietly.

This was one of the two main corridors which ran from front to back in the *Earth's Fury*. It was meant to be kept clear at all times, though at this moment it was anything but clear. Dead Vraxar were piled in both directions as far as the eye could see. Their huge, torn bodies covered the floor and in places there were so many dead, they came close to the ceiling. Blake stared numbly in the direction of the bridge and could see no end to the butchery. The greasy fluids which ran through the Vraxar's veins were splashed liberally over the floor, the walls and the bodies of the dead, making the floor treacherous.

"Best watch your footing, sir," said one of the soldiers. "It's slippery."

"The visor blocks out the smell," added another.

"What...?" asked Lieutenant Pointer, emerging from the maintenance tunnel.

A gentle whirring sound made Blake look up and he found himself looking into the slowly-spinning barrels of a ceiling minigun.

"That single gun did this?" asked Quinn. He put a hand to his throat and retched violently.

"*Earth's Fury* is filled with them, Lieutenant. In the walls and the ceiling." Blake swallowed. "I didn't expect them be quite so effective."

"This is awful," said Hawkins. "It's like the Vraxar thought they could get through if they only ran hard enough."

Blake's eyes were drawn to the face of the closest Vraxar. It had once been Estral, as had all of the bodies he could see. The alien's skin was smooth and unlined, pristine and untouched by the minigun slugs. The Estral's eyes were closed and the closest word Blake could find to describe its expression was *peaceful*.

"Tassin-Dak on *Ix-Gorghal* told us the Estral meant little to him," said Blake in disgust. "Here's the result. The Vraxar have their slaves and their masters. Look at this and remember."

A soldier approached along the corridor, doing his best to pick through the pieces. "Clear to the bridge," he called.

"Let's get away from this," said Blake. "I've seen enough."

It was a grim journey to the bridge and one or two of the squad vomited. Blake felt his gorge rising more than once and it was an effort to keep it down. They passed beneath several more miniguns, a couple of them still warm, and each one tracked the group passing below. It made the soldiers even more jumpy and they muttered amongst themselves.

"This has got to make us stronger," said Hawkins.

"How much stronger do we need to be, Lieutenant?"

She had no answer and fell silent.

The number of bodies lessened until there were only a few here and there – the fastest or luckiest of the Vraxar. By the time they came to within fifty metres of the bridge, there were none.

"I don't want to walk that walk again," said Pointer, close to tears.

"Shut it out, Lieutenant," said Blake. "Come to terms with it later – we've got a tough time ahead of us and we can't be distracted."

The bridge door whisked open and the crew entered. Corporal Bannerman was inside, fiddling with the comms console. He looked up guiltily when the crew approached.

"I'm just checking it out, sir. Professional interest."

"Don't worry about it, Corporal. Where's Lieutenant McKinney?"

"Scouting the ship, sir. To see if we're alone."

"This is the only room which matters."

"He doesn't want the Vraxar planting explosives on the door while we're inside."

"Fine. Lieutenant McKinney knows what he's doing." Blake

turned to his crew. "There's no time to lose. Find your seats and let's get this spaceship in the air."

With that, the crew found their stations, leaving the soldiers with the task of eliminating any pockets of Vraxar which may have escaped the withering fire of the internal defence systems. Blake pushed the memory of what he'd seen in the corridor from his mind. He accessed the main console on *Earth's Fury* and got to work.

CHAPTER TWENTY-FOUR

THE BRUTAL ATTACK on the *Sciontrar* and its subsequent disappearance into lightspeed had a sobering effect on the crew of the *Ulterior-2*. The destruction of the Vraxar battleship was a victory of sorts, yet only really a sideshow to the main event.

"Have the Ghasts abandoned us?" asked Ensign Park.

"I might not be trained for ship duty, but that damage to the *Sciontrar* looked fairly terminal to me," said Sergeant Li.

"It was," Duggan replied. His voice rose. "Lieutenant Cruz, where is *Ix-Gorghal*?"

"I'm looking, sir. Their stealth modules are just as good as ours."

"They're somewhere close," said Duggan. "I can feel it. After that engagement, they'll know we're here as well."

"Captain Blake can't fire at them if he can't see them, can he?" asked Li.

Duggan shook his head in answer. *Ix-Gorghal* was nearby and maintaining its stealth cloak. The *Ulterior-2* was also hidden and this was the only thing keeping the crew alive.

"What are they playing at?" He didn't expect anyone to respond and they didn't.

The answer came to him with a certainty he couldn't shake. The Vraxar were enjoying this – to them it was a game; a hunt in which they stalked their far weaker prey. *Until they get bored.*

Duggan didn't enjoy games, particularly when they put the lives of billions of people at risk. Somehow, he had to play for time until Captain Blake got *Earth's Fury* ready, and then he would need to figure out how to bring *Ix-Gorghal* out of stealth. The odds were far lower than he would have liked.

"I've located the *Sciontrar*," said Cruz. "They got dumped out of lightspeed close to the moon. They're going to impact."

The Oblivion was too far away for the *Ulterior-2*'s sensors to produce a pin-sharp image. The view was good enough to show the *Sciontrar* heading down at high speed. If the battleship's life support was active, the crew might live. Otherwise, there'd be nothing left to scrape off the walls and the only monument to their deaths would be a thousand-kilometre crater in the middle of New Earth's moon.

Just then, all hell broke loose.

"A big gauss slug went past our nose," said Cruz. "That one was close. Holy crap, dozens of them!"

Duggan pushed at the controls. "Time to get out of here."

He didn't hold back and took the *Ulterior-2* up to full speed. The battleship wasn't only loaded with weapons, it was also the fastest ship in the fleet excepting the spy craft *ES Blackbird*. It burst away from New Earth, reaching a velocity of 2600 kilometres per second. Gauss slugs from *Ix-Gorghal* tore through space in their hundreds, some coming perilously close to the *Ulterior-2*'s shields.

"They don't know exactly where we are," said Cruz.

Duggan had been in this position before. The enemy would gradually narrow down the precise location of the fleeing battleship until eventually one of those massive projectiles would score a direct hit. "They soon will."

"They're right where we want them," said Li. "Hot on our tail."

Li spoke the unpleasant truth. They had a good idea where *Ix-Gorghal* was and all they had to do was keep it in pursuit until Captain Blake got *Earth's Fury* into a position from which he could fire. *As easy as that,* laughed Duggan bitterly.

"I can tell you exactly where the enemy ship is, sir," said Cruz. "It's hard for them to conceal their location when they're firing a thousand guns at us."

"Hold fire," warned Duggan. "If we open up, it'll give the game away."

The *Ulterior-2* sped through space, heading for the New Earth moon. The satellite was a bleak, cold rock and the *Sciontrar*'s impact had produced a vast crater near to its northern pole. The Ghast battleship lay at the bottom. It had flipped over during the impact and its nose pointed at an angle towards the sky. Aftershocks from the collision spread outwards for thousands of kilometres.

"I'm going to bring us around the moon in a tight circuit. It'll prevent them from seeing the *Earth's Fury* when it takes off," said Duggan.

"If we make it. That last slug missed our shield by fifty metres," said Cruz. "Their average miss distance is less than a thousand metres."

Duggan had a sudden thought. "Can you communicate with the *Earth's Fury* now *Ix-Gorghal* is away from the surface?"

"Negative and they're still on the ground. Whatever was jamming the comms, it's still in place."

"Send them our coordinates and keep sending them updates. We're stealthed, but they should be able to locate us from that."

"Yes, sir, I'll set up an automated update."

Cruz made an exclamation of surprise.

"What is it?" asked Duggan sharply.

"An open channel from the *Sciontrar!*" she said excitedly. "Tarjos Nil-Tras says hello!"

"Well I'll be..."

An idea appeared in Duggan's mind, slotting in with the sort of perfection he didn't believe existed. His breathing deepened and his heartrate quickened at the sheer audacity of it.

"Tell Nil-Tras to warm up the Particle Disruptor and be ready to fire!"

Cruz talked quickly. Before she was done speaking, the *Ulterior-2*'s approach towards the moon took it out of comms sight and the connection with the *Sciontrar* went dead.

"Did he get the message?" asked Duggan.

"I don't know if he got it all, sir."

"The *Sciontrar* is badly damaged," said Park. "Do we know if their Particle Disruptor is even working?"

"We call this *taking a chance*," said Duggan.

"I've heard it called many things, sir," said Sergeant Li.

The *Ulterior-2* came within a thousand kilometres of the moon. A series of huge craters caused by the fire from *Ix-Gorghal*'s guns suddenly appeared on the surface below, each impact throwing up a fountain of rock shards. Before Duggan could adjust the battleship's course, disaster struck and one of the slugs crashed into the spaceship's energy shield, sending the primary Obsidiar core's power reserves plunging.

"I don't think we can take another," said Ensign Bailey.

They didn't have a choice in the matter and a second projectile followed the first, depleting the shield entirely. With its momentum almost spent by its passage through the shield, the eighty-thousand tonne ball of alloy thudded into the *Ulterior-2*'s rear section with insufficient force to rupture the armour plates, and then spun off into space.

"That's got to have given them a big clue about where to aim," said Bailey.

Duggan knew it as well. He hauled the *Ulterior-2* into a much tighter arc around the moon, coming to within a few hundred metres of the barren surface.

"Whoa, shit!" said Cruz.

Ix-Gorghal's gauss slugs drubbed the surface, creating another storm of rock which clattered against the battleship's hull. Duggan increased their speed and altered course again, hoping to throw off the Vraxar ship's aim.

"We're coming up on the *Sciontrar*, sir," said Cruz. "They won't be able to see what they're aiming at."

It was possible the Ghast comms team would be able to identify the location of *Ix-Gorghal* in a split second and then fire the Particle Disruptor. On the other hand, they might be too late and this opportunity be forever wasted.

This was the moment. Duggan saw it clearly – the fulcrum upon which everything was balanced. Success and failure at opposite sides of the scales. Success could not exist without failure, but sometimes the scales could be given a push to disturb their equilibrium.

Duggan took the *Ulterior-2* higher above the moon's surface and then, when the *Sciontrar* appeared on the sensors far below, he gave the order.

"Target *Ix-Gorghal* and fire Shimmers."

Park had been slow the first time. On this occasion he was like lightning.

Sixteen upper and rear Shimmer tubes launched their missiles. The enemy ship was under cover of stealth, but it was huge and presented a far bigger target than the *Ulterior-2*. The Shimmers detonated in less than a second and their explosions spread outwards and around *Ix-Gorghal*'s energy shield, defining its shape and betraying its location.

Duggan was shocked at how close the enemy was to them - the Vraxar spaceship was within five hundred kilometres and its fearsome size made him experience a wave of terrible doubt. *We can't beat that.*

He didn't allow weakness to consume him. "Lieutenant Cruz - if the *Earth's Fury* is listening, let them know it's time to fire. We don't have long."

"Yes, sir."

The Shimmer launch was the final piece of the puzzle for the Vraxar and a series of gauss slugs skimmed across the *Ulterior-2*'s hull. Another struck the battleship's upper section, knocking one of the Havoc cannons free and leaving a furrow in the armour plating.

Duggan and his crew stared death in the face.

"Captain Blake, don't let me down."

Meanwhile, on the surface of the moon, a bright blue light glowed fiercely at the nose of the *Sciontrar*.

CHAPTER TWENTY-FIVE

EARTH'S FURY wasn't ready to join the Space Corps fleet and it showed. The comms was the only main system fully tested and functional. Everything else was partway there, some of it more partway than others.

"No sign of the *Ulterior-2* on our sensors," said Pointer. "Or anything else, for that matter."

Lieutenant Quinn had the most difficult job and he spoke with Blake to try and figure out how to get the *Earth's Fury* off the ground.

"Four of the main engine modules are missing, sir," said Quinn. "The shipyard wasn't finished tying the others in yet, because they were waiting for the life support."

"As long as we can get off the ground, Lieutenant, that's what matters. Without the life support, we won't be able to utilise a fraction of the engine output before we get spread across the rear bulkhead."

"True enough. This is still a heavy ship and we need ten or fifteen percent to get into the air." Quinn drummed his fingers. "I'm going to activate modules ZF and ZR."

"What will that give us?"

"Eight percent."

"Not enough."

The two engine modules kicked into life and sent a vibration through the walls, which quickly died away to a steady hum.

"Those are good ones," said Blake.

"Yep, we're at two percent of maximum and rising."

"Which other modules are ready?"

Quinn grimaced and rubbed his face. "Some of these other tie-ins look finished, just not tested."

"Do whatever it takes, Lieutenant."

"Let's see if modules RC and LLQ will come online. Here we go."

This time, the result wasn't so good. The entire ship shook and rumbled, accompanied by the sound of one inconceivably heavy object colliding with another. Quinn hammered a hand onto an area of his console to shut it down.

"I guess LLQ wasn't tied in after all."

"You reckon?" said Hawkins.

"How are you getting on with the weapons?" asked Blake. "We need more than just engines."

"What weapons, sir? If they fitted anything other than the main gun, they haven't been linked into our consoles."

"Don't worry about that – Earth's Fury was meant to carry one thing and it's up on the roof."

"The Shield Breaker has extensive test records, sir. They haven't sent live ammo through it yet."

"We're fully loaded now, right?"

"Absolutely. There are twelve Obsidiar projectiles in that magazine."

"Are you comfortable with targeting and firing?"

"I wouldn't say I'm exactly comfortable, sir. See these

numbers on this screen? That's how much time it takes the barrel to re-target."

"That isn't good."

"We can hit *Ix-Gorghal*, as long as it stands in one place long enough."

The walls of *Earth's Fury* shook again and the entire vessel shuddered.

"I'm getting a response from module RC," said Quinn. "ZF and ZR are warming up nicely."

"What's our estimated output with those three?"

"Ten percent."

"Is it enough?"

"Do you want me to do the sums right now, sir?"

"Bring module LLR up," said Blake, ignoring the question. "That one is tied in – I can feel it."

"You can feel it, huh? Who am I to argue?" said Quinn. He activated module lower-lower-rear and sat back to watch.

Blake grinned. "Well?"

"Like I said – LLR is a good one, sir."

"Output?"

"Twelve percent when fully warmed up."

Blake watched the available power climbing steadily on his console. *Earth's Fury* vibrated like a thousand-year-old diesel engine and the lumpy note of its gravity drive didn't inspire confidence. One console screen showed only amber warning alerts and a red symbol flashed distractingly. He turned the display off.

"This would never have been ready in five weeks," said Hawkins.

Blake clicked his harness into place - it felt strange having to use one. "It's going to fly now, Lieutenant. Time to buckle up."

With no life support it was *definitely* time to buckle up.

"Engine output is only nine percent of maximum, sir," said Quinn, trying to get his fastenings in place.

"I'd rather start slow and see what falls off."

Pointer laughed. "Truly inspiring words, sir."

Blake took hold of the control sticks and fed power gradually into the gravity drive. The vibration increased and the engine note climbed louder and louder. At maximum available output, the *Earth's Fury* remained planted on the ground. Blake didn't let up and watched as the active engine modules slowly reached normal operating levels.

"Up we go," he said.

Earth's Fury lifted off on its maiden flight. The positioning of the active engine modules made it unbalanced and the levelling systems hadn't been calibrated. Neither was the autopilot available.

"There go the trench airlifts," said Pointer.

"They can build new ones."

Slowly at first, the *Earth's Fury* cleared the sides of the construction trench. It climbed ponderously, whilst Blake struggled to correct a list to one side. In normal circumstances it didn't matter even if a spaceship was upside down, since the life support would keep the occupants firmly on the floor. On this occasion, it made things harder for the crew and Blake heard one or two comments about the quality of his flying.

He adapted and got the spaceship level. The available engine power peaked at slightly more than twelve percent and he accessed the new reserves. *Earth's Fury* accelerated and the crew felt the crushing effects of it pressing them into their seats.

"You forget what it's like," shouted Blake over the engines. The muscles in his neck pulled and his shoulders ached. He clung onto the controls and kept the spaceship climbing.

"Twelve thousand klicks per *hour*," said Hawkins. "This thing is fast."

The acceleration went on and on. The *Earth's Fury* reached escape velocity and pulled free of the planet. New Earth dwindled slowly on the sensor feed as the spaceship drew further away.

"Find *Ix-Gorghal*." Blake's jaw was hurting now and it was hard to speak.

"I'm trying," said Pointer, fighting the words out.

Blake was conscious of his promise to Fleet Admiral Duggan that he would take *Earth's Fury* far from the planet before he did any shooting and he left the spaceship's engines on full until he felt his sight dim.

"Time to back off!" yelled Hawkins.

Blake relented and pulled down on the control sticks. The relief was instant and he felt blood rushing into his head. Nausea followed and then his body adjusted once more.

He checked the navigational system, which was only connected to a quarter of the sensor arrays. The spaceship was heading on a rough course towards the moon, with an estimated arrival time of five hours at their current speed.

"Lieutenant Pointer?"

"I'm looking, sir." Then, "I've located the *Ulterior-2*!"

"Where?"

"They're cloaked. Lieutenant Cruz is sending us a series of coordinates to show their vector."

"Put it into my screen. Quickly!"

The details appeared as a constantly changing series of eighty-digit numbers.

"I've pinpointed them, sir! You should be able to see them on your console."

A dot appeared, showing the *Ulterior-2* moving at high speed across the surface of New Earth's moon.

"Can you predict their course from this?"

"I don't think so, sir. They could change direction at any moment."

"They've been around the moon and they've come out the

other side," Blake mused. He snapped his fingers. "They've got *Ix-Gorghal* following them and the Vraxar have their stealth modules activated."

"I can't shoot what I can't see," said Hawkins, frustration spilling over.

"Admiral Duggan will know that, Lieutenant. He's going to do something."

"The *Sciontrar* must have crashed into the moon!" said Pointer. "The *Ulterior-2* is on an intersecting course."

"I know what he's going to do!" said Blake. "Lieutenant Hawkins, aim the Shield Breaker towards the *Sciontrar*. Get ready to fire!"

"The barrel is moving too slowly. You'll need to turn the ship, sir!"

It took all of Blake's skill and concentration to pull it off. He made the tiniest of adjustments to the controls and the *Earth's Fury* began the slowest of rotations.

Quinn thumped the arm of his seat. "Where the hell are they?"

A comms message reached the *Earth's Fury*.

"Lieutenant Cruz says get ready!" shouted Pointer.

The sensor feed picked up signs of warheads detonating above the surface of the moon and the front section of an immense shape was highlighted briefly. A new fire came, flooding over the intensity of the Shimmer fires. Suddenly, *Ix-Gorghal* was surrounded by the blue heat of the *Sciontrar*'s Particle Disruptor. The ovoid shape of the Vraxar capital ship was cast in relief against the grey background of New Earth's moon, the colour as pure and deep as an Atlantis sea.

"Fire," said Blake.

With a sound no louder than a whisper, the Shield Breaker fired.

CHAPTER TWENTY-SIX

THE *ULTERIOR-2* WAS in a bad way, its plating battered, crushed and split by *Ix-Gorghal*'s gauss turrets. Duggan's console was covered in red alerts and the control bars were unresponsive. He roared in anger, refusing to give up hope.

On the viewscreen, *Ix-Gorghal* burned, not for a moment letting up in the bombardment. Duggan raised his fist towards the image and then...

Something crashed through *Ix-Gorghal*'s weakened shields, leaving a black plume through the disruptor fire. The Shield Breaker's projectile struck the flank of *Ix-Gorghal*, travelling just shy of lightspeed. It punched through the spaceship's thick hull, leaving a tiny, insignificant hole in one of the outer structures.

The unstable Obsidiar didn't quite explode. Rather, it ruptured into a vast arc of unstoppable energy, which burst through the centre of *Ix-Gorghal*, reducing metal and a quarter of a billion Vraxar into their individual atoms. At the opposite side from the entry point, the depleted remains of the projectile smashed free, its speed hardly diminished. In its wake was a huge, gaping hole, two hundred kilometres across.

Incredibly, *Ix-Gorghal* was not destroyed. It stopped firing at the *Ulterior-2* and began turning, slowly and ponderously. Duggan saw into the depths of the weapon tube at its nose and watched the green light building within. The Vraxar ship turned inexorably towards New Earth.

"Fire!" said Duggan.

The *Ulterior-2* unleashed its arsenal, sending wave upon wave of missiles into the damaged enemy ship. With its energy shield burned out, there was nothing to prevent the Shimmers exploding against *Ix-Gorghal*'s dark armour. Havoc slugs tore through, each hit doing untold damage. It wasn't enough – the Vraxar capital ship was far too large to succumb to a single salvo.

A second round from the Shield Breaker crashed through the enemy ship. The effects of the unstable Obsidiar were difficult to model and this second projectile had an even more catastrophic effect than the first. It caught *Ix-Gorghal* at an angle and this time the disintegration arc travelled lengthways through most of the structure, before finally blowing out the rear third of the ship.

The green light faded from the front tube and gradually *Ix-Gorghal* began to break up.

"Should I hold fire?" asked Park.

"Never stop until you're sure, Ensign."

Sergeant Li knew the truth of those words and he fired the Havoc guns as quickly as they would reload. Another turret ripped free and still the soldier didn't stop.

Blake knew the truth as well and when the third round from the Shield Breaker hit *Ix-Gorghal*, it was finally clear the job was done.

Scarcely able to believe it, Duggan didn't know whether to laugh or cry. He felt a hand rest gently on his shoulder. He looked into the eyes of Lieutenant Paz.

"We got them, sir."

He nodded. "In the end."

"Is this how it always is?"

He choked back the tears. "Mostly."

"Time to go home."

The return flight was difficult. The *Ulterior-2* was badly damaged, though not so much that it couldn't launch two of its shuttles to find out how many of the *Sciontrar*'s crew still lived. The battleship limped towards New Earth with only a fraction of its engine power available. There was little conversation and not one of the crew dared to mention that *Ix-Gastiol* was still somewhere in Confederation Space.

A million kilometres behind, a vast cloud of debris slowly scattered, the pieces spinning and turning on their journey to nowhere. Duggan couldn't bring himself to look at it.

The comms were still jammed and Duggan ordered a circuit of the planet, shooting down each of the remaining Vraxar satellites.

"Only 12% oxygen remaining," said Cruz.

"We have generators," Lieutenant Paz replied. "Old Estral technology."

The comms returned with the destruction of the final satellite. Duggan spoke to Blake and wasn't surprised to discover the *Earth's Fury* was back on the ground.

"Our turn next," said Duggan.

"A fine job, sir."

"From every one of us, Captain."

"You haven't forgotten, have you?" asked Paz.

"No, I haven't forgotten about Benediction."

"We should hurry."

"There must be hours left."

"Three hours, sir. These satellites took a long time, and there are plenty of Vraxar on the base."

"Very well, let's get a move on."

There were still twelve thousand Vraxar on the landing strip and in the shipyard, as well as thousands more in the streets and buildings. Those in the vicinity of Trench Two lacked guidance and waited patiently while the *Ulterior-2*'s bulwarks cut them to pieces. A few minutes later, the battleship joined *Earth's Fury* on the landing strip. One spaceship looked incomplete, whilst the other looked like it had been struck a thousand times by a billion-tonne mallet. Duggan boarded one of the remaining shuttles and got on his way, bringing Lieutenant Paz and an escort of soldiers with him.

BENEDICTION

Benediction was exactly as Duggan remembered it. His brain didn't register the shape or the colour, so much as the terrible promises it whispered.

"The ultimate trade," he said.

Paz knew exactly what he meant. "I get the feeling it's desperate to be used. I don't know why."

"It's not evil, Lieutenant."

"I don't think it's evil, sir. It's just...chaos. The unfettered joy of destruction for the pure hell of it."

Duggan glanced at Paz, wondering just how much she knew of his own feelings on the matter. She didn't say anything else and he didn't ask.

"There's the timer."

000:000:02:21:09

"No joking around, sir. Can you just turn it off so we can get out of here?"

Duggan accessed the bomb's security computer and disabled the timer. The display went blank, awaiting input. His shoulders sagged and he sensed the relief in Lieutenant Paz.

"You have to carry the weight of this around with you all the time." The words were neither a statement or a question.

"Someone's got to do it."

"You won't let us down."

"No, Lieutenant, I won't let us down."

They exited the facility. The defeat of *Ix-Gorghal* was a monumental achievement, but Duggan couldn't allow himself the time to celebrate. The war wasn't over and there was still so much to do.

———

Follow Anthony James on Facebook at
facebook.com/AnthonyJamesAuthor

ALSO BY ANTHONY JAMES

The Survival Wars series

1. Crimson Tempest

2. Bane of Worlds

3. Chains of Duty

4. Fires of Oblivion

5. Terminus Gate

6. Guns of the Valpian

7. Mission: Nemesis

The Obsidiar Fleet series

1. Negation Force

2. Inferno Sphere

3. God Ship

4. Earth's Fury

Printed in Great Britain
by Amazon

43391843R00168